$\mathcal{R}$

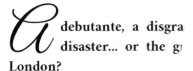 debutante, a disgra
disaster... or the g_]
London?

MISS DELILAH BANCROFT HAS A PROBLEM. A sizable and rather bloody one. Namely, a dead man on the library floor. She'd only wished for a moment of solitude out of the glaring eyes of Society. Instead, she's caught red-handed (unfortunately, literally) by an attractive stranger. Is he her salvation or ruination?

Marcus, Lord Wyndam has inherited a decrepit castle and a tainted title. During his desperate search for evidence to silence whispers of treason against his father, he stumbles across a woman holding a deadly stiletto over a body. Is she murderer or pawn? What he knows for sure is that she is his only link to the truth. With enemies beating down the door, he spirits her from the scene before she is discovered with blood on her hands— and her pretty white debutante dress—to unearth her part in the grisly plot.

Delilah proves herself to be a woman of wit and courage as well as beauty, and as the only person who might be able to identify the man behind the plot that ruined his father, Marcus must keep her close. Even if he has to ruin her to do it.

WARNING: Contains a lady who longs for adventure, a man of honor who longs for respectability, and a head long rush through London's ballrooms on the hunt for both. Will they live to love another day?

A SINFUL SURRENDER

SPIES AND LOVERS

LAURA TRENTHAM

ALSO BY LAURA TRENTHAM

*H*istorical Romance
Spies and Lovers
An Indecent Invitation Book 1
A Brazen Bargain, Book 2
A Reckless Redemption, Book 3
A Sinful Surrender, Book 4
A Wicked Wedding, Book 5
A Daring Deception, Book 6 (Coming Soon)

CONTEMPORARY ROMANCE
Highland, Georgia Novels
A Highlander Walks Into a Bar, Book 1
A Highlander in a Pickup, Book 2
A Highlander is Coming to Town, Book 3

HEART OF A HERO Novels
The Military Wife
An Everyday Hero

. . .

COTTONBLOOM NOVELS
Kiss Me That Way, Book 1
Then He Kissed Me, Book 2
Till I Kissed You, Book 3
Christmas in the Cop Car, Novella 3.5
Light Up the Night, Novella 3.75
Leave the Night On, Book 4
When the Stars Come Out, Book 5
Set the Night on Fire, Book 6

SWEET HOME ALABAMA Novels
Slow and Steady Rush, Book 1
Caught Up in the Touch, Book 2
Melting Into You, Book 3

FOREWORD

This book reads as a standalone story, however, if you've read the first three Spies and Lovers books, you will have met one secondary character, Lord Rafe Drummond. In fact, A Sinful Surrender takes place chronologically at the same time as An Indecent Invitation. Marcus and Delilah attend some of the same functions as Lily and Gray, although their paths do not directly cross.

If you've read A Brazen Bargain, which takes place the fall after An Indecent Invitation and A Sinful Surrender are set, then you've already met Marcus and Delilah a few months after the events of A Sinful Surrender.

I love the entangled storylines of the Spies and Lovers world and how it is expanding!

CHAPTER 1

*M*iss Bancroft is not hideous, I suppose, but she is only just passable. Don't you agree? So quiet and... and *boring*. I'm afraid those novels she's fond of are rotting her brain. She reminds me of this brown paneling." Sir Wallace Wainscott rapped the wall.

Hiding farther down the shadowy hall, Delilah Bancroft felt the vibrations in her cheek as she did her best to disappear into said paneling. Even more mortifying than overhearing something dreadful about oneself would be getting caught doing it. Especially by a man whom her mother had been sure was ready to come up to scratch.

"But her father has coin and lots of it if the latest on-dit is to be believed. Her wardrobe is certainly ostentatious enough." Lord Nash sniffed as if Delilah's white debutante dress carried a certain eau de commonness because her papa's merchant money had purchased it.

She ran a hand over the skirt and fisted the muslin. Perhaps the extra flounces and ribbons bordered on extravagance and didn't suit her, but other girls wore dresses with an equally garish number of fripperies. One unfortunate girl even now pranced around the dance floor with a chartreuse sash that matched her sallow complexion tied in an enormous bow.

"I overheard Mr. Bancroft boasting about his new ship. Can you imagine?" For the first time, Delilah heard the malicious whine that had garnered her suitor the nickname Whiney Wainscott among the more seasoned ladies.

She had done her best to catalog Sir Wallace's finer points— good hygiene, a full set of teeth, and most of his hair—when he'd come to call. A glass was always half-full in her estimation. Although her outlook was most likely a consequence of being the pampered daughter of a wealthy man with no worries over food or having a roof over her head. Her childhood had been full of carefree adventures.

For most of her life, she'd not faced significant hardships, but now they piled up, threatening to crush her. Her illness two years earlier had come on the heels of the death of her brother fighting on the Peninsula. Entering the marriage mart hadn't been the fun distraction she had expected. It was riddled with unexpected pitfalls and proved difficult to navigate.

"The Bancrofts' connection to Lady Casterly—and their vulgar money—are the only reasons they aren't given the cut direct." A bronze statue of a rearing horse on a pedestal blocked her ability to see his expression, but Lord Nash's tone dripped with disdain.

"Miss Bancroft will have a sizable dowry settled upon her." An opportunistic lilt in Sir Wallace's voice turned the statement into a half question, as if he were seeking Lord Nash's approval.

"Common coin is still common." Lord Nash's attitude tarnished the sense of muted welcome she had received from the ton under Lady Casterly's wing. How many lords and ladies tittered behind their cheroots and fans at her ostentatious frocks and common coin?

Beneath the tears that burned up her nose and blurred her vision was a feeling she had a hard time quantifying. Yes, Sir

Wallace and Lord Nash's opinions hurt her terribly. Embarrassment was rife that she had mistakenly assumed the ton's acceptance of her family into their ranks was genuine. But another feeling trumped her hurt and embarrassment.

She was mad. No, not mad. She was furious. At the two gentlemen—although neither man qualified for the moniker in her eyes anymore—for discussing her in such a manner. At herself for being a question and answer away from accepting a lifetime in purgatory with Sir Wallace. And at her mother for convincing Delilah that Sir Wallace was the best she could expect.

Delilah quelled the urge to march over and plant a facer square on Sir Wallace's aristocratic nose. It would be ruinous to her reputation and was exactly the kind of impulsiveness her mother had worked diligently to smother out of her with tonics and compresses. After all, her impulsive behavior was what had landed her at death's door, and she had no wish to put herself or her mother through any more trauma, physical or social.

With the discussion shifting to gaming losses and horseflesh, Sir Wallace and Lord Nash retreated to the far end of the hallway where the stairway descended. Delilah remained pressed against the wall for a few breaths, hoping the two men would return to the party, but they tarried.

She'd been searching for the retiring room before coming across the two men. Now the thought of smiling and making polite, meaningless conversation with her mother or any of the ladies was untenable. Yet neither could she lurk in the hallway for Sir Wallace or some other gentleman to discover and mock.

If she were as brown and bland as Sir Wallace intimated, no one would notice her. She slid away from the men with her hands flat against the wall. Could she escape down the servants' stairway, feign tiredness, and beg to go home? A new novel awaited her on her bedside table. Adventure between the covers of a book was as close as she'd come in recent memory to true excitement. She'd arrived in London with hope she'd broaden her world, but if Sir Wallace and his ilk were the inhabitants, she'd rather retreat to her bedchamber alone.

Her fingers brushed a metal latch inset into the wall. She pulled, and a door swung open with nary a squeak. She backed into the room, closed the door, and turned. It was a small library, intimate, welcoming, and most importantly, empty. Four braces of lit candles cast wavering circles of light around the room. Books covered two walls, and the air held the scent of beeswax and parchment.

She examined the door she'd entered through. It was flush with the wall, and if she hadn't felt the latch, she might have overlooked it. Which meant, with luck, anyone in the hallway would overlook it as well. She could gather her wits and confidence in private.

Most debutantes would be devastated by being categorized as *barely passable*, but Delilah had long ago accepted her brown hair and freckled complexion didn't incite the composition of love poems. She was unfashionably hardy-looking compared to the blond-haired, pale-skinned, delicate English roses in vogue with Society. But she'd received compliments on her eyes, rich chocolate with shards of amber, and her smile had been referred to as beguiling once or twice.

Quiet? She would admit to veering toward silence, especially when expected to converse on inanities like the rise and fall of bodice lines or horseflesh. She didn't care for riding and preferred to get around the countryside on her own two feet.

But *boring?* That stung like a patch of nettles. And she knew of which she spoke. She had endured her fair share of scrapes as a child wandering the hills and woods around their village of Stoney Pudholme. The villagers had called her wild, most of the time indulgently, sometimes less so. Her last ill-fated adventure had quelled her wildness. She'd been as boring as a crypt mouse since her illness, no matter that she felt back to her hale, healthy self.

A half-full decanter of what she could only assume was illegally procured brandy from France sat beside four glasses on the sideboard, candlelight sparking off the crystal. She wrangled with her conscience only a moment before pouring herself a finger of liquor, anger at herself and all Society burning hot in her chest.

She tossed the brandy back like a shot. While it wasn't her first experience with liquor—her beloved brother had indulged her curiosity more than once, and her father allowed her the occasional glass of after-dinner port—she'd never experienced the river of fire she'd ignited with her rashness.

She coughed until her eyes watered. The blaze subsided and took on the feel of a warm bath in her belly. She straightened, wiped her eyes, and poured herself another finger. This time she sipped and savored her small rebellion.

A high-backed settee faced an ornate fireplace. The fire behind the grate had burned down to glowing coals. She sank onto the cushions and slipped her fan off her wrist. The names of her dance partners for the evening were scribbled along each rib. More than half were empty. Sir Wallace would be looking to claim his second dance of the evening soon. He could cool his heels and wonder where she was, because she was unavailable. A laugh of evil-tinged glee escaped at the picture she painted.

The solitude washed over her and banked her anger like the remains of the fire. Yet she wasn't at peace. Expectation crept through the room with each tick of the clock on the mantel. The lit candles and brandy made her wonder if the room would be used for an assignation this night.

The hairs on the back of her neck quivered and sent a shiver down her spine. She whipped around, but no one had sneaked in on her unawares. Shaking her head, she resettled herself on the cushion, but her senses remained on alert and her back refused to bend.

Delilah should have outgrown such nonsense. Her imagination had been the bane of her mother's existence. Her romp on the moors with only her daydreams as company had led to getting stuck in a mire for hours in the rain. A chest infection had taken root and had nearly finished her off, but she'd survived. Instead, it had been her honorable, brave, rule-following brother who had died on a battlefield in Portugal.

She quaffed the remaining liquor, plunked the glass on top of a leather-bound book lying on the mantel, and meandered to a set of windows flanked by heavy, dark curtains. She unlatched one side and pushed the pane open a few inches, breathing in coal-tinged night air. She missed Stoney Pudholme. London was dirty, raucous, and less welcoming than she'd thought.

The back garden appeared smaller from the second floor. A couple stealing a kiss behind tall shrubbery settled a melancholy sadness in her chest. Would she ever experience a loving embrace, or was she destined to marry a toad like Sir Wallace, not for love, but because it furthered her parents' ambitions?

She deserved one more tot to bolster her courage before returning to face a ballroom that secretly viewed her and her family with contempt. As she reached for her glass, a noise made her freeze. The latch of the hidden door jiggled.

She had a breath to decide what to do. Unable to tolerate the thought of being caught and giving an explanation, she tucked herself behind the brocade curtains. The rustle of a person entering the room rushed through the silence with the force of a flood. Her heart hammered through her veins and echoed in her head.

The embarrassment at Sir Wallace's assessment of her boringness would pale in comparison to her humiliation if she were caught hiding behind a set of curtains. Why hadn't she tittered an excuse and slipped away instead of acting like she was guilty of some misdeed? Her stomach gnawed on a stew of nerves. If luck shone upon her, whoever had entered would exit none the wiser to her existence.

She pressed her back against the wall and tried to control her trembling knees. The sliver of moonlight from the window on her right did nothing to illuminate what was going on beyond the curtain. She closed her eyes and reached out with her other senses.

Papers crinkled. Was the person reading? A book snapped shut. Delilah started. The curtains wavered, and she ceased breathing, expecting to be exposed.

"Damnation, where did he put it?" a male voice muttered. More papery noises. She grew light-headed and allowed herself shallow breaths.

The door snicked shut. Had the man left? No. A second set of footsteps.

"What are you doing here?" the first man whispered.

"Have you found it?" The raspy voice of the second man was edged with impatience.

"Do you suppose I'd be ransacking Harrington's bookshelf if I'd found it?" More rustling followed. "Well? This would go faster if you helped."

The curtains fluttered as one of the men passed within inches of her. On the stirred air, the scent of expensive cologne tickled her nose—spicy and masculine. The noise increased, and the thumps of books hitting the floor matched the uneven pounding of her heart.

She prayed they'd find whatever blasted book they were seeking and leave so she could rejoin the ball. She would be missed soon, if she hadn't been already. Her mother would worry herself into a fit of vapors. Lady Casterly, on the other hand, might well organize a search party, which would be even worse.

"I found it." While the first man's voice was low, it vibrated with triumph.

Delilah let out a slow breath of relief. It would all be over in a moment.

"Excellent. Hand it over." The second man's accent resonated with an upper-crust education and a penchant for intimidation. In other words, like most of the gentlemen of the ton.

"Hawkins has been after this information for a year."

"Give it to me, Quinton. I'll make sure he gets it. You can trust me."

Delilah shook her head slightly and bit the inside of her mouth until she tasted blood. *Don't trust him, Quinton!*

"I was tasked with this mission. I will see it done." Something that might have been suspicion hitched Quinton's voice, but she could also hear his uncertainty.

"I'll ask once more. The book, if you please." A threat lurked behind the man's politesse.

"I'm duty bound to deliver the information to Hawkins."

"Your loyalty will be your downfall. I'm rather sorry for this." The man's voice was cold and distant and didn't sound sorry in the least. Like a mouse sensing the flight of a hawk overhead, Delilah pressed into the wall, seeking a protection the unforgiving wood could not offer. Danger permeated the room.

"What in blazes? *You* betrayed us? But why?"

No answer was forthcoming. Grunts and curses punctuated the sound of fists hitting flesh. A fight, perhaps to the death, was occurring beyond her hiding place, and all she could do was clamp her hand over her mouth and remain still. Although her knees had turned to water, she was nowhere near a swoon.

Her expectations of what gentlemen did and did not do had been shattered by the evening's events. Perhaps she was boring and common and only just passable, but she wasn't dense. Not in the least. Whatever Quinton had found was worth more than her life. If the cold stranger found her, a polite offer to escort her back to the ballroom would not be offered.

A keening sound and a loud thud were followed by a spate of silence. Was it over? Was she alone? Her blood raced, and her mind picked over possibilities. Drowning in the tension, she peeked around the side of the curtain. Legs clad in black satin breeches were splayed on the floor, and a torso was hidden behind the settee. One of the man's silver-buckled shoes had come off, leaving his stocking-covered toes pointing toward the ceiling.

"Foolish, young pup," the other man said with his back toward her. The timbre of his voice fingered him as the man who had entered second, which meant the man on the floor was the unfortunate Quinton.

The second man's fine black evening clothes and polished riding boots indicated wealth, and his bearing spoke of maturity. Strangely, he wore a hat even inside. Not the tall hat of a gentleman, but a slouched hat more common with country gentry. It also did a fair job disguising the man's hair and face, which she supposed was the point.

What shot bone-chilling fear through her was the man's calm stillness. The fight had not left him with latent aggression or panic. In fact, he wasn't paying any attention to the man sprawled behind the settee. No, he stared toward the mantel. What was so interesting?

He tapped the edge of the glass she'd been drinking from before lifting it to the light and examining the small amount of liquor at the bottom. His black gloves cast long shadows against the bright crystal facets. Her heart crimped. She ducked her head back behind the curtain and curled her toes, hoping her slippers weren't sticking out. Her feet weren't exactly petite.

Light, nearly soundless, footsteps tread. In which direction? She squeezed her eyes shut, expecting to feel the whoosh of the curtains being drawn. Instead, the click of the door closing clanged like a bell of freedom. For a dozen more beats of her heart, she remained hidden. At the continued silence, she drew the curtain aside.

The intimidating man was gone. She shuffled from behind the curtains and stared at the legs of the man on the floor. They didn't so much as twitch.

"Sir? Mr. Quinton, I presume? Are you well?" Her mouth and throat were dry, and her voice was thin.

She felt like an utter nincompoop. Quinton obviously wasn't well, and he would need more help than she would be able to provide. Girding herself to seek Lord Harrington, she side-stepped to the door. The full sight of the man on the floor stopped her short.

Crimson spread over his white shirt and cravat like an ink stain, and his gray and silver waistcoat was wet with blood. Although no wound was visible, a five-inch narrow blade with a very pointy, deadly-looking tip had been discarded on his chest. But it was his eyes, staring vacantly at the ceiling, that shoved her closer to a swoon than she'd ever been.

The shake started in her legs and spread to every part of her. Even though her head told her there was nothing anyone could do to help the man now, she fell to her knees at his side. She picked up the knife between her thumb and forefinger. Her gaze shifted between the face of man and the knife.

Who was Hawkins? What book had Quinton been tasked to retrieve, and why was it worth killing for? The biggest question of all was what was she to do now? Find her parents or Lady Casterly? Seek Lord Harrington? What would the murderer do if she confessed all to the constable?

Another question popped into her head. Why *wasn't* she swooning or screaming or having a fit of hysterics like a normal young lady? A numb coldness held her frozen and distanced her from the moment as if she were immersed in a nightmare.

"Am I dreaming?" Her whisper echoed in the empty room.

~

"YOU AREN'T DREAMING." Marcus Ashemore, Lord Wyndam, stood with his back to the window.

A window that had been conveniently left cracked for his uninvited intrusion. The tools to pry it open weighed heavy in the pocket of his jacket, and he'd been overjoyed not to have to use them while perched on the narrow ledge too far off the ground for his comfort. Unfortunately, his joy was short-lived.

Much like the dead man bleeding out on the Aubusson rug.

The lady in white holding the deadly stiletto knife over the man's body was certainly a surprise. And not a good one. A drop of blood fell from the tip to spatter on her gown, the sight malevolently poetic and disturbing.

"Who in the blazes are you?" Marcus kept his voice low so as not to give her cause to scream the house down upon them. Although, seeing as how she was unfazed by the dead man, he assumed she didn't want to be caught red-handed either—literally, in her case.

"Who are *you*?" She scrambled to her feet, the knife still dangling awkwardly from her fingers.

When he stepped forward, she stepped back. A sprinkling of freckles across her nose lent a naivete that contrasted with the intelligence projected in her sharp dark eyes. Chestnut ringlets of hair drooped over her ears, the curls unspooling. Her hair was too thick and straight to conform to the current style. Her dress was high-necked, white, and demure with a blue sash, yet her womanly curves contrasted sharply with the childish bows and ruffles.

Pure innocence splashed with the blood of sin.

"Why did you kill him? Lover's spat?" Marcus gestured to the dead man but never took his eyes off her or her knife.

"No! Of course not. I didn't do anything. Why would you

18

think such?" Her voice sailed into a high squeak of shock, her fear palpable.

"Dead man. Knife." He pointed from the body to her. "Natural conclusion, wouldn't you say?"

"I didn't kill him. I was hiding when it happened." She gripped the handle of the knife more firmly now and pointed it at him. The assassin's instrument of death looked incongruous being held by this young woman in her debutante's dress. The way the blade wavered gave credence to her assertion of innocence.

Now that he was closer, Marcus recognized her calm was, in reality, shock. Her eyes were wide and her face pale. He knelt, keeping the body between them, and lay his fingers along the side of the man's neck. No rush of blood through veins could be detected. He sat back on his haunches and let his hands dangle between his knees. The complications piled up by the day.

"Did you see who did kill him?" He looked up at her.

Her mouth opened and closed, and her tongue darted out to daub her lips. She was weighing how much to tell him. Wise. "I was behind the curtain."

She had seen or heard something. The horror scrolling across her face hinted at a story. A story he needed to hear. Excitement quickened his heart. This was as close to a piece of the puzzle as he'd found since he'd vowed to clear his father's name of treason.

"What did you see? *Who* did you see?"

Her gaze darted to the dead man. Her face matched the white of her dress, and her trembles amplified. If she swooned, he would get nothing from her.

"Don't look at him. Look at me." He rose and injected a soft croon into his voice he usually reserved for his dog or his horses. "I won't hurt you."

"How can I possibly trust you?" Although suspicion ran rife through her words, her gaze was glued to his. Was she merely an innocent in the wrong place, or was she a player or pawn in the deadly game afoot?

"I'm all you have at the moment, lass."

"You're Scottish?"

He grabbed his heart as if she'd wounded him. "Half Irish, and I'm appalled you'd suppose otherwise." His attempt at humor did nothing to ease her mounting panic.

Muffled voices drifted from the hallway, and he mouthed a curse. Were they merely on the hunt for the gaming room, or were they searching for the book too?

The lady turned in a circle as if seeking an escape, her skirts floating around her ankles. He glanced over the wall, nearly missing the door. They couldn't be found. Not like this. One or both of them might be hauled off to Newgate for murder, and considering his tarnished family name, he would be hanged before the week was out.

Stalking by her, he grabbed a chair and shoved it under the door latch. It wasn't a terribly sturdy chair, but it would slow their discovery. Back at the window in a trice, he swung his leg over the sill.

The climb had been precarious enough for him in breeches and boots. How would a lady manage in skirts? She would have to manage though, because she was coming with him. While he was confident enough in her innocence of the murder, she was in possession of valuable information. Information the men on the other side of the door might view as a threat to be eliminated.

He couldn't allow it. She might very well hold the key to unlocking the mystery of his father's downfall and death. He needed time to coax it out of her. Time they could ill afford to waste.

The lady faced the door with the knife out, looking ready to fight to the death.

"Come on, then." He tried to quell his urgency, but it sneaked into his voice nonetheless.

"What?" She glanced over her shoulder at him.

He held out a hand. "We don't have much time."

"I can't... What about him?" She pointed at the dead man with the knife.

"There's nothing we can do to help him, and if we're caught, questions neither one of us wants to answer will be asked. Not to mention, it will be more than your dress that's ruined."

She blinked and swayed, as if the thought hadn't occurred to her, then she ran her free hand down her skirts, smearing more blood.

"My dress," she whispered.

Marcus couldn't have her swooning at this point. He pulled his leg back inside, grabbed her elbow, and tugged her toward the window. "You can fall apart after we've reached safety."

"But my mother. Lady Casterly." She planted her feet with more determination than he'd given her credit for and shifted as if she planned to exit the study and reenter the ballroom.

"You can't go back. Not covered in a dead man's blood," Marcus whispered as kindly as his impatience allowed.

The handle jiggled, and a voice called out, "I say, who's there? Let us in this instant."

Marcus gave her a little shake. "Make your decision. Are you coming with me or staying to face the consequences?"

CHAPTER 2

*D*elilah stared at the man's mouth. It had moved, and she was fairly certain he had asked her to follow him out of the second-story window. "Are you addlepated, sir?"

Those same lips twitched into the briefest of smiles. How could he find a smidgen of humor in the situation? One man was dead, his murderer might very well be dancing downstairs, and other men were beating down the door.

"There are some who say I most certainly am."

The door shook with the force being applied to open it. Did she dare go with a stranger out the window and into the unknown? Did she dare stay to attempt an explanation?

The murderer would no doubt hear her tale through the gossip mill, and then what? He wouldn't balk at killing a woman with a loose tongue. The man in front of her might be a scoundrel, but he was a scoundrel offering her an escape. A means to save herself and her reputation.

She could make her way home, sneak into her room, and burn her dress. She'd think of a story to satisfy her mother later. One involving a headache or tossing up her accounts and, most assuredly, *not* involving a murder.

Once upon a time, she would have been able to concoct a corker of a tale, but it had been a long while since she'd had an adventure outside her books. Adventures were dangerous, and people could die.

She could die.

For the past two years, her mother had drilled the importance of safety, decorum, and following a strict set of rules. Delilah was never to leave their rented town house without a maid and a footman. She was never to be alone with a gentleman. She was never to let herself get lost, because she might never be found.

Yet, even with the care she'd taken to follow her mother's rules, here she was covered in one man's blood and being urged out a window by another. She had landed herself smack in the middle of the kind of danger her mother lamented about. A tingle of excitement, despite the dire circumstances, had the hair on her nape wavering.

"I won't hang for this. Are you coming with me or not?" The man retreated to the window and gracefully swung a leg over. His vibrant green eyes drew her closer. Keeping her gaze on his as if they were tethered, she took a step, short and hesitant. Her next step was longer and more resolved. Her choices were bad and worse.

Banishing her mother's voice, she closed the distance between them and slid her ungloved, blood-smeared hand into the man's. His clasp was firm, his hand rougher than she'd imagined a gentleman's would be. But what did she know? Not counting her brother and father, she'd never touched a man's bare hand before. Perhaps all strange men's hands were this warm and strong and reassuring.

He swung his other leg over and stood on a foot-wide ledge. "Come out with me. I'll close the curtains and window to buy us some time."

The notes of a waltz drifted into the night air from the ballroom below. With any luck, the dance would draw everyone from the garden, leaving their unorthodox exit unobserved. She lifted her leg to cross the sill but hesitated. More than her ankle would be exposed.

"Look away, if you please."

She didn't miss his eye roll heavenward, but that's where his gaze stayed. She raised her skirts to her knees and scrambled over the sill to the ledge, her fingers seeking handholds on the rough bricks. Her foot slipped once, sending debris to rustle the bushes. Her entire body shook as if an earthquake was centered in her heart.

He pulled the draperies and closed the window. The barrier quieted the banging and distanced her from the dead man inside. She could almost convince herself she'd imagined it all. Except for the blood on her skirts. And her precarious position on the ledge.

The man shuffled to the right, toward the corner of the house where it was darkest. When he had gone six feet, he looked over at her and nudged his head in an unspoken command to move.

She did. One foot followed the other, her hands clamping onto the rough stone. The situation had spiraled out of her control as if she had been caught by a river current, one she wasn't strong enough to fight. So she didn't.

She matched the man's movements until they reached the corner. A downspout to catch rainwater ran to the ground. Another step, and she came face-to-face with the devilish face of a gargoyle standing sentinel.

Death. Hell. Purgatory. Which had she earned tonight? Her hand slipped off the stone. Unbalanced, she teetered, her other hand scrabbling for purchase. A garbled cry for help emerged.

The man pressed a hand against her back and pushed her against the wall. "Steady, lass." His whisper was as soft as the night breeze. "I'll shimmy down the pipe first."

The implication of his words did nothing to steady her. If he was to shimmy down first, that must mean she was next. She made the mistake of looking toward the ground. While it couldn't have been more than three body lengths, it felt as high as London Bridge. Dizziness swamped her, and she lay her forehead against the rough stone. "I can't."

"You must." He trailed his finger down her cheek.

The simple touch drew her attention from the bricks to his face. Light-colored stubble dotted his jaw, and laugh lines creased the corners of his eyes. His face had been burnished by the sun.

He is handsome. The thought registered with some surprise. She hadn't been in a state of mind to notice inside. Not that clinging to the side of a lord's town house during a ball while escaping a scene of carnage was a better locale to draw such a conclusion.

"Who *are* you?" she asked.

"I'm your only hope." Like a spider, he traversed down the pipe in only a few of her quickened breaths, making it look easy.

She glanced back at the window. The men must be in the room by now. They could look outside any second. The man stood under her, gesturing with both hands, his urgency pulsing to her. Although she was sure hours must have passed, the waltz was still playing. When it ended, the garden would flood with people.

She grabbed hold of the gargoyle's hooked nose but couldn't get her feet to move. Dear Lord, this is where her mother and Lady Casterly and the ton would find her. Dangling from a gargoyle's proboscis.

"You can do this." His voice lilted up to her. He wouldn't sound so confident if he knew her last adventure had ended in catastrophe.

She took a deep breath. Still holding on to the gargoyle, she dropped one foot down and wedged it into a crack in the stone.

Her slippered foot was pinched but stable. She did the same for her other foot. She lowered herself another few feet in the same method. The tiniest of smiles broke through the panic. She was going to make it.

A crack sounded. Untethered from the stone, she fell through nothing. A scream tore through her chest, but before she could free it, she made impact not with the ground but the man. She opened her eyes to the sky and felt as much as heard the man's groan.

"Blast and damn."

She was prone on top of him, her back to his front. "Are you injured, sir?"

His answer was to put them into motion again. This time, thankfully, they remained earthbound. He rolled her until she was on her back, partially hidden under some shrubbery, sticks poking her in various places. He scooted on top of her and pressed her down into the grass and dirt, his body lean, hard, hot.

It was scandalous, embarrassing, and… something else. Something that sent heat rushing through her body.

"Get off." She squirmed.

"Be still. They'll see us. Your dress is a bloody beacon."

She wasn't sure if he was being literal or had used a blasphemy. Did it really matter? She could hear voices now from above. The men were standing in the opened window. They had escaped by mere seconds.

"Did they take it?" The clipped words were emotionless.

"It's gone. How could this happen in my home?" It was Lord Harrington then, and he sounded truly horrified. "I only did this as a favor to Edward. What was in the damn book?"

"Not your concern."

"What are we going to do with the poor boy's body?"

"My people will handle the body and clean the mess before your servants see. Tell no one. This incident is not to make it to the gossip mongers, is that understood?" The threat was clear even to Delilah on the ground.

"Yes. Of course."

What sort of men killed without remorse, disposed of bodies, and threatened lords? And what kind of man was on top of her? If he was in search of the same book, what methods would he stoop to in order to obtain what he wanted? Murder? Lies?

"Should we give chase?" Harrington asked.

"Whoever he was, he was an experienced assassin. He'll be halfway across London by now."

"Gilmore should be warned."

"Let the office handle Gilmore. Forget this ever happened, Harrington."

She closed her eyes and wished she could do the same. She would spirit herself into her corner room and cozy canopied bed. She'd be safe with her mother on constant guard. Or would she? The danger Delilah had stumbled into wasn't like catching a chill, being caught alone with a gentleman, or getting lost on the moor.

The men's voices faded. Delilah pushed at the man's chest. This time he rose and held out a hand to her. She stared at it for only a heartbeat before allowing him to help her stand. Calluses along his palm made her suspect he was familiar with reins.

"We can slip out the side gate with none the wiser." He was already on the move, as quiet, graceful, and dangerous as the lion she'd seen pacing at the Tower menagerie.

She followed him not because she trusted him but because his plan was expedient. She could be home before her parents and send a note back for them. Her family had a rented town house only a brisk walk away. Alone. At night. It wasn't ideal, but needs must.

She stayed close to him. When he stopped, she bumped into

him. A wrought iron gate stood six feet tall, the hinges rusted and the ironworks peeling.

He shifted and examined her head to toe. "Your dress will attract undue attention on the streets."

Not only were her skirts covered in drying blood, but with dirt and grass stains as well. A shot of anger made her stand up straighter. She hadn't asked to bear witness to a murder.

"As soon as we step outside this garden, we will go our separate ways and pretend this never happened," she said.

Instead of launching into the argument she sensed brewing behind his narrowed eyes, he shrugged out of his jacket and swept it over her shoulders. "That should distract from the worst of the damage."

She slipped her arms through the sleeves, the cuffs brushing her fingertips and the shoulders drooping down her arm. The jacket was of quality superfine, but it was well-worn and headed toward shabby given another season of wear. She tugged the lapels close together and buried her nose in the collar, noticing one of the buttons was loose. It was warm from his body and smelled of green rolling hills, not the smoky, foggy city. Goose bumps rose along her arms even though she wasn't cold.

The gate swung open with nary a squeak, and as they passed through, the faint aroma of animal fat drew her attention to the hinges. They were shiny with grease. She cast a sideways look at the man by her side.

On his heels, she slipped through the mew's alley toward the bustle of the main thoroughfare. Carriages clogged the fashionable street. The mundane, familiar noises of horses and coachmen and the rattle of wheels calmed her racing heart. She matched his brisk pace, shoulder to shoulder now and heading away from Harrington's.

What excuse would fool her mother? Her mind whirled. An upset stomach was the only reasonable option. A sliver of the truth would make her tale go down with fewer questions. She could relay the conversation between Sir Wallace and Lord Nash. Her mother would understand her humiliation.

The man took her elbow and steered her toward a shadowy lane. She shook him loose and pointed. "My family's town house is this way."

"You must accompany me. I need to hear everything you observed. You are the lone witness to the night's dark deed."

"I only saw the back of the man for an instant, and he wasn't known to me. Neither was the dead man." She held her breath and his gaze. His eyes held no trace of the humor that had carved the lines at the edges.

"You can't traipse down this street in a bloodied dress with my jacket as your only protection." Although he tried for cajoling, there was a desperate sharpness she didn't like. "You'll be recognized, and then what? My rooms are just—"

"You are most definitely addlepated if you think I'm going to accompany you to your rooms. There's still a chance I can avoid ruination by returning home now."

"You care about your reputation when a man is dead, and a killer is on the loose?" The exasperation in his voice only fired her own ire higher.

The passions and impulses her mother had dedicated herself to stamping out in Delilah had never been extinguished, only dammed, and the night's events had punched countless holes in her control. The onslaught of emotions was overwhelming. Anger, sadness, and terror all jockeyed for dominance.

"What do I have except for my reputation, sir? What does any young lady have? If my reputation is ruined, my family loses their foothold into good Society where my father might expand his business. If I lose my reputation, my life will be forfeit to others' whims. If I lose it, what will I be?" She was regurgitating one of her mother's most recent lectures, "The Importance of a Reputation."

"What will you be? By my estimation, you'll remain a woman with quick wits and staunch courage."

Her mouth opened, but no retort was forthcoming. Tears burned her nose and eyes, and she blinked furiously. "I wasn't courageous at all. I cowered behind a curtain in fear while a man was murdered."

"Balderdash." He chafed her arms. "Most ladies would have swooned dead away and not had the presence of mind to hide. You would have been killed along with the poor man in the library."

"Quinton. His name was Quinton."

He ceased his soothing ministrations and gripped her arms. "The dead man?"

"Yes."

"I thought you didn't know him."

"I didn't. The second man—the killer—called the first man by that name."

"What else can you tell me about the killer?"

"He wore a slouched hat like a country squire." She needed to get home before her mother and father raised the alarm. Plus she didn't want to dissect and relive the moment. "I must go."

He gave her a little shake, not releasing her. "What did the killer sound like?"

"Normal, I suppose."

"What do you mean, normal?"

"Like anyone at the ball. His evening clothes and boots were very fine, and his voice..." She looked away and bit her bottom lip.

While his accent was that of a thousand other well-bred gentleman educated at Eton, something intangible and cold, like an etching in stone, set it apart.

"You believe he is part of the ton?" he asked.

"*He* didn't need to come in through the window. I assume he was invited." She raised her brows.

"Point taken." The small flare of amusement in his face faded quickly. His mouth was set in a grim line, and he nodded as if coming to a sudden decision. "Wait here while I hail a hackney."

A sigh of relief gusted from her. She would be home with no one to bear witness to her scandalous behavior. Except the strange Irishman, of course. He returned and herded her to the curb and into the waiting hackney.

"I have no coin, I'm afraid." She settled onto the lumpy squab and rattled off her address.

The man spoke to the jarvey, but his words dimmed under the roar in her ears as a sudden realization jolted her. She hadn't brought her reticule to the ball, but she was missing something else. Her dance fan. She'd left it on the settee. Who had found it? The killer or Lord Harrington? Neither scenario boded well.

The hackney rumbled on its way. Only when the blur of fine townhomes gave way to an unknown section of town did the reality of her situation hit her. She wasn't pointed toward safety and her home. She was being kidnapped.

"Where are we going? Take me home immediately!"

"Now, lass, I can't do that." His mild, apologetic voice sounded as though he were informing her the kitchens were out of scones, not that he was abducting her.

She judged the distance to the door and wondered if she could throw herself free of the hackney without getting run over by another carriage or trampled by a horse. The way her night was progressing, it was doubtful. "I've told you everything."

"You may believe that to be the case, but shock is keeping you from remembering everything. Besides that, a killer roams. A killer only you can identify. You may well be in danger."

"But… but he didn't see me. I was hidden." While what she said was true, she pictured the man examining the glass she'd discarded, and what of her fan? Had he found it? Could the man deduce her identity based on her dance partners or lack thereof? Would he feel the need to eliminate even the slightest connection to the murder?

The hackney jerked to a stop. The man glanced out the window. "My rooms."

She tightened his jacket around her. "I can't accompany you to your rooms, sir."

"I'll take care no one recognizes you." He swung out of the hackney and looked up and down the street. "You can't return home in your state."

She didn't move. "Are you telling me you have a spare dress in your rooms?"

A small twitch at the corners of his mouth betrayed a natural good humor the night's events had stymied but not smothered. "I will procure you a clean dress."

She had no coin for a hackney and no idea how to navigate the streets home. Plus he was correct. Her dress would draw too much attention. Still, she hesitated.

He cocked his head and lay a hand over his heart. "My word as a gentleman, I have no evil designs on you. Anyway, we'll not be unchaperoned. My valet is upstairs and will vouch to my good character."

She knew what his bare hand felt like in hers and what his body felt like stretched out over hers, yet she didn't have a notion who he was. "I don't even know your name," she whispered.

"Marcus Ashemore." He executed a bow. "And you are?"

"Delilah Bancroft."

"Delilah. How charming."

The use of her given name was a breech in etiquette her mother would never forgive, but hearing it lilt off his tongue stopped her knee-jerk reaction to correct him.

She slid her hand into his once more and allowed herself to be guided into the darkened building and up a flight of stairs to the second floor like they were a pair of birds in flight. Male laughter and conversation filled the hall and stairways, but no actual man spotted her. Breathless, she kept her head down as he unlocked the door and ushered her inside.

A single candle on the mantel cast a half circle of wavery light, revealing a worn brocade chaise, a squat bookcase with only a few volumes, and a faded rug with frayed tassels. The room might be cramped and the furnishings shabby, but it was neat and smelled fresh.

Marcus made straight to a small table holding a bottle of liquor, poured himself a tot, and knocked it back with relish. Still holding his glass, he wiped his mouth with the back of his hand and raised his brows. "Would you like a glass?"

Remembering the warmth the liquor had imparted in the study before everything went to hell, she nodded. However false, she needed a small measure of comfort. "Please."

He poured a glass and handed it to her before refilling his own. Instead of quaffing the entire amount as he was doing, she took a sip and blinked against the burn.

Faint whistling grew louder, and an older man with flaming-red hair entered the room. His surprise to find them there was comical. He clutched his chest, his thick, fuzzy eyebrows jumping high. "Ach, lad. You crept in without me knowing." His voice was a hair too loud and echoed through the room.

In turn, Marcus raised his voice. "You wouldn't hear an elephant breaking down the door, O'Connell."

While the man was obviously hard of hearing, there was nothing dull about his blue eyes. "And who might this be? Surely you haven't involved her in your mischief? Is that blood on the lass's frock? Ach, laddie." He shook his head in a parental disappointment so familiar to Delilah she almost smiled.

"Why do you assume I'm to blame?" Marcus's Irish lilt thickened as he spoke to the man. "I saved her from certain ruin and possible death, thank you very much."

"Death seems a bit dramatic, don't you think?" Delilah interjected.

"No, I don't. You would have been sacrificed without a second thought by these men." The solemn truth in his voice had her taking a larger sip of her drink.

"O'Connell, may I present Miss Bancroft. It is miss and not lady?" At her nod, Marcus continued, "And this is Mister Conn O'Connell, horse trainer, valet, and my trusted companion since I was in short pants." Affection warmed Marcus's voice. A man who held a servant in such high regard couldn't be all bad, surely? Her inclination to trust him gained momentum despite the detour he'd forced upon her.

The old man dropped his voice to a stage whisper. "Whose blood does it be?"

"A man named Quinton. I'm not sure of his role, but he was killed this evening by an unknown player." Marcus rubbed his stubbled jaw. "Miss Bancroft needs a clean dress. Any ideas on how to acquire one?"

"A secondhand shop?" The man sent an assessing gaze over her frame as if sizing her up.

"We need something tonight, so she can return home before dawn."

O'Connell hummed. "Lemme see what I can scrounge up." He slipped out of the rooms, leaving them alone.

The lack of a proper chaperone was the least of her worries. She had witnessed a murder, climbed out the window, accompanied a stranger to his rooms, ruined her dress and possibly her reputation, and lest she forget, her dance fan might be in the hands of a killer.

Her stomach gave a heave, and she directed her focus on what she could control. "Whether my dress is bloody or not, how am I to avoid ruin? When will you take me home? My parents will be frantic."

He topped off their glasses and gestured toward the settee.

Delilah hesitated until he sat, and then she took the opposite end. He sprawled in the corner, his head lolling on the back.

"It's a bloody awful mess, and I'm not referring to your pretty frock," he said softly. The lilt in his voice softened the curse. He raised his head. "I need you to relay what happened in that study. Every word that was said. Every detail, even if it seems inconsequential." Lines had deepened around his mouth. He was a desperate man. What would he do if she denied him?

"I want to forget it ever happened." She took a sip and gripped the glass tighter. In contrast to her threadbare surroundings, the glass was heavy and expensive. Perhaps a family heirloom.

He leaned closer but didn't touch her. "Please, Delilah."

"Who is the Edward who gave the book to Harrington for safekeeping? Do you know him?" What sort of "mischief" was Marcus involved in?

"Edward is—" Marcus paused and cleared his throat, "—*was* my father."

Feeling as if any words were inadequate, she settled for a softly whispered, "I'm so sorry."

"These men framed my father for treason. I want to make them pay and clear my father's name, but I can't prove anything. Yet." Pain and anger squat next to him like guests who had long overstayed their welcome. "Please help me."

O'Connell banged through the door with an emerald-green dress draped over his arm. The fabric was shiny and thin-looking. "It's the best I could find, laddie."

"It will have to do." Marcus rose and held out his hand. "Would you like to clean up and change?"

"Water should still be warm. Come with me, lass," O'Connell said.

She followed O'Connell into a bedchamber with the same shabby feel as the sitting room. A man's bedchamber. *Marcus's* bedchamber. Her face heated.

O'Connell laid the green dress at the foot of the bed, rumbled a fake-sounding cough, and backed toward the door without meeting her eyes. "I'll leave you to change, shall I, lass? Give us a shout if you need anything."

She nodded, but he was already gone, the door snicking shut behind him. With only a moment's hesitation, she locked it. Trust had become a scarce commodity.

She held up the green dress and gasped, surprised she could still be shocked after the events of the evening. The bodice scooped lower than anything her mother had approved for her at the modiste. Which was worse—a bloodstained frock or a scandalous one?

It took some maneuvering and flexibility and a torn seam, but finally her ruined dress puddled around her ankles. Her chemise also bore stains. She daubed at them with the warm water and ended up smearing them. Giving up, she focused on her hands and scrubbed long after they were clean, feeling as though Quinton's blood had worked its way under her skin, leaving her forever tainted.

In the small looking glass propped on the wash stand, she gasped at the sight of her hair. The clustered curls that had looked so jaunty at the start of the evening drooped like flowers left to wilt in the sun.

She yanked the pins out and left the thick mass to hang loose around her shoulders. She'd been vain about her chestnut-colored hair before coming to London and being confronted with the elegant blond, blue-eyed English roses with smooth porcelain skin, willowy bodies, and perfectly coiffed hair.

The trauma of the evening reflected in her pale face and shadowed eyes. She pinched her cheeks to bring some color back, and finger combed her hair, trying to instill order, but it was hopeless. From her hair to her freckles to her frame, she was woefully out of fashion in every way. Plain. *Barely* passable.

What did it matter? Marcus certainly wasn't a suitor but a…

what? A captor? A savior? He'd promised to escort her home, but he wanted something from her in return. Information. Did the little she knew hold value? What would he do if she refused him?

She shuddered and looked around to discover more about the man. The room was as spare and neat as if he were a monk. His shaving implements were lined up next to the basin, cleaned and ready for their next use.

The bed was made, and she picked up the single book on the stand and flipped through it. Detailed drawings and descriptions of horses lined the pages—different breeds' musculature and organs.

She opened the wardrobe and riffled through a stack of shirts. They were unremarkable except for several lines of tidy stiches along the sleeves of almost every one. Did the man routinely enter into knife fights?

A jacket in a similar state to the one he'd draped over her shoulders hung on a hook alone and forlorn. A pair of patched leather breeches were folded underneath. She checked the pockets and the crannies of the wardrobe but turned up nothing that shone a light on whether Marcus Ashemore was a villain or her hero.

Unable to procrastinate any longer, she stepped into the green dress, slipped her arms into the puff sleeves, and pulled the bodice up. There was too much fabric at her slippers and not enough at her bosom. She tugged and shimmied, but the top swells of her breasts remained exposed. Even worse, she couldn't reach the tapes, leaving a sizable draft along her shoulders.

Holding the too-scant fabric to her chest, she unlocked and cracked the bedchamber door open. Marcus stood to the side of the window, peering around the edge of the curtains. She cleared her throat. He looked over his shoulder, then fully turned, never taking his eyes from hers.

"I can't reach the fastenings." She swallowed and presented her back to the crack in the door.

His footsteps were light and quiet. She tensed, her insides squirming in dread at his touch. Or was that anticipation? Her world had gone topsy-turvy over the course of a few hours, and she couldn't categorize her emotions.

His fingers made contact with her skin, warm and glancing. Gathering her hair, he pushed the mass over one shoulder and made deft work of the tapes, as if this wasn't the first time he'd played a lady's maid. The bodice hugged her chest. She dropped her hands and looked down.

"Dear Lord," she murmured. Perhaps it wasn't as risqué as the dresses of the more daring ladies of the ton, but it was far beyond the pale for a debutante to wear such a revealing dress in a color reserved for married women.

Marcus remained behind her. Strangely, she could feel his heat even though he wasn't touching her. "Are you well?"

"To be honest, I've been better."

"I'm sorry you got mixed up in this sad, sorry business." He moved away. "I have tea if you'd like some."

"Yes, please."

She gathered her bloodied dress and joined him in the sitting area. Marcus and O'Connell were in discussion close to the window. She guessed Marcus would have preferred it to be private, but O'Connell was incapable of whispering.

"Eh? Special characters?" O'Connell asked. "What makes them so special?"

"Not special. *Suspicious*. Anyone loitering in the street or alley. Don't speak to them. Just make a note and come back."

"Aye, lad." O'Connell's eyebrows were low over his eyes, almost camouflaging them as he slipped out the door.

She was alone with Marcus. Again.

CHAPTER 3

*T*roubled, Marcus scrubbed a hand over his jaw as he surveyed the street from his third-floor window. The man standing at the mouth of the alley might have nothing to do with the evening's events, but his intuition told him otherwise. His quest to discover the truth and clear his father's name had not gained him admirers, and he realized now he'd been foolish to bring Delilah to his rooms. If he was being followed, then he'd put her in even more danger.

"Is something amiss?" Her voice trembled, and he turned to give her assurances he couldn't support with facts.

He froze. He swallowed. He blinked. Words deserted him when he needed them desperately to finesse the truth from her.

The shiny green fabric of the dress looked cheap and was far too revealing for an innocent like her. But in the dress and with her hair loose, Delilah looked far from innocent.

The expanse of skin and curves had his mouth drying and gaping open, words a foreign concept. The dress skimmed her body and puddled at her feet. Her thick hair was no longer forced into ridiculous clusters of curls but tumbled past her shoulders in waves. Striations of chestnut and caramel sparked in the candlelight.

With a jolt, he concluded she was pretty in the way of a milkmaid. His mind skidded back to the moment in the garden when he'd rolled her under him. It had been a necessary ruse, but he hadn't been completely unaware of the way their bodies fit together.

She shifted and crossed her arms under her breasts, emphasizing their shadowy curves. "What's amiss?" she asked again more stridently.

He cleared his throat. "Nothing. Nothing at all."

"You're lying to me, aren't you?"

If a young woman of little experience could see through him so easily, how was he to ferret out the information he required from England's trained spies?

"We should burn your dress." He took the crumpled, bloody mass of white.

Stirring the remnants of coal in the fireplace, he used a poker to shove the dress under the ash. It caught in a hot blaze.

He gestured to the worn settee, and they sat and stared at the licking flames eating the fabric.

"Will you tell me again? Every word. Everything you remember." He tried to keep the desperation out of his voice even though he was feeling quite desperate indeed.

"Were you close with your father?"

Her question felt like a test. How to answer? His father had been his hero. A giant of a man. Important. Too busy and away too often. His visits with Marcus in Ireland had been filled with fun and adventure, but what did he really know of his father? Very little, he was coming to understand.

"I loved him." Embarrassingly, his voice cracked, but his answer seemed to satisfy her.

"Were you meeting with Quinton for information?" Her stare was intense and slightly accusatory.

"Of course not. I would have picked a less dangerous and easier-to-reach assignation if that were the case. Tonight was the first I've heard his name."

"Were you on the hunt for the mysterious book then?" At his reluctant nod, she asked, "What's in it?"

"I'm not entirely certain, but I hope it holds the truth." He sighed and ran a hand over his jaw.

"The truth of what?"

"The truth of what my father was involved in during the last months of his life."

"Why would the book be hidden in Lord Harrington's library?"

"Lord Harrington and my father were friends. My father must have been in fear for his life. Quinton was killed because the book points the finger at those who would commit treason against England."

"Treason?" Delilah sounded suitably appalled.

With the war against Napoleon dragging on, the strain on English institutions had begun to show cracks with discontent welling out, but there were some who never wanted the war to end. It had become too profitable.

"The information in that book is the key to my father's death. Now it's been taken, and I don't know where else to look. Did you hear anything else? Names or places or… *anything*?" He was ready to fall to his knees and beg when she rose to pace, the borrowed dress swirling around her legs and feet like liquefied emeralds in the snapping firelight.

"Quinton was to deliver the book to someone named Hawkins."

"Hawkins!" Marcus popped to standing with a sudden burst of energy.

She spun to face him. "You are acquainted with him?"

"By name only. He doesn't often circulate among Society, but he casts a long shadow across Westminster."

"He works for the good of England then?"

Did he? While Hawkins was rumored to be England's spymaster, could he have been lured by the promise of coin to commit treason? "Ostensibly, yes, but I trust no one."

"Quinton had been tasked to retrieve the book and said he was honor bound to deliver it to Hawkins. Once the man in the hat confronted him, Quinton turned accusatory. 'You betrayed us,' he said."

"Those were his exact words?" Marcus gripped her upper arms and squeezed to draw her gaze to his. He could detect no guile, only a sincerity born of fear.

"Yes. Quinton seemed shocked, as if he'd trusted his killer. What does it mean?"

"It means I must find the man in the hat. He has the book, is most likely a traitor, and he's definitely a murderer. What do you recall of him?"

She closed her eyes, tipped her face up to his, and tugged her bottom lip between her teeth in an unconsciously sensual way. Anyone observing them might assume they were lovers on the cusp of a kiss. "He was tall and elegant, and except for the rather unfashionable hat, he was well-heeled."

"Anything else?"

"His scent was distinctive."

"How so?"

She leaned in to sniff him. "You smell of the outdoors. Fresh and green. This man smelled of spices and darkness."

Marcus blinked while he wrapped his head around her lyrical description. "Would you recognize him if you happened across him in a ballroom?"

Her gaze skated to where her dress had turned to blackened ash in the grate. "I might."

It wasn't a no. His urge to hug her close in gratitude was almost too strong to deny.

The creak of the door opening cut him away from her. The

anxiety pulling O'Connell's mouth into a tight frown told Marcus enough.

"Three blokes, laddie. All rough-looking sorts. One in the alley. Two on either corner. Who sent them?"

"Someone who doesn't like the questions I've been asking. Hawkins perhaps."

"Or the killer," Delilah said darkly.

Marcus met her gaze and swallowed hard. "Perhaps. Although I don't see how he could have known of my involvement tonight. And you were hidden."

"Whoever sent them, how are we to sneak away? I must return home."

"If we assume they know what I look like and that my only companion is my valet, then perhaps we don't sneak away." Marcus rubbed his jaw and shot a meaningful glance toward O'Connell. "It's time for the case."

"Ach, yes, I think you're right, laddie." O'Connell bustled into the bedchamber.

"What case? And what if one or both of your assumptions are incorrect?" Delilah stared at the door O'Connell disappeared through.

"These men are after me, not you. If they nab me, they'll let you go." He tried to sound confident, but the narrowed gaze she swung toward him told him he'd failed.

"That's being rather optimistic."

"You haven't even heard my plan." At the rise of her brows, he continued. "In my experience, people see what they expect to see. What they wouldn't expect is to see a drunkard exiting the building with his doxy."

Her mouth dropped open with a gasp. "I assume the part of doxy is mine to play?"

"I'm afraid the dress won't fit me." He tried on a smile that had been called charming once or twice, but he was obviously out of practice, because she remained stony-faced.

"I'm not a… a… whore," she whispered.

"Of course, you aren't. And I'm not a drunkard, but if we put on a good enough show, we'll fool the men outside and escape unharmed. The other option is to scale the rooftop to an adjacent building."

She shook her head with a vehemence that made her hair swing around her shoulders. "Oh no. I've had a lifetime's worth of inching along ledges. You really think they wish to harm us?"

Best-case scenario had the men kidnapping and questioning him. Marcus assumed it wouldn't be in a drawing room over tea and biscuits. Worst case, he would end up like Quinton. He couldn't bear to think what they would do to Delilah. "I'm afraid so."

"But won't they recognize you even pretending to be a drunkard?"

On cue, O'Connell returned holding a black leather case a foot square and six inches deep. It had been acquired from an actor on Drury Lane. Marcus set the case on the table, unlatched it, and opened the lid. Hair pieces including a mustache and beard and pots of various tints were arranged neatly inside. Everything an actor might need to assume a variety of stage roles.

Marcus plucked out a wig of jet black and used his reflection in the window to position it over his sandy brown hair. The wig was surprisingly comfortable. The hair was longer than his own and tickled the back of his neck and swept over his forehead. He turned and held his hands up. "Different enough to throw them off the scent?"

"Very different. If it weren't for your eyes…" She stared at him and blinked, her lips parting before giving a brisk shake of her head. "What do I need to do to convince them of my role?"

"The dress is a fine start, and once we're out the door, you only need to follow my lead."

Marcus sprinkled the brandy left in his glass over his jacket and then gave O'Connell a hug. He didn't need to tell O'Connell what to do if he didn't return. Contingency plans had been made long before. It didn't stop O'Connell from looking worried and whisper-yelling, "You take care, laddie, or I'll whip you meself."

Marcus took Delilah's hand and tugged her out the door and to the first-floor landing, stopping to reassess the situation. A shadow moved across the lane.

"You reek of liquor," she whispered.

"That's the point, lass," he whispered back before wrapping an arm around her waist and pulling her flush with his body. He raised his voice and added a slur. "What a pretty thing you are."

He slapped the front door open with the heel of his hand and stumbled down the stairs in fits and starts. Delilah clutched his shoulders to maintain her balance. Perfect. Once at street level, he spun Delilah so she was pressed against the stone wall. He hoped her gasp was one of surprise and not pain. He pushed his leg between hers and dropped his mouth to her ear. She arched against him and tilted her head so he could access her neck. Excellent.

"Almost there." He tangled his fingers in her hair and forced her head back. Maintaining an inch between his lips and her heated, feminine-scented skin, he trailed his lips down her throat to her collarbone.

He tried to ignore the quickened pulse of his heart and concentrated on the threat surrounding them. A breathy moan escaped her lips, and she writhed against him. An unwelcome reaction occurred. His cock stiffened to half-mast. Delilah was too good of an actress.

"Do you keep a room close to the market?" His voice, forced absent of any Irish lilt, echoed off the stone. "We'll have no privacy for a good tupping on the street."

"Y-yes. Close to the market." Her breathlessness could be

attributed to fear or arousal or nerves, but he couldn't allow her to say more or her genteel accent would give them away.

"Good. I'm near to bursting. Let's not dawdle." He put his arm around her shoulders and stumbled against her.

From the corner of his eye, he could see one of the men on the corner take a hesitant step toward them and then another. They were almost to the circle of light cast by the lantern hanging from the post. It would be their downfall. He tugged Delilah into a doorway carved into the stone. The shadows afforded a small amount of cover. It also afforded them no escape.

Once again, he nuzzled her ear. "One of the men is coming closer."

Her chest jerked against his in a sharp breath that only made him more aware of the swell of her breasts, milky white and ever so tempting in the darkness. "What should I do?" she whispered.

"Hold me. Act like you want me." Marcus didn't need to act like he wanted Delilah. In spite of the danger—or perhaps because of it—his blood pounded through his veins, heightening his every sense.

"I've never…"

Of course she hadn't, but neither of them had a choice if they wanted to meet the sunrise alive. "Pretend you want me, or we're lost, lass."

She snaked one of her arms inside his jacket to clutch the back of his shirt and wrapped her other hand around his nape to pull his face down to hers until they were cheek to cheek and her breath stirred the fake hair at his temple.

Her body molded against his from chest to thighs, and he had a moment's disquiet knowing she could feel the semi-hardened length of him against her hip. If she was new to a man's embrace, she might not even realize the significance of his body's reaction.

And that's all this rush of desire was. A natural reaction to having a woman in his arms after too long. Not having to pretend to be off-balance, he stumbled and landed with his back against the side of the alcove, his legs braced wide and bearing her weight.

He cupped her head, his fingers caught in the silken web of her hair, and stared down at her shadowed face. Her eyes were half-lidded, and her lips parted on her quickened breaths.

No woman deserved her first kiss in a stinking lane under duress. A lady like Delilah should be kissed for the first time under a sun-dappled oak with a spring breeze ruffling her hair.

His nose glanced hers in a caress, once, twice, three times. She nuzzled closer, and her lips skimmed his jaw an inch from his lips. The hairs on the back of his neck prickled. His nerves vibrated with the overwhelming desire to press her against the stones and do wicked, depraved things to her body.

"Delilah." Her name emerged on a begging, whispering groan. His lips came within a butterfly's wing of touching hers, but he restrained himself. Barely.

"Marcus." Her whisper-hiss of his given name sent shivers down his neck. "Is it working?"

"Working?" If she was asking whether her touch was driving him to the brink of madness, then, yes, it was working spectacularly.

"The men. Are they fooled?" She clutched his nape, but when she inched her hand up to grasp his hair, he reached around and stopped her. Their precarious situation registered like a gong. He'd almost lost control of the situation and himself. If she pulled the hair piece off his head, their only option would be to run for their lives.

The man was halfway across the lane and shuffling closer, peering at them. How far did Marcus have to go to throw the brutes off the scent? A tupping in the alley? While his body was all in, a heaviness he recognized as his tattered honor stamped the idea into oblivion.

"He's coming closer. I apologize most profusely, Delilah."

"For wha-a-a-a—"

He interrupted her query by smoothing his hand down the elegant curve of her spine to cup her buttock. Squeezing the firm mound, he tucked her closer, his cock cradled against the softness of her belly.

Any other gently bred woman would have swooned a thousand times over confronted with the gauntlet fate had assembled for Delilah this evening. The woman in his arms only arched her back and gasped in a distinctly non-horrified way that injected more heat in Marcus's blood.

The man from the corner retreated, a lecherous smile across his face. It was time to make good their escape, yet he didn't have the strength to separate them. She was the Delilah to his Samson.

The thought kindled enough humor to get his brain churning on their problems and not the attraction burning between them. His lips moved against her temple. "It's now or never."

Her response wasn't as urgent as he'd hoped. Or rather, it was urgent in an entirely different way. She hummed and clamped her fingers on to the muscle of his shoulder. His eyes closed instinctively as tingles shot to every extremity.

A glance to his right showed a second man had joined the first to watch them. They had fooled the men, but for how long? He scraped his gentlemanly resolve from where it had taken an undignified dive to the pavers and put inches between them.

"Follow me," he whispered for her benefit. For the men watching, he said, "Let's fly to your rooms, my ladybird."

His knees were embarrassingly shaky, which gave his stumbling, weaving gait an unexpected authenticity. In a stroke of good luck, a hackney plodded toward them and stopped to disgorge two very drunk gentlemen. Marcus handed Delilah up, gave the jarvey the address she'd given earlier, and joined her in the stale-smelling cab on the opposite squab. She was silent, giving no clue as to her state of mind. Did she want to kiss him or kill him?

He took her hands and chafed them between his. "How are you bearing up?"

Her voice, when it came, was bitten short with what might be frustration or fury. "Bearing up? My life was a simple one until I met you."

"Your life had become complicated before I climbed through the window."

The fight leaked out of her like water in broken crockery. She sagged on the squab and covered her eyes with a hand as if that would help her hide from the reality of her dire situation. "Ugh. You're right, of course. I only have my bruised feelings to blame."

"How are your bruised feelings to blame for any of this?"

"I was hiding in that blasted room because I overheard something rather unflattering about myself."

"Who said what?" All Marcus's frustration—sexual and otherwise—was directed at whoever had hurt Delilah's feelings.

"It's not important. Not anymore."

He grasped her wrist and pulled her hand away from her eyes. Her gaze met his for an instant before skating away to watch the passing town houses through the grimy window, but for an unguarded moment, he could see the hurt she had been running from.

"It's important to me." He forced a calmness he didn't feel into his voice.

"Is it?" She swung back around to glare at him. "Why? You're only interested in what I've seen and how I can help you clear your father's name."

"That's not entirely true."

"But it is mostly true." Bitterness flavored her words. "It seems the *gentlemen* of London only wish to use me to their ends."

"Delilah…" What could he say? She was the only one who could identify Quinton's killer. He had to find the man by whatever means possible.

But that was for the morrow. Tonight his mission was to return Delilah unharmed and unruined. The hack slowed to a stop. The town house was more than respectable and far more elegant than his ramshackle rooms.

When she made a move to push the door open, he barred the way with his arm. "Do you have a plan?"

"I'll sneak through the gardens and to my room up the servants' stairs."

"What excuses will you offer?"

She heaved a sigh and looked over at him, her mouth tight. "I'm a bit out of practice, but I'll think of something satisfying, I'm sure."

With that, she was gone in a flash of green.

CHAPTER 4

*D*elilah only made it as far as the first step of the servants' stairs. The quick tap of shoes along the hall was only too familiar. Her mouth dried, and her mind shuffled through excuses, discarding one after another. The risqué dress she wore was a problem she had no idea how to explain away. On the other hand, her bloodied white frock would have been an even bigger problem.

"Where have you been? You disappear from Harrington's and turn up hours later. I almost had a fit of the vapors," her mother hissed at her.

"It's nothing to worry about. I can explain everything." Two lies told. How many more would leave her lips?

Her mother moved closer, the light from the candle she held spilling onto the shiny green fabric. Delilah's hand twitched with an urge to imitate a piece of fichu and cover her décolletage.

"Come with me." Her mother whirled, her flower-embroidered dressing gown whipping around her. Delilah lifted the hem of the too-long dress and followed her mother into the study, which was thankfully absent her father.

"Did anyone see you?" Her mother's voice was strangely calm as she paced in front of the cold fireplace. Even though her father possessed a fortune, he retained the frugal mentality of a butcher's son.

"No one." While it wasn't strictly true, Marcus wouldn't count in her mother's mind. He wasn't an important member of Society.

"Perhaps we can salvage this."

"Does Father know?"

"He believes you left early because of a stomach indisposition. Only Lady Casterly and I know you disappeared without a word to anyone." Her mother stopped, grabbed the edge of the desk, and stared off to the side as if she couldn't bear to look at Delilah. "Who is he?"

"My dress was ruined. I couldn't return to the ball without causing a scandal. My new acquaintance procured me this dress and put me in a hackney. Nothing happened." Delilah swallowed. Even though the bones of her excuse were true, it sounded ridiculous even to her own ears. Had word of the murder reached the gossipmongers? "Was there any excitement after I left?"

Her mother ignored the question to fire back one of her own. "Are you still a maiden?"

"Of course! I'm not ruined." The half-truth kindled a wildfire in her cheeks.

While she was still a maiden, she was no longer wholly innocent. The feel of Marcus's body pressed into hers had altered her forever. He had imprinted on her. Yet he hadn't even kissed her. Much to her shame, she would have welcomed the liberty. She had craved a taking that had never come.

Later, in the darkness of her room, she would dissect every nuance of their embrace, from the tickling of his whiskers against her lips to the delicious grip of his hand on her bottom.

For now though, she had to lock the blazing memory away and hope it didn't burn her to cinders.

"You can be ruined by rumors even if you weren't ruined by deed," her mother said with a calm coldness that was more worrisome than anger. No tears or wrath or guilt would be laid on her shoulders? "You missed your dance with Sir Wallace. He was most disappointed."

Delilah was filled with remorse. Not because of the missed dance, but because she understood the pain her recklessness had inflicted two years ago on top of the toll her brother's death had taken.

"I'm sorry, Mother," Delilah said softly, backing toward the door. "It won't happen again."

As quick as a snake, her mother took hold of Delilah's wrist in an implacable grip. "Indeed, it will not. We will never speak of this night again. Go to your room and burn that monstrosity of a dress. It's obvious to me now that you need a settling hand as soon as possible."

"What does that mean?" Dread overtook her remorse.

"You need a husband, gel." Her mother's demeanor softened, and she touched Delilah's hair so lightly it felt like a butterfly landing. "Don't fret. Sir Wallace will make a fine husband, and once you have a babe or two, your life will make sense. You're too high strung and not at all strong since your illness."

Her mother had used the same excuse over and over the past two years to keep Delilah under her watchful, protective gaze. Delilah had even been grateful for the mothering she'd received those first months while recovering from the lung malady.

When news of Alastair's death in Portugal fighting Napoleon arrived while she was in the throes of her own battle, her mother's grief had transformed into an all-consuming need to keep Delilah safe.

Once Delilah was recovered, however, it hadn't taken long

for her mother's restraints to chafe, but guilt had kept her obedient.

Until now. She refused to marry Sir Wallace.

"We'll have callers tomorrow. You need sleep to look your best." Her mother's forced lightness grated. "We don't want Sir Wallace to question your ability to bear him strong sons."

Her mother spoke from a place of love, but it had been twisted into something ugly. Panic made Delilah want to run away and play pretend the way she had as a child. She missed the easy innocence of the days when her father was a modest merchant, her brother's laughter boomed from their cottage, and the smell of her mother's baking would draw her home.

"I'll go to my room now, Mother." Delilah slipped away and padded up the stairs.

Thankfully, no servants witnessed her duck inside wearing the garish dress. She struggled to remove the dress, finally wrenching herself free. Kneeling in front of the grate with the fabric spilling from her outstretched hand, she hesitated as the orange glow made the green dress sparkle. A shiver ran through her body. Changing her mind, she folded the dress and tucked it onto a high shelf in her wardrobe.

After slipping into a night rail, Delilah climbed under the covers and closed her eyes, but they immediately popped back open when all she saw was the dead man staring vacantly back at her. Did Quinton have a family who would miss him? A mother, a sister, or perhaps even a wife and children?

She grabbed a pillow and hugged it to her chest, which summoned a different set of eyes. Green eyes that were very much alive, dancing with mischief and beckoning her with a promise of adventure.

When she finally drifted to sleep, her dreams were plagued with danger and excitement and secrets.

~

SHE DIDN'T RISE until noon, and even then she did not feel truly rested. The events of the previous evening took on an unreal cast, as if Delilah had only read about the murder and not semi-witnessed it. Had Marcus been only a dream?

She clambered out of bed and went straight to her wardrobe. The green dress was tucked behind her folded chemises, exactly where she'd left it. A scratch at her bedroom door, as soft as it was, made her heart jump.

"Come in," she called.

Millie, the lady's maid hired for the London season, bustled in with a pitcher of water. "Good morning, miss. Are you feeling well enough to dress and receive callers?"

Delilah stumbled over her words. "Erm… Yes, I'm feeling better."

Millie glanced her direction while filling the basin with steaming water. "Are you sure? Your color is rather high. You're not feverish, are you?"

The looking glass revealed tangled hair and reddened cheeks as if Delilah had been out walking a windswept countryside without a bonnet. "No, I'm quite well."

"Your mother said I wasn't to bother you last night as you were feeling poorly." It was obvious by the lilt in her voice that Millie hoped for details.

"The ball was hot and crowded, and I felt faint."

"Your mother made mention of your weak constitution."

Delilah didn't feel weak in the least. In fact, her body hummed with energy. She felt alive. Perhaps that's what seeing death at close quarters did.

Millie bustled to the wardrobe, and Delilah tensed until the maid pulled out a pretty blue frock with pleats along the bodice and embroidered flowers along the hem and cuffs. Her secret remained safe. For now.

After dressing and choking down tea and toast, Delilah commandeered the morning paper from her father's desk and skimmed the headlines. Nothing about a murder at Lord Harrington's. Nothing about a suspect in a bloodied white frock.

She dropped the paper to her lap, her hands crinkling the newsprint. Was the lack of news a good or bad omen? Relief and worry battled.

"Everything all right, my dear?" her father asked, peering at her over his spectacles. "Still feeling peaked?"

She pasted on a smile, rose, and kissed his cheek, returning his paper a little worse for wear. "I'm feeling much restored after a good night's sleep, Father."

He smiled absentmindedly, the crux of his thoughts always on his business, and returned to scratch in the ledger lying open on the desk. It was a leather-bound affair several inches thick and at least a foot and a half in width. The book stolen from Harrington's library must be considerably smaller in order to be concealed in a gentleman's frock coat.

With a final look over her shoulder, Delilah joined her mother in the drawing room to poke a needle through the cloth stretched tightly in her embroidery hoop. Before she realized what she had done, the cow she embroidered had two heads. One uncommonly small, the other freakishly large. She put the work aside and tapped her toe.

What would have satisfied her the day before—sitting quietly with her mother and daydreaming—now knotted her stomach. It wasn't nerves exactly, but something closer to impatience or anticipation.

What was she expecting to happen? Stumbling upon a scene of murder and intrigue didn't happen every day, thank goodness. Waiting was a woman's lot, after all. Waiting for a dance, a visit, a proposal.

She remembered this feeling. This feeling had driven her to explore the moors around their cottage. This feeling had led to pain and suffering for herself and for those she loved. She stilled her foot, took a deep breath, and began to pick out the stitching of the cow's extra head. She would fix her mistake.

Her mother's gaze could examine and diagnose as well as any physician. "Perhaps Kirby should inform visitors we're not receiving."

"I'm quite well, Mother."

"Sir Wallace is sure to call and question your whereabouts last evening."

"Yes, I suppose he will." She accidently jabbed the needle into her finger. Blood spread on the cloth, turning her bucolic pasture into a scene of carnage.

Kirby opened the door. "Sir Wallace Wainscott, ma'am."

Her mother stood, smoothed her skirts, and ran a critical eye over Delilah. "Don't forget your smile, dear. Men prefer demure, agreeable wives."

The words sent a shudder through her. Imagining her life as Sir Wallace's wife left her weak in the knees and sick to her stomach. Nevertheless, she pasted on a smile and put her work aside. *Work.* As if the sampler would add anything worthy to the world.

Sir Wallace stepped across the threshold wearing a pair of buff-colored breeches, a dark blue frock coat, and a cream waistcoat with a gold stripe. His hair was pomaded into an artful style, and his cravat was so elaborate and high not even his knobby Adam's apple was visible. No doubt Mr. Brummel would have approved.

At one time, she would have said his expression was aristocratic. Now, he just looked priggish. The angry spark he'd ignited the night before with his ungentlemanly comments turned into a blaze with astonishing speed.

"Ladies." He performed a courtly bow and stepped forward to take Delilah's hand for a kiss. "I've been aggrieved since I heard you'd taken ill. Indeed, I hardly slept a wink, but you look as fresh as a flower, Miss Bancroft."

Delilah pulled her hand from his and clenched her skirts to keep from giving into the compulsion to slap the smile off his face. "What kind of flower, pray tell? A blooming lily, or do I remind you of dull, common bird's-foot?"

His smile faltered. "An English rose, of course, Miss Bancroft."

Delilah barely stifled a snort. Most likely, Sir Wallace had spent the evening at a gaming hell or brothel with Lord Nash.

Her mother glided over to greet Sir Wallace, her face reflecting her disquiet. After she covered the pleasantries, the three of them took their seats. Delilah sank into a corner of the settee across from Sir Wallace while her mother settled beside her.

Sir Wallace perched on the edge of an armchair, one leg extended as if proud of his slender limb and elaborately embroidered stocking. Although Marcus had been wearing boots, based on the breadth of his shoulders and chest, Delilah could extrapolate and pictured a well-muscled limb to go along with the rest of him.

Sir Wallace cleared his throat. Delilah's gaze flew from Sir Wallace's string-bean leg to meet his knowing smirk. Lord help her, the man thought she was admiring his form.

Sir Wallace's long, thin—one might even say skeletal—fingers brushed his cravat. A shudder coursed through her, imagining him touching her the way Marcus had. "I was distressed to miss our waltz last evening, Miss Bancroft."

"We don't always get what we want, do we?" Her tongue had been marinated in lemon juice and infused her words with a tart sass most unlike her. Or, more accurately, most unlike the young woman she'd been these past two years and much more like the old her.

Her mother's eyes were huge as they swung from Delilah to Sir Wallace and back again to stare pointedly at Delilah. Her mother tittered. "It was quite the crush at Harrington's.

It's no wonder Delilah got overheated and had to depart early."

"I noticed you conversing with Lord Nash last night. Were the two of you school chums?" Even though Delilah's lips were turned up in a smile, no resulting good humor filled her.

"Indeed, we were. Same class at Eton." Sir Wallace tucked both feet closer together and shifted on the cushion.

"We've never been properly introduced. Perhaps you could do the honors?" Delilah tread on perilous ground.

Bringing up, however obliquely, the conversation she'd over-heard could place her close to the scene of the murder if the events of the evening came to light, but she needn't worry. Sir Wallace's total confusion verified his status as rather dim as well as whiney.

"Nash will be delighted to make your acquaintance."

This time she didn't bother to muffle her incredulous snort.

Kirby rapped twice and entered the drawing room. "Earl Wyndam requests an audience, ma'am. He has no calling card."

"An earl?" Her mother popped up, her hand stealing around her neck. She turned to Delilah. "You neglected to tell me you made the acquaintance of an earl last night, my dear."

"That's because I didn't. He must be here to see Father on business."

Her mother nodded to Kirby. "We'll receive him."

"Lord Wyndam, ma'am." Kirby made the announcement and bowed his way out of the room.

The man Delilah knew as Marcus Ashemore paused in the doorway. Every nerve in her body vibrated. Even her hair felt alive. His secretive, teasing half smile hit her like an arrow through the heart. Unaware of even moving, she found herself within touching distance of him.

Marcus was dressed in serviceable buckskin breeches, boots, and the navy frock coat she'd seen in his wardrobe the night before. His cravat wouldn't have passed muster with Brummel, but the peek of tanned skin at his neck was masculine and attractive.

He took her hand and skimmed his lips over the back. His forefinger brushed the pulse point of her wrist. If it was any reflection of the way her heart beat at her ribs, he would see through any ruse of calm she attempted.

"Marcus Ashemore, Lord Wyndam at your service, Miss Bancroft."

"You are the late Lord Wyndam's son?" Sir Wallace sat up straighter, looking like he'd smelled something distasteful but was too polite to mention it.

Marcus's face shuttered as if preparing for a storm, and his hand, still gripping hers, tightened. "Obviously."

Delilah caught her mother's hard stare and pulled her hand from Marcus's—Lord Wyndam's—grip. Surprised her legs could still carry her, Delilah returned to sit on the edge of the settee cushion.

"The earldom passed to you." Sir Wallace's tone reflected his surprise.

"I'm his only son. His heir. Why wouldn't it pass to me?"

"I would have thought it impossible, considering…" Sir Wallace made a sweeping gesture.

Marcus shuffled his feet wider, his shoulders straining the seams of his well-worn jacket. "Be very careful with your next words, Wainscott."

Although he was the same man from the night before, next to Sir Wallace's prancing, effeminate nature, Marcus's edge of danger and raw masculinity was enhanced a hundredfold. He was nothing like the men who claimed her for dances, brought her lemonade, or remarked on the weather at the gatherings she attended.

Trapped in the somber blandness of their drawing room, Marcus exuded a potent energy that threatened to upend every-thing. She couldn't take her eyes off him. Not because she was fearful but because she was fascinated, which was even more dangerous.

When Sir Wallace said nothing, Marcus took a step closer to him. "My father was never accused of any wrongdoing."

Not sensing the possible peril to his person, Sir Wallace picked a piece of lint off his sleeve and said, "Not formally perhaps, but—" He shot a glance at Delilah and her mother, then winked and tapped the side of his nose. A nose Marcus looked ready to break.

"Lord Wyndam is inordinately fascinated with botany, and I promised to show him our garden. If you'll excuse us?" Delilah smiled at Sir Wallace and her mother.

Her mother's mouth opened and closed, but she didn't voice an objection, and in the moment, Delilah wasn't sure she would have heeded one. She rose and hastened to the drawing room door, sending a glance over her shoulder. "This way, Lord Wyndam."

The menace on his face had been replaced by a familiar spark of humor. "I am eager to acquaint myself with your bushes, Miss Bancroft."

"Delilah, stay within sight, if you please." Her mother had regained her voice, adding a dose of sternness.

"Of course, Mother." Delilah took the arm Marcus offered, and they strolled to the garden door, not speaking again until they were outside. She dropped his arm and any pretense as soon as they were alone.

"An earl?" She propped her hands on her hips. "Why didn't you tell me that last night?"

"You didn't ask, and honestly, I'm not used to using the title."

"Why on earth did you enter the library through the window and not as a guest?"

"Unfortunately, Wainscott is somewhat correct. The Wyndam name is tarnished, hence the reason for my interest in the book. My father was a good man, and I intend to prove it."

"I skimmed Father's newspaper but saw no mention of last night's incident. Have you heard anything?" Delilah took a step closer to him and lowered her voice even though no one was within earshot.

"Not a peep." Marcus sounded more worried than relieved.

"What does it signify?"

"It means someone in power has hushed it up. Hawkins, most likely."

Delilah plucked a leaf and stripped it to its veins. "I can't help but wonder if Mr. Quinton has a family missing him."

"My thoughts have dwelt on the possibility as well." Birdcalls and the rattle of carriages from the street broke the lengthy silence. "I've tasked O'Connell to search for any crumb of information."

"I suppose it's over then." The finality should have calmed her nerves, but she was still on edge. Delilah turned back toward the house, but Marcus caught her hand.

"It's not over for me. Have you remembered anything else that might help my quest?" His desperation was palpable and spread to her like a contagion. No, it bound them like iron forged by the trial they'd endured together.

She closed her eyes and hugged herself around the waist, putting herself back behind the curtain in her mind. She reviewed the events once more for Marcus, but nothing new came to mind.

"I don't. I'm sorry," she said in a thickened voice, the slug of emotion taking her by surprise. Tears clouded her eyes, and she wasn't sure why. Whatever nerve had held her together through discovering the body and fleeing into the night with a stranger had frayed. Who would cry for the dead man if not her?

Marcus's face was blurry with her tears, but his hands were firm on her shoulders, a grounding force. Warmth infused her. "You've been so strong, Delilah. Any woman—any man, for that matter—would be forgiven for falling apart. I wish…"

"What do you wish?"

"I wish I could take you in my arms and comfort you. I wish we hadn't met over a dead body. I wish I could claim a waltz in front of all polite Society." He touched her cheek lightly.

She wished she could nuzzle her cheek into his palm and step into the hard, comforting warmth of his body, but she was aware of her mother's promise—threat?—to keep them under her watchful gaze.

Delilah took a step away from him and sniffed. Marcus produced a soft handkerchief. She dabbed her eyes and blew her nose. It smelled of fresh sunshine and country air. When she tried to hand it back, the corner of his mouth quirked up. "Keep it. Save your tears for later. If your mother and Wainscott think I made you cry, I won't be allowed inside the front door next time."

She blinked, her thoughts a chaotic whirl. "You plan to call again?"

"You're the only one who can identify the killer."

"But I didn't see his face."

"Last night you thought you might recognize him. If he was at Lord Harrington's, then he is part of Society and will eventually show himself."

"What will you do if I actually manage to locate him?"

"Doesn't Quinton deserve justice?" His nonanswer didn't go unnoticed.

"Why not go straight to Hawkins? At least we know he hasn't killed anyone."

"Based on his reputation, I wouldn't be too confident about that," Marcus said darkly.

"You're sure whatever is in the book can clear your father's name?"

His hesitation was answer enough. "That's what I hope, yes."

She daubed her bottom lip with her tongue and asked softly, "What if it doesn't?"

"Then I'll keep hunting for information that does."

She recognized the futility in arguing about his father's honor. "If I see the man in the hat, I'll send word."

"I would be most appreciative." He paced in front of a rose bush whose buds were beginning to form. Picking one, he twirled it between his thumb and forefinger.

She had never been around a man so at ease with his body. He'd swung himself out of the window to traverse the ledge and descend the water pipe as if such things were natural.

The gentlemen she'd met at the balls and soirees moved with stiff formality, even when dancing. How would it feel to be waltzed around the dance floor in Marcus's arms? How would it feel to kiss him? A blush heated her face and made her long for a fan or a cool breeze, but neither was on hand. Her missing fan popped into her mind. Should she tell Marcus?

"They mentioned another man," he said.

The direction of her thoughts veered. "Who? When?"

"Lord Harrington and his companion when we were lying on the ground under the bush outside the window." His gaze remained on the flower in his hand. "Gilmore. I did some digging and discovered he's a lord and circulates among the ton regularly. Are you acquainted with him?"

"Only by reputation, which is said to be dissolute."

"Harrington insinuated he needs protection. We can only assume from the killer, which means he might know or be in possession of something useful."

"Was he a friend of your father's as well?"

"Not that I'm aware, but there is much I don't know about my father's personal and business dealings."

"Does Gilmore work for or against England?" she asked, not expecting an answer.

"Either way, I would wager my horse on the possibility either the killer or Hawkins will send someone for Gilmore. And if the killer gets there first…" Marcus shook his head.

"Lord Gilmore is hosting a soiree in a week's time. It seems a good opportunity to search."

Marcus stopped and stared. "You received an invitation?"

"Yes, but Mother is set to decline."

"You must change her mind."

She huffed and rolled her eyes. "You don't know Mother."

He took her hand in both of his and squeezed. "Please, Delilah."

The air around them snapped with the energy of a great storm on the horizon. She welcomed the chaos.

If her mother had an inkling of what Delilah had witnessed and what Marcus was asking of her, she would lock Delilah in a nunnery to keep her hidden and safe—or marry her to Sir Wallace by special license that very afternoon.

Yet Delilah would take the risk. From the moment Marcus had appeared in their drawing room, she knew she would do whatever it took to obtain justice for Quinton's murder and help Marcus clear his family name.

"I'll ensure we attend Gilmore's soiree," she said.

"I'll finagle an invitation. Or make my way inside somehow." Marcus glanced toward the house. "Is Wainscott a serious suitor?"

"Mother believes he's ready to come up to scratch." She dropped her gaze and bit the inside of her lip. The overheard conversation between Sir Wallace and Lord Nash ached like a bruise to her heart.

"Two minutes in his company and it's clear he's a dunderhead. You'll surely decline." At her silence, his voice harshened. "Won't you?"

Her breath caught at the intensity reflecting in his green eyes. "Mother and Father are encouraging the match. An advantageous marriage would give my family a foothold into polite Society and widen my father's business contacts. Father is a merchant who only recently came into a fortune."

"Is he the one?" Marcus's shoulders bowed up, and he pointed toward the drawing room.

"The one what?"

"The man who hurt your feelings last night." Marcus's hands were balled into fists, and color burnished his tanned cheeks. He fairly vibrated with murderous intent, which she was more of an expert on recognizing than she had been the day before.

"Yes, but—"

"I'll teach him a lesson he won't soon forget."

She gripped Marcus's biceps. It was hard as stone. "Considering everything that's happened since, he's not worth adding to our troubles."

He relaxed a fraction. "You plan to refuse him."

She dropped her hand from his arm. "Mother caught me returning last night."

"What did she say?"

"She informed me I need to be taken in hand by a husband as soon as possible."

"Your mother plans to wed you to Sir Wallace to avoid scandal and climb higher in Society." At her brusque nod, he asked, "What do you want?"

Not even her mother had asked her what she wanted. "What I want doesn't matter."

"Of course it does. It's your future in the balance."

How could men be so ignorant to women's plight in the world? "Are you mad? My reputation and dowry are my only possessions of value. My dreams and ambitions are worthless. Even worse, they're a hindrance. I must keep my reputation pristine, hand over my dowry to my husband, and provide heirs like a broodmare. It's all I'm good for, and it's bloody well not fair."

Speaking her mind for the first time in two years left her dizzy and breathless. A wound had been excised and drained of rot. While her body had healed long ago, her soul had remained in convalescence, but finally, strength rushed through her in full measure.

Politeness dictated she should immediately apologize for her outburst, including the profanity she'd overheard Alastair use on many an occasion. Instead, she raised her chin and glared at him because she wasn't sorry.

If she had to quantify the emotion flashing in Marcus's green eyes, it wasn't disdain, but something akin to admiration. "I agree. It's bloody well not fair a woman such as yourself is reduced to a tally sheet."

The understanding radiating off him reminded her painfully of Alastair. Her brother had encouraged her and even joined in her explorations before his interests had veered toward village girls, gaming, and war.

Unable to control herself, she leaned closer to Marcus, close enough to catch his scent—the earthiness of the countryside and the pleasant tang of his shaving cream. The same scent had enveloped her the previous evening when he'd rolled his lean body on top of hers under the cover of the bush and again in the street.

He raised his hand, and for a few skipping heartbeats, she froze, sure he was going to touch her. Instead, he cleared his throat, took two giant steps backward, and smoothed a hand down the lapel of his jacket.

"Your mother and Wainscott watch us," he murmured.

Delilah stole a glance toward the window. Sir Wallace peeked around the curtain, but her mother felt no such compunction. Her thunderous face was framed by the dark curtains like a portrait of a Shakespearean fury.

"I wonder what poison Sir Wallace is feeding my mother," Delilah said.

"Wainscott is only repeating what is on everyone else's lips." The hurt in his voice spread like an indelible stain, the kind she feared would never be truly clean no matter what he discovered in the infamous book he sought. "We should return."

They strolled side by side out of the garden. At the drawing room door, out of sight from both her mother and Sir Wallace, he caught her forearm, the calluses along his fingers finding the bare skin at the edge of her sleeve. It was not the touch of a gentleman's hand, but she didn't pull away. A shiver crawled up her arm to stir the hair at her nape.

"I'll see you at Gilmore's," he murmured. Although it wasn't a question, he waited for her answer.

"I'll be there." Even if she had no idea how to change her mother's mind.

Her mother stared at them from where she stood in the middle of the drawing room. Marcus smiled gamely and raised his voice. "I'll take my leave. Thank you for the tour of the gardens, Miss Bancroft."

"You're most welcome, Mar— Lord Wyndam. Good day to you."

Marcus shifted his grip to her hand and brushed his lips across the back. His index finger stroked over her palm and ignited a path of heat like flint. It was over before Delilah could react, and he disappeared out the door without a backward glance.

There was nothing untoward about his actions, and yet... And yet they had been intimate and sensual. The neck of her gown seemed to shrink two inches. Her lips, still in the curl of a smile, trembled as she returned to the drawing room.

Sir Wallace pulled out a pocket watch and made a show of checking the time before closing it with a snap. "I must take my leave. I'm meeting Nash at White's."

Delilah considered the problem of Gilmore's invitation. Under only one circumstance could she imagine her mother accepting an invitation from an avowed rake. With as much warmth as she could muster, which truthfully wasn't enough to register as a northerly spring breeze, Delilah offered Sir Wallace her hand. In contrast to Marcus, Sir Wallace's grip reminded her of a dead fish.

"Will you be attending Lord Gilmore's soiree? I would be most pleased to save you a waltz. Or even two to make up for my absence at Lord Harrington's."

His eyes sparked—with excitement or avarice?—and his lips twitched but never reached the curve of a smile. "I will indeed be attending, and I would be very happy to claim the first waltz."

Delilah ignored the warning she saw in her mother's tightened expression. "We will be accepting Lord Gilmore's most gracious invitation, won't we, Mother?"

A refusal hovered at her mother's mouth, but her lips reformed and said, "Yes, of course," albeit reluctantly. Farewells were exchanged, and Sir Wallace departed, leaving Delilah and her mother facing off like prizefighters.

"I feel as if my daughter has been replaced by a changeling. What has gotten in to you?"

Spirit? Nerve? Courage? Along with more than a dash of terror? "Nothing. Everything is fine."

Her mother's gaze attempted to strip Delilah to the truth, but the truth would only endanger her family. Delilah didn't crumble or look away but pasted a vacuous expression on her face.

"When and where did you meet the earl?" her mother asked.

"Last night, at Harrington's."

"You met the man last night, and he lured you into a liaison?"

"Of course not! Marcus was a complete gentleman." That was mostly true.

"Marcus?" Her mother snorted. "According to Sir Wallace, Lord Wyndam's father is a traitor to the Crown."

"Merely rumors."

"Are you aware of what the whispers entail?" Anguish twisted her mother's mouth, aging her a decade in a blink.

Fingers of foreboding grabbed hold and squeezed the air from Delilah's lungs. "No."

"It's said the old Lord Wyndam was behind the commission that sold tainted gun powder to the troops."

It was suspected Alastair had died not from heroics on the battlefield but a misfire of his rifle attributed to a bad stock of powder. His burns had turned putrid, and he'd died in a field hospital a continent away.

A lump in Delilah's throat made it difficult to swallow, so her words emerged gruff and not at all convincing. "You can't lay the sins of the father onto the son."

"That man inherited money earned by selling the gunpowder that killed Alastair." Her mother stifled a sob and left the drawing room at a quick, half-stumbling walk. If the past held true, her mother wouldn't come out of her rooms until dinner.

Delilah paced and chewed on her thumbnail. A habit her mother had tried to quell since Delilah's childhood. The loss of Alastair was an emptiness she confronted every day. What if Marcus's father was to blame despite his belief in his father's innocence? Marcus's judgment was clouded by affection and couldn't be trusted.

What now? Did she cut all ties with Marcus to spare her mother's feelings? Or could she help discover the real culprit and bring justice for Quinton and Alastair and countless others who had been killed or maimed by the tainted shipment of gunpowder?

Far from discouraging her, the revelations about Marcus and Alastair only strengthened her resolve. She would continue her quest for the man in the hat, but if the information proved the old Lord Wyndam was guilty, could she trust Marcus to do what was right?

CHAPTER 5

*M*arcus smoothed the collar of his best jacket and hoped the fraying around the cuffs wouldn't be noticeable in the crush and candlelight. Logic and self-preservation told him to leave London and pursue his plan to breed horses, but would anyone buy a horse from a peer with a sullied lineage? His estate and name were in shambles, with no clear path to redemption for either. The longer he remained in London searching for the truth, the more he began to doubt himself.

Yet here he was at a soiree with no invitation. His excuse of delivering a message to his master had gotten him through the kitchen door without the threat of a skewering. Now it was up to him to not get caught and face the same fate as the unfortunate Quinton.

Even if he managed to corner Gilmore and ask pointed questions as to his involvement, it might not prove anything. If the information did miraculously clear his father of wrongdoing, the tangle of loyalties and betrayals made it impossible to know who would even believe him. And even if he found someone to believe him, the Wyndam name would remain tainted in the eyes of Society. The rumors were too entrenched in the mud to be purified.

The killer was merely one more shadow to chase. One more lead that would disintegrate or get yanked away by whatever puppet master controlled the game Marcus had yet to learn the rules to.

While the faint hope of salvaging his family's honor was fading, a new objective was driving him. Delilah was in danger. The inevitable approach was like a storm on a chill breeze.

He stopped on the dais leading into a large room converted to a ballroom for the occasion. It was early, but the party was already awash with lords and ladies—and some women in low-cut evening dresses who appeared to not be ladies at all—sparkling under the hundreds of candles burning in the chandeliers.

A man dressed in severe black evening clothes and white gloves stood at the entrance. "Your name, sir?"

Blast. He hadn't considered being announced to the room. His title would draw a bull's-eye on his chest. He murmured, "Mr. Ashemore."

As his name floated over the crowd in the butler's sonorous voice, Marcus slipped into the crowd with his head bowed. His shoulder clashed with another gentleman's as he attempted to lose himself in the crowd.

The man shifted around, his expression supercilious and cool, like many gentlemen of the ton. Although his hair was silver, it was thick, and his face was unlined. Marcus guessed he was nearing his fourth decade.

"Pardon me, sir," Marcus murmured, ready to duck into the crush and lose himself.

"You look familiar, sir. Have we been introduced?"

"I don't believe so." Marcus didn't offer his name, and neither did the gentleman.

"Perhaps we share Etonian connections?"

"That must be it," Marcus said even though he hadn't attended Eton. He slapped on a smile, nodded, and excused himself before the gentleman—because there was no mistaking his blood for anything but blue—outright asked his name.

Growing up in Ireland with his maternal grandparents meant he had no connections with the lords of London. Eton had neither been offered nor desired. The village rector had tutored him in a variety of subjects. His life in Ireland had been full of adventure and love, and his only pain had emanated from missing his father during his extended absences.

He weaved through the crowd on the hunt for Delilah. Her name whispered through his head like a caress. At first, he'd thought the exotic name unsuited to her. Except for the scenario in which he'd found her, she'd seemed unremarkable. Brown hair, pretty figure, freckles.

But the moment she'd followed him out the window, her extraordinary eyes locked on his, she'd revealed herself to be the opposite of unremarkable, and he didn't understand why her drawing room wasn't filled with gentlemen wanting to claim her.

If she hadn't managed to attend, all his machinations were for naught. His heart stumbled, and his feet followed when he spied her standing between her mother and an older lady wearing a severe frown. Delilah had forgone a snow-white gown in favor of buttercup yellow. The neckline scooped low enough to reveal the top swells of her bosom and constellations of freckles along her shoulders.

Her hair had been pulled back and weaved together in a series of braids. The elegance suited her better than the affectation of curls. Amber hues in the strands sparked in the candlelight.

She was brave and intelligent and deserved better than a clod like Wainscott. If he were being truly honest, she deserved better than a man like himself. A man whose fortunes and family name were in tatters. A woman like Delilah deserved a duke, but only if that's what she desired.

He put the crimp in his heart down to anxiety at the night's planned skullduggery. Squaring his shoulders and putting on his most charming smile, he circled to the front of their little group, bowing with what he hoped was the perfect amount of deference. "Mrs. Bancroft. Miss Bancroft. It's lovely to see you again so soon after my visit."

"You as well, my lord." Delilah inclined her head, not bothering to hide an alluring, secretive smile, and then turned to the stately lady on her left. "Lady Casterly, have you made the acquaintance of Lord Wyndam?"

The white-haired dowager held up a quizzing glass and squinted in his general direction. She let the glass drop to swing on a thin gold chain and rapped her cane on the floor like a magistrate giving judgment. "So you're Edward's son. You have his look about you."

Nothing in her tone gave him an indication how she felt about his father except for her familiar use of his given name. Marcus had managed to avoid confrontations such as this until now. "Indeed, I am."

"Your mother was a fine lady, despite being Irish."

His mother had died soon after giving birth to him, so the loss wasn't as keen as it might have been. Her absence had been a gentle ache, like the residual pain from a poorly knitted bone. "Thank you, Lady Casterly. I was raised by my mother's parents in Ireland. They were fine people."

"Have they passed on?"

"A fever took them both last winter."

"I'm so sorry, Mar— Lord Wyndam." Delilah's voice overflowed with sympathy, and she lightly touched his arm, the gesture unfitting and forward in the context of the social situation, but it was appreciated nonetheless.

If Mrs. Bancroft hadn't been eviscerating him to the spine

with her gaze, he would have taken Delilah's hand and laid it over his heart.

Lady Casterly gave another rap of her cane. "Are you here to claim a dance from Miss Bancroft?"

He nodded. "Indeed, I am."

"I'm afraid she has no free dances, Lord Wyndam." Mrs. Bancroft's tone was one of satisfaction, not regret. She linked her arm with Delilah's as if he might try to drag her to the dance floor. "Ah! Here comes Sir Wallace, Delilah. Look lively."

Sir Wallace performed a smart bow and jabbed an elbow into Marcus's arm to force him aside. Marcus tempered his anger and ceded the field. Imagining planting a facer on Sir Wallace called forth a smiling grimace, but Marcus couldn't afford to bring more scandal upon his head.

"Ladies. You are looking lovely this evening." Sir Wallace wasn't even looking at the trio of ladies but smiling and nodding at other guests. Finally, he swung his attention to Delilah, but it was fleeting and dismissive. "I believe I have a claim on the first dance, Miss Bancroft."

"Yes, Sir Wallace, I believe you do." As Sir Wallace turned away, she muttered, "Unfortunately."

Marcus camouflaged his laugh with an unconvincing cough, earning him a reproachful glare from Mrs. Bancroft. Delilah shot Marcus a veiled, unreadable look before joining Wainscott on the edge of the dance floor, her hand on his arm.

Taking a deep breath, Marcus fisted his hands to keep from pulling Delilah away from the other man. How could Lady Casterly and Mrs. Bancroft seriously consider him a suitable match for Delilah? While his social pedigree was adequate, Wainscott had no brains, bravery, or humor. In short, he was a priggish boor.

The opening strains of a country dance swelled through the room, and Delilah took her place in the line of ladies.

"Perhaps you'd be so kind as to fetch me a lemonade, Lord Wyndam?" Lady Casterly raised an eyebrow toward him.

"Yes, of course. It would be my pleasure."

His plan had been to scout the first-floor rooms as soon as possible. Now though, he was having trouble tearing his gaze away from Delilah. She was similarly distracted, it seemed. On every turn, she met his gaze and trod more than once on Wainscott's deserving toes, resulting in charmingly flushed cheeks on her part.

A tap on his shoulder drew him around. He'd stepped conspicuously toward the dance floor without realizing it.

"A lemonade, my lord?" Lady Casterly nudged his foot with the end of her cane, a gleam in her eyes.

Staying in Lady Casterly's good graces was a necessity. It seemed she had considerable influence over the Bancrofts.

"Immediately, ma'am." He went in search of refreshments and returned with two glasses, one for each lady. Mrs. Bancroft waved hers off as if he might have spat in it and turned away in conversation with another matron.

Marcus gripped the glass too tightly and glared across the dance floor until he spotted Delilah. The steps of the dance had taken her to the other side of the room.

"Sir Wallace has shown a marked interest in Miss Bancroft. It would be a suitable match," Lady Casterly said speculatively.

"She could do better. Much better," Marcus said, feeling disturbingly combative.

"I'm not so sure. While she is reasonably pretty, and her dowry is certainly admirable, her family is common. Their money new. You know how Society looks down upon such things."

He gulped his drink to cover his agitation but only ended up choking on the barely sweetened drink.

Lady Casterly took a sip, unbothered by the tartness. Perhaps because it matched her personality. "The Bancrofts are a fine family, and Mr. Bancroft is a good friend and business partner to my husband, but even under my protection, the Bancrofts will never be truly accepted by the ton unless Delilah makes a good match."

"And Wainscott will be a good husband?"

"Heavens, no!" Her laugh was tinged with incredulity. "I imagine once Miss Bancroft provides an heir and a spare, they will hardly see one another. It is the way of most marriages."

He couldn't imagine marrying for such mercenary reasons. While he had no memory of his mother, his gran had weaved a love story between his parents. A dashing young lord falling in love with a squire's daughter while on holiday and sweeping her into a life she'd never dreamed possible.

As if reading his mind, Lady Casterly murmured, "I was sorry to hear of Edward's passing."

The familiar use of his father's name pricked his instincts once more. This time, there was more than a little affection in her voice. "You knew him well?"

"The Wyndam estate is only a few hours' ride from my ancestral home. We've known one another since we were small. Edward was a lively dancer. An excellent horseman. There was even a push for us to marry, but then he met your mother, and I met Casterly."

"Had you spoken to him in recent years?" How delicately did he have to tread?

"I've heard the rumors, but I don't believe them. Unlike some." She swung her cane to point at Mrs. Bancroft before putting it back on the floor and leaning onto it. "Edward was still a man about town right up until his death. His illness must have taken hold quickly."

"Indeed, it did." The bullet to his head would certainly classify as sudden. The magistrate, an old friend of his father's, had classified the death as a fatal apoplexy. Although Marcus was relieved the true manner of his father's death hadn't made the rounds of gossip, he was more interested in the other bit of news she'd imparted. "My father was a man about town?"

"He did love a game of whist and a good laugh, bless his soul." A fond smile softened his face.

That didn't fit with the sober, serious man Marcus had come to know through the writings he'd left behind. "I didn't know him as well as I would have liked."

"You've been in Ireland all these years? Edward never thought to present you?"

"I suppose he assumed there would be time. But I was happy in Ireland and reluctant to leave my grandparents in their dotage. I have little choice in the matter now."

"You have the taint of scandalous family rumors about you, and Edward left you the decrepit family estate." Lady Casterly's bluntness was growing on him.

"That's the gist of it."

"It would be better for all involved if you stayed away from Miss Bancroft, you know. You will only hurt her chances, and her parents will never give their blessing, earldom or not."

The assessment knocked his heart into a new rhythm. One that was uncomfortable. Lady Casterly couldn't know their association went far deeper and was more dangerous than a dance or a morning call. He faced a dilemma.

Did he selfishly use Delilah to further his own aims of clearing his father's name and possibly ruin her chances with Wainscott or other potential suitors?

Delilah circled Wainscott, their hands touching, but her gaze belonged to Marcus. He murmured, "Lady Casterly, would you make my apologies to Miss Bancroft?"

"Wise decision, Wyndam." The lines around Lady Casterly's eyes and mouth deepened with what might classify as regret. "I wish you well. Truly."

She inclined her head and shifted away, effectively dismissing him from her sphere. Marcus broke eye contact with

Delilah and retreated to the entry door to survey the room. It was impossible to cull the crush of finely dressed lords and ladies for a gentleman he had no way to identify without Delilah's help.

What he did notice was several hired bruisers wandering the edges of the crowd. Excitement quickened his nerves. Gilmore was worried enough to hire protection. Was he feeling vulnerable after Quinton's murder? Or was he protecting something else? Could Gilmore possess physical evidence that might clear Marcus's father? The most likely place to house such evidence would be the study.

The musicians struck up the waltz. A pang of remorse had him scanning the dance floor. Delilah was not among the couples whirling across the parquet. Part of him reveled in the fact no other man had claimed her, but the other part cursed the longing he couldn't afford.

Lady Casterly was correct. Using Delilah for his own ends would only lead to her ruin, and even if he wanted to do something honorable, he had nothing to offer her but a tainted name, a rundown estate, and a dream.

Determined to put her out of his mind and concentrate on the mission, Marcus strolled into the entry, past a footman who stretched the shoulder seams of his jacket, and down a hallway warmly lit by sconces.

Gilmore's study was not on the first floor, although Marcus had accidently located the ladies' retiring room, which precipitated many apologies and a quick escape. The study must be located down the darkened hallway at the top of the stairs.

Did he dare make a break up the stairs? His title would earn no boons from Gilmore's hired brutes or Quinton's killer if he were caught. A late arrival swung the brawny footman-cum-guard's attention to the door, giving Marcus a heartbeat to make a decision.

He took the steps two at a time and pressed himself deep

within the shadows above. The sprint upstairs plus the stress of the situation sent the blood skidding through his veins like a bolting horse. He didn't have time to catch his breath or gather his wits.

Voices sounded on the stairs. Well-educated male voices speaking in low tones. Marcus slipped into the nearest room. It was dark, but shadows in the shape of a settee and a small table marked his location as a sitting room. He could only hope the men weren't planning on seeking its privacy.

Marcus peered through the cracked door. At first, he saw no one, but then a man he didn't recognize moved in and out of view before Marcus could set his features to memory, leaving an impression of dark hair and a wiry frame. Could he be Quinton's killer?

Gilmore sidled into view, his hair thinning and his stomach straining against his waistcoat. He had the reputation for heavy drinking and excess gambling. He rocked on his feet and mussed his hair with jerky movements of his hand.

"You made a copy of the bloody book. It's of no use to anyone. Take it," Gilmore said with clenched teeth. "I want out."

"I'm afraid that's not possible, my lord." The unknown man's voice was as cool as Gilmore's was furious. It also niggled at Marcus's memory. Was this the man who had been in the window with Harrington the night of Quinton's murder?

"The devil it's not. A man is dead. You assured me I would be safe, and then Quinton turns up half-eaten in the Thames. I won't end up as fish food, do you hear me?" Gilmore's attempt at sounding authoritative descended into full-throated fear.

"You're overreacting. No one knows who killed Quinton or why. It might have been a jealous husband." The other man's voice was soothing, but considering the subject, he came across as disingenuous. "Anyway, our quarry doesn't know we are in contact and have copied the book in your possession. He is desperate to obtain it, and we are desperate to unmask him. You are our only connection to him."

"My connection is tenuous at best. Old Wyndam is the only one who dealt with him face-to-face, and look where he is now —worm food. If you expect me to keep the meeting with this cove, then I want more coin." Gilmore did his best to gather his emotions and appearance, smoothing his hair and waistcoat.

"What day has it been set for?"

"Tuesday at Fieldstones."

"Fieldstones? At your suggestion, I suppose." Distaste flavored the stranger's voice. It was obvious he didn't care for Gilmore.

"It was at his suggestion," Gilmore said defensively.

"What manner of man is he? I wonder." Hawkins spoke as if not expecting an answer, but he got one anyway.

"I hope not the murdering kind," Gilmore said darkly. "If he wishes to remain anonymous, I can't see him turning up at all."

"This meeting is our only solid lead. Once you hand over the book, I'll have a man waiting to nab and question him."

"I might be more motivated with extra coin in my pocket. I've had a bad run at the tables." Fear blunted the wheedling whine in Gilmore's voice.

A silent negotiation seemed to commence until the unidentified man murmured, "Expect a courier with half the payment, but if you can't deliver me the identity of the traitor, consider my protection withdrawn. Now, point me toward the servants' stairs."

Gilmore moved out of Marcus's view, and a nearby door creaked. Marcus grabbed the doorjamb, straining to see and hear.

Gilmore called out, "Hawkins!"

Marcus started and bumped the door. The slight squeak froze him in place, but neither man swept it open with an "Aha!" The stranger was Hawkins. The puppet master. Marcus had imagined a larger, more imposing fellow, but he couldn't deny Hawkins had dominated Gilmore.

"I'll expect a boon from Prinny if I succeed. Another estate, perhaps?" Gilmore's voice was oilier now he had seemingly won their skirmish.

Marcus couldn't hear Hawkins's reply. Gilmore and Hawkins were working in tandem, and Marcus could only guess the man Gilmore was set to meet at Fieldstones was the man in the hat who'd pinched the first copy of the book and killed Quinton and perhaps his father. A traitor, Hawkins had called the killer, which meant his father was not a traitor. Unless he had been in league with Quinton's killer. While questions still swirled, Marcus finally had a handle on the players of the game.

Gilmore muttered, "I need a drink and a distraction."

Marcus heartily concurred. Tossing Gilmore's study was too risky now. Instead, he would crash the assignation at Fieldstones where he would have the opportunity to identify the killer, pinch the book, and hopefully, discover the truth within its pages.

The man's heavy footsteps grew quieter, and the whoosh of a door opening down the hall moved the air around Marcus. Instincts told him he was alone. After verifying with a quick peek, he slipped out of his hiding place, keeping to the shadowy edges of the hall.

With the top of the staircase in sight, his heart danced along his ribs, and a rush of relief made him sick to his stomach. Cloak-and-dagger games weren't his specialty, and as soon as this debacle was resolved, he would retire to the country to breed horses the rest of his days.

A bundle of yellow dashed up the stairs. *Delilah.* She held her skirts, her trim ankles flashing with every step. Hesitating at the top, she looked around, her chest working with her quickened breaths and drawing his attention downward to her rather magnificent décolletage.

He stepped out of the shadows, drawn to her like a planet to the sun.

"Marcus," she whispered urgently and ran to him, catching his arms and drawing close. "There are runners about."

"I noticed. I overheard Gilmore and Hawkins in a tête-à-tête."

She gasped softly. "What did you discover?"

"Gilmore has another book in his possession. It's here but too dangerous to seek out at the moment. There was mention of an upcoming meeting at a place called Fieldstones in order to pass the book to Quinton's killer."

"What is Fieldstones? An inn, perhaps?" A crinkle appeared between her brows.

"More likely a gaming hell."

"'Ere now, she was a pretty little thing and giving you the eye, if you know what I mean." A man with a Cockney accent was ascending the stairs, the top of his pomaded hair coming into view, a compatriot close behind. If he and Delilah were caught, ruination would be the least of their worries.

Marcus looked over his shoulder at the sitting room he'd vacated. Could they make it? He tensed, prepared to pull her to relative safety.

As if she sensed his thoughts, Delilah murmured, "There's no time for retreat. Forgive me, Marcus."

Before he could respond, she took his face between her gloved hands and pulled him to her, mashing their lips together. His eyes remained open in shock, her face blurring. The bulk of the two men cleared the top of the stairs.

Her lips remained planted on his. As his shock faded, his body roared to life. He'd been thinking and dreaming of kissing her, and now she was offering the one thing he would have never taken on his own.

A kiss.

Simple, yet infinitely complicated.

He wrapped an arm around her waist and fit her curves against him. His other hand cupped her nape, his thumb grazing the satiny skin of her jaw and tilting her head to take control. Tendrils of her hair sneaked under his cuff to tickle the skin of his wrist. He moved his lips over hers, exploring and coaxing a response.

Her response was a breathy moan, her arms twining around his neck, her body molding even closer. He glided his hand up her arm, the satiny fabric of her glove giving way to the heated, soft skin of her upper arm. His rough, rein-calloused fingers caught on the delicate yellow fabric of her frock. The urge to unwrap her like a piece of candy and relish the sweetness underneath nearly overwhelmed him. It would be a sweet, sinful surrender to his desire.

Time pushed and pulled and ceased to have meaning. Danger was an abstract concept. The feel of her in his arms blurred out the sharp edges and urgency of his mission.

He sucked her bottom lip between his teeth and nipped it gently. Her tongue darted to touch his lip. He groaned and was ready to push her against the wall when the sound of a throat clearing brought him out of the trance her kiss had cast over him.

He looked over his shoulder. The two hired men stood behind him, smirks on their faces.

"'Ere now, sir. You and the, er, lady will have to find somewhere else for your peccadillo. This floor is off-limits."

"Do you mean there are no private areas? Even for a bit of coin?" Marcus's blasé, rakish tease sounded more like the croak of a frog. Or a man rocked to his core.

"Not here, sir. You and your young miss need to return to the ballroom."

Marcus offered Delilah his arm as if he hadn't been ready to strip her lemon-yellow dress off her body in the middle of a hallway moments ago. She lay her hand on top, her tremble vibrating through his arm. Her hair was decidedly less neat than when she'd arrived, and her lips were red and slightly parted as if she were having a difficult time catching her breath.

His lungs didn't seem to be working properly either. The two men escorted them to the bottom of the stairs. One touched his forelock and winked at Marcus. A yell came from upstairs, and the two men started and exchanged a telling look before bolting upstairs.

Marcus froze and stared up the stairs. What was happening? Had the killer come for the book and for Gilmore? Had Marcus's last best chance been lost? He swayed, wanting to follow, sure the commotion had something to do with the mystery he had yet to untangle.

"No." Delilah tugged him into the fringes of the crowd and stood on tiptoes to glance around the room. "We can't afford to raise suspicions any higher. I need to return to Mother and Lady Casterly before I'm missed, and you need to lose yourself in the crush before suspicions arise."

As she brushed by him, he caught her hand. "Be careful, Delilah. Please."

Her lips parted as if she wanted to say something, but she only gave his arm a squeeze before slipping away. He stayed rooted until the bright yellow of her gown was snuffed out by the crowd. The stuffy air and wall of people pressed down on him like a giant hand, the weight unbearable. He needed night air and solitude.

The men who had been guarding the door were gone. A backward glance showed movement at the top of the steps. It would be safer all around—to Delilah's reputation and his mission—if he disappeared. For now.

CHAPTER 6

*L*ady Casterly paced in front of the settee, each tap of her cane a strike to Delilah's temple. The previous evening had alternated between tedium and tension. Marcus had nearly gotten himself caught, as had she, the results of which would have been dire for them both.

And the kiss. *The kiss.*

It was the kiss that had troubled her sleep the most. In all her imaginings—and she had imagined much after their playacting in the lane—she couldn't have fathomed instigating such a kiss.

In her novels, the hero was the one who attempted to ravish the lady while she protested in vain. Granted, she had nothing to compare her kiss with Marcus to, but it had been raw and invigorating. *Very* invigorating.

In fact, kissing Marcus might count as the greatest adventure she'd ever had. So far. Delilah felt like a baby bird, a little wobbly and unsure but determined to fly. Her mother and Lady Casterly, however, were even more determined to clip her wings and keep her confined to her cage.

"You have made it a habit to wander off at events, Delilah. I realize you were not raised in polite Society, but you must understand not only is it bad form, but as an unmarried young lady, you must be accompanied by a chaperone at all times." The disapproval in Lady Casterly's voice would have had her knees quaking a week ago.

Everything had changed. Her worries were no longer about how many available lords—young or old—filled her dance card or doing her best to conform to her mother's expectations. She was part of something bigger. She was helping untangle a web that had claimed at least one life. She might help clear Marcus's family name and possibly bring justice to her brother Alastair and the other men who'd died as a result of the tainted gunpowder.

"It was an awful crush. I needed to compose myself." Delilah did her best to keep her expression impassive.

Lady Casterly turned to face her with military precision. Her stare did funny things to Delilah's insides, as if the older woman had special powers to strip away her bluff to reveal the truth. "You were not in the ladies' retiring room. Where were you?"

"Nothing happened." A quiver of defensiveness took up in Delilah's voice.

Her mother piped up from the corner of the settee. "She wasn't gone long enough for anyone to notice, Lady Casterly."

Lady Casterly's gaze didn't waver from boring a hole through Delilah. "The same can't be said about Lord Harrington's. People noticed when you didn't return. These disappearances are becoming an unfortunate habit."

"My constitution is weak, isn't it, Mother?" Delilah's hands grew clammy, and she drew them into fists around her skirts. As a matter of fact, she was feeling rather sick with dread at the moment.

Lady Casterly harrumphed and banged her cane on the floor. "Don't pretend weakness with me, gel. You might have played the simpleton when I agreed to sponsor you, but you are neither weak nor insipid. I recognize the rebellious fire in your blood."

"Fire?" Delilah's mother straightened. "Delilah is demure and sweet and pliable."

Lady Casterly barked a laugh. "Then she has you fooled. This gel—" she jabbed her cane in Delilah's direction, "—is none of those things. As a matter of fact, I loathe demure and sweet and pliable. I much prefer a little passion in a person. However, not so much that it gets you ruined."

"I'm not ruined." *Not yet, at least*, a little voice sniggered inside Delilah's head. Very little scandal was required to ruin a lady's good name and blacken her reputation. It would take the fingers on two hands to count the ruining offenses she had partaken in over the past week.

"Lord Wyndam is a handsome devil, is he not?" Lady Casterly cast raised brows in Delilah's direction, no doubt hoping to hook a reaction.

Nothing could prevent the heat flooding from her chest into her cheeks, but she injected coolness into her words. "He's not an ogre, I suppose."

Another short, disbelieving laugh was Lady Casterly's response.

Her mother drew herself up, lay her embroidery hoop down, and put on a somber face. "Lord Wyndam is not to be considered. Earl or not, he doesn't have two farthings to his name. Even worse, his father left the title tainted."

"I was well acquainted with the old Lord Wyndam. He was a good man, and the rumors are just that. Scurrilous and unproven whispers." Lady Casterly sniffed dismissively.

"I also heard tell his death was not due to sickness." Delilah's mother spoke in hushed tones befitting the blasphemous gossip. In a more normal tone, she added, "Lord Wyndam has no proper connections, whatsoever. He's half-Irish, for heaven's sake. For all we know, he's even a Catholic."

"Are connections all that matter? Is my happiness not a consideration?" Delilah scooted forward on her seat.

"Has Wyndam made overtures of marriage?" Lady Casterly asked.

"Of course he hasn't. I'm speaking in general terms. Sir Wallace, for instance."

"A fine young man and very well connected. He's so polite and gentle, my dear. You and Sir Wallace would be quite content." Her mother's smile sent a shiver up Delilah's spine.

"Sir Wallace is a prig. And a deceiver. He cares naught for me, only for my dowry. He views our family as—" Delilah couldn't bring herself to crush her mother's aspirations of acceptance in genteel Society.

Her mother popped up and loomed over her. She went from delicate matron to intimidating harridan in a blink. "He has never been anything but a gentleman, and you should count yourself lucky he's considering a match with you."

Maybe at one time she would have counted herself lucky. Lucky to still be alive. Lucky to be presented in Society. Lucky anyone wanted to marry her. She had forgotten how big and wide and exciting the world was, but she was remembering.

She stood and faced off with her mother. "I'll not marry Sir Wallace."

"You will if your father and I decree it."

"You would force me into an unwanted marriage?"

"If it keeps you safe? Yes."

Safe. Her mother's obsession.

As a child, Delilah had relished the monikers their neighbors had bestowed upon her—fearless, a hoyden, an adventurer—and her parents had indulged her high spirits. After all, they had Alastair to carry the family name. Everything had changed after Alastair was killed.

"Put the question of whether Sir Wallace will come up to scratch aside for the moment. It is early in the season. More gentlemen may yet show interest." Lady Casterly did her best to defuse the swirling tension.

It had been two long years of Delilah deferring to her mother's directives. "Even if no other offers are forthcoming, I will not marry Sir Wallace."

"Time will tell," Lady Casterly said cryptically. "There is one thing your mother and I agree upon: Lord Wyndam offers nothing but trouble."

What if trouble is what I crave? Delilah fisted the delicate fabric of her skirts.

"Promise me you'll not see or talk to Wyndam again, Delilah." Her mother reached out a hand.

With only a slight hesitation, Delilah met her halfway for a quick, conciliatory squeeze. "I… promise," she finally whispered, knowing yet another lie had left her lips.

"Excellent. I'll inform Kirby we are not at home for Lord Wyndam." Her mother bustled out, her relief palpable.

"Your mother loves you." Lady Casterly took a seat but remained perched on the edge, her back ramrod straight. Did the woman lie down to sleep, or did she have a contraption to keep her regally upright?

"As I love her and Father."

"I have nothing against Lord Wyndam, you know, but he would make a terrible match. Unfortunately, whether it is deserved or not, Edward left his son a scandal."

The use of his first name jolted Delilah to prod for more information. "You knew Marcus's father well then?"

"Quite well. A fine man." Lady Casterly gazed out the window but seemed to be looking even farther beyond. Years beyond. "Wilomina, the current Lord Wyndam's mother, was a delightful girl as well. Sadly, their love story was doomed from the start."

"Because she was Irish?"

"Yes. To make matters worse, her father was merely a squire.

A common horse breeder. Nevertheless, I enjoyed her and hoped Edward might find some happiness with her. He did for a time, I suppose, but she died soon after giving birth."

"If Lord Wyndam is an earl and you approved of his parents, why are you adamant about me not associating with him?"

"Because I understand the ways in which he wants to associate with you. He's too fierce and wild for a gently bred young lady." Lady Casterly leaned over her cane, her gaze like a set of pins on a butterfly's wings. "I wasn't always an old woman. I've had a husband and lovers."

Delilah prayed for a giant hole to open and swallow her whole.

Lady Casterly had slammed through polite barriers, and it was only strength of will that kept Delilah from squirming. When Lady Casterly spoke again, her voice was low but sharp with warning. "I see the way your gaze follows him. He fascinates you. Were you off with him at Harrington's? Gilmore's? Are you truly ruined?"

Delilah clutched her neck while her throat worked to get words out. "I didn't... I'm not... Nothing happened," she repeated inanely.

If one discounted murder, escaping out a window, retreating to a gentleman's rooms, and a kiss that had both saved and changed her life, nothing had happened. After all, she was still untouched in the ways that would concern a husband.

"Make sure it remains so." Lady Casterly gave her one final knee-quivering look before turning a banal smile toward Delilah's mother on her return.

"It seems I caught Kirby in the nick of time. Lord Wyndam presented himself as I hid behind the door." Her mother sat, arranged her skirts, and picked up her embroidery, seemingly content everything was worked out to her satisfaction.

Delilah popped up and strode to the door, her nerves

jangling. "I'm feeling quite wrung out. May I be excused to read and rest for a bit?"

"Certainly, dear. We want you looking your best tonight at the Underwood's musicale." Her mother favored her with a smile, but it was tinged with worry. Delilah felt suffocated by her mother's machinations and was relieved to make her escape.

She went to her window and twitched the draperies open. London, dirty and magnificent, stretched out under a brilliant blue sky. How was she, a sheltered debutante with an overprotective mother and a shrewd sponsor, supposed to locate Marcus without bringing about her own ruination?

CHAPTER 7

The Underwood musicale was as tedious and bereft of talent as Delilah had expected. Her mind wandered and worried during the cringe-inducing missed notes of Miss Underwood the elder's plodding rendition of Beethoven's "Moonlight Sonata."

Sir Wallace, snoring to her left, snorted and jerked upright, drawing stares and titters. Delilah pinched her lips together to stem her own laughter. After the piece ended, Lady Underwood announced a break in the entertainment. A few young bucks in the back clapped more enthusiastically at the announcement than for the performance.

Delilah remained seated, hoping her cool demeanor would send Sir Wallace off for more scintillating company, but since she'd taken to ignoring or outright rebuffing him, his interest had grown keener. She would never understand gentlemen.

Her mother and Lady Casterly hadn't helped matters when they conceived of ways to force them together. Resentment wedged its way into her heart like a festering splinter. Her vociferous opposition to Sir Wallace meant nothing.

"Are you enjoying the music, Miss Bancroft?" Sir Wallace reached into his jacket for a snuffbox with a scantily clad woman painted on the lid and took two pinches up his nose.

"Quite. How was your nap?" The smile she turned on him felt a bit vicious. A proper lady wouldn't have mentioned his lapse, but she feared she would never qualify as such.

Sir Wallace tugged at the points of his collar and smoothed a hand down the front of his jacket. "Miss Bancroft, I regret if I've done anything to offend. You must know I hold you in the highest regard, and I hope to speak to your father as soon as he is returned from seeing to his ships in Portsmouth."

Fear and dread fed the kernel of anger she'd nurtured since she'd overheard his hurtful assessment of her. She met his gaze, her brows rising, not sure her show of nonchalance was successful. "You don't think me too quiet and boring? Too much like brown paneling?"

"Certainly not. You are exceedingly—"

"Passable?" She'd gone too far. The cogs of his brain started to turn, and his eyes dulled with the effort. With luck, they were rusty. A change of subject was required. Perhaps his self-professed connections would prove useful after all. "Sir Wallace, are you familiar with Fieldstones?"

For a moment, he was still, and she assumed he must not have heard of Fieldstones. Then his eyes turned bug-like. "Familiar? I should say not. And I'm surprised to hear a lady such as yourself mention such a club."

She'd unwittingly stepped onto a perilous conversational ledge. Still, she did her best to pick up the scattered crumbs of information. A club, and a scandalous one at that if the mere mention threatened to bring down the wrath of genteel Society.

He continued as if her moral character was impugned now. "The debauchery associated with that place should never be associated with a young innocent such as yourself. Put it out of your mind. Where did you hear the name?"

"Merely an overheard conversation. Pray, excuse me. Lady Casterly is gesturing me over." Lady Casterly was doing no such thing, but Delilah needed to escape before Sir Wallace asked more questions.

She rose, but her attempt at an elegant retreat was marred when her foot looped around the leg of a chair in the tightly packed drawing room. Momentum kept her moving, her feet stumbling to keep up, until she caught herself on the instrument of the previous hour's pain—the pianoforte. Her forearm landed on the keys, the jolt of a multitude of discordant notes silencing the room.

Every gaze swung to her. The blush heating her face could have started a fire. She straightened and did the first thing that came to mind. She pasted on a smile and curtsied as if the Prince Regent himself were present. Soft laughter rolled through the room. She raised her chin and glided straight down the aisle, ignoring the sound, knowing it was at her expense but not maliciously so.

The crowd was almost impenetrable. She pardoned and excused her way through the finely dressed members of the ton. As she sidled between the backs of two gentlemen, the elbow of one man jostled her, and she dropped her fan.

The man turned and murmured an apology. It was Lord Whitmire, a gentleman she'd been introduced to at a ball early in the season. He had silver hair and was clad in a fine jacket of bottle-green velvet.

Although he was handsome, his smile held no warmth, and instead of attraction, she experienced only discomfort under his gaze. His attendance at the musicale was surprising because she'd heard he was discriminating and spent most of his time at Westminster or with Prinny and his circle.

He broke eye contact, retrieving her dropped fan and holding it out to her with a small bow. "Yours, I believe?"

"Yes, thank you." She took the fan and tugged. Whitmire held on a fraction too long before letting go. Delilah favored him with a small smile and made an escape, flicking her fan open as soon as the crowd thinned.

Refreshments were being served in a room at the back of the town house, but by the time she arrived, no lemonade remained, only champagne. She took a glass, drank it in three swallows, and allowed a footman to refill her glass.

A breeze tickled the hair at the back of her neck. Doors thrown open to the garden outside beckoned. There was no sign of her mother, Lady Casterly, or Sir Wallace. With her luck, Sir Wallace was informing her mother of her unmaidenly interest in a club she shouldn't even be aware of. She sidled outside the door, seeking a moment's peace before being subjected to another round of torture by Beethoven.

"You certainly know how to make an exit." The wry, lilting voice had her spinning for the source.

Marcus stepped out of the shadow of a pillar, dressed in the same set of formal clothes he'd worn to Gilmore's soiree. The earthiness of a cheroot weaved among the sweet scent of spring flowers in the air.

"You saw?" Delilah's fan picked up its pace.

"The curtsy was a nice touch."

"Mortifying."

"It was actually quite charming."

He was humoring her, and she didn't appreciate it, but more pressing matters took precedence. "I discovered Fieldstones is a scandalous club."

He shushed her, glanced over her shoulder, and took her hand. He led her down the garden path until they were hidden between thorny rose bushes and the back wall. He propped his shoulder against the bricks, one foot over the other, his stance casual, his green eyes anything but.

"You haven't put yourself in danger, I hope?" he asked.

"Of course not."

His raised eyebrows cast doubt on her knee-jerk denial.

"I merely inquired about the place while conversing with Sir Wallace," she added with a little hitch to her words.

He covered his mouth, his fingers muffling his words. "I can only imagine how that went."

"Hence my graceless escape."

"Fieldstones is a private club that caters to the debauched tastes of the upper classes." He stroked his chin and stared up at the blackened sky.

"Are we going?"

Marcus straightened, his nonchalance vanished. "Hold right there. *We* are not going anywhere near Fieldstones."

Her feelings were inexplicably pricked. "You're going without me?"

He made a guffaw of disbelief. "A young lady can't be witness to such vulgarities."

"Pray tell, what is more vulgar than murder?"

He ran a hand down his face and gave a slight shake of his head. "Point taken."

"Without me, how will you identify the killer?"

"I refuse to subject you to the danger and debauchery that a foray to Fieldstones may entail. Anyway, Gilmore will be my unsuspecting guide." Marcus made debauchery and danger sound entirely too appealing.

"Being a woman is tedious." Her frustration was trumped by a sad sort of resignation.

"I would have you at my side if it were possible, Delilah." Earnestness roughened his voice. He took her shoulders in a squeeze, his thumbs dancing over her collarbones. A delicious shiver shimmied down her back, which suddenly and inexplicably arched.

He glided a hand up her shoulder until he cupped her nape. "The braids suit you. You remind me of a rampaging Boadicea."

"Curls are de rigueur this season. I'm terribly out of fashion."

"Current fashion is overrated. You're lovely." He fingered a tendril of her hair that had come loose in the back, the slight tug whirling a strange sort of pleasure through her like a storm, the thunder settling in her lower belly.

"I'm barely passable." Her voice cracked like rotten wood.

"Balderdash." His eyes twinkled as if they had captured starlight. "I'm surprised you don't have dozens of suitors camped in your drawing room, lass."

"I'm the unaccomplished daughter of a merchant with a rich dowry."

"Don't marry Sir Wallace, Delilah," he said softly.

She couldn't imagine kissing Sir Wallace, much less begetting his heirs. Not like she imagined kissing Marcus. She feared she would not be given the choice.

"Mother made me promise not to see or speak with you," she said. "She and Lady Casterly think you are a harbinger of disaster."

"Yet here you are." He brushed the pad of his thumb along her cheekbone.

She closed her eyes and nuzzled into the palm of his hand like a kitten. "Here I am."

DELILAH'S BODY SWAYED CLOSER, her breasts a hairbreadth away from his chest. He craved her softness against him. He wanted to explore her lips and tongue and teeth with his own. He wanted to take his time with her. All night wouldn't be enough.

But even more, he wanted to take her hand and explore London at her side. Wanted to sit across the dinner table and discuss topics ranging from the weather to the state of the world. Wanted to whirl her around a dance floor and have her grin at him.

It was madness. Utter and complete madness.

He dropped his hand back to her shoulder and put distance between them. "Your mother and Lady Casterly speak the truth."

Her eyes fluttered open, trusting and confused. He fought the urge to toss her over his shoulder and spirit her away. She grabbed the lapels of his jacket. "What?"

"Even if I manage to clear my father's name—*my* name—the rumors are entrenched, and polite Society will forever look askance at me."

She batted his arm away. "I should accept Sir Wallace's suit then?"

No. The word reverberated in his head, but his mouth remained clamped shut. Anything else would be selfish considering he had less than nothing to offer her. The estate was in shambles, his name incited the cut direct, and his mission to clear his father of wrongdoing might well see him on the pointy end of a knife.

A throaty sound of disgust preceded her spin and march away. He reached out a hand but drew a fist of air and let her go. She disappeared inside as one of the Underhill ladies butchered another classical masterpiece.

He rubbed his chest and wondered at the crushing loneliness besetting him. He'd lost his beloved grandparents and his father less than a year apart, but the thought of losing Delilah—a woman he had no right to claim as his—hollowed him out and left him bereft for something that could never be.

Instead of chancing a run-in with Mrs. Bancroft or Lady Casterly, Marcus toed himself over the brick wall separating the garden from the mews. Strolling toward the main thoroughfare, the knicker of a horse stopped him.

The musky scent of the stables drew him like the Pied Piper. A black gelding with a distinctive white star on its forehead was tied to the post, its saddle still in place. The horse snuffled in Marcus's palm as if looking for a treat, and it shook its head when it realized Marcus had come empty-handed.

"Rude of me, but I didn't realize I would be meeting a beauty such as yourself this evening." Marcus rubbed the horse's muzzle.

Horses were Marcus's first love. His dream was to breed horses and sell them to the very men who considered his name tainted. None of his protests otherwise had made a difference. Perhaps, over time, he could whitewash the stain of his father's supposed treachery, but the ton had a long memory. Even the decades-old scandal of his titled father marrying an Irish squire's daughter had the power to still resonate.

He leaned his forehead against the horse's white blaze. "What's next for me, do you suppose?"

As if in answer, male voices twined their way from the narrow alley. Instinct had him ducking inside the mews and crouching down in the first stall. He gently shouldered the resident horse aside with a soft shush. Although he hadn't done anything wrong, being found hiding would make any prostrations of his innocence less than believable.

Two men approached, their accents fingering them as part of the ton.

"I prefer to conduct business at the office. My wife and daughter are inside." It was Hawkins. Marcus recognized the crisp, cool tone.

"I apologize, sir, but I'm afraid we have a problem."

Hawkins's long, loud sigh spoke his exasperation. "Go on, then."

The second man's voice dropped in timbre, and Marcus strained to hear him. "Old Lord Wyndam's son has been sniffing around."

"And?" Impatience clipped the word.

"And?" The man's voice contained a vibration of anger even

as it dropped in timbre. "What if he killed Quinton for the book? He certainly has the motive to bury the truth."

The instinct to pop up and claim his innocence warred with the wisdom to stay hidden and ferret out as much information as possible.

"I understand you want to avenge Quinton's death, but I'm not convinced young Wyndam is to blame. We have been unable to decode the pages as of yet. The cipher used is complicated. It might clear the old earl, not damn him." Hawkins's voice had lost its impatient edge, and while Marcus wouldn't call the man's tone warm, it bordered on sympathetic.

"He's the most likely suspect. Who else has the motive?"

"Someone who has much to lose."

"The simple truth is that Edward, Lord Wyndam, betrayed his country for a quick profit."

Marcus gripped the stall door so tightly splinters dug into his palm. Hawkins was silent, and Marcus couldn't help himself. He peeked around the edge of the stall. Hawkins's back was to Marcus, so like at Gilmore's soiree, his face remained a mystery, but the impression of a small, neat man of middle years and excessive confidence was reinforced. The other man carried himself with the air of a Corinthian, but he was a stranger to Marcus.

"You're young. One day, you'll learn nothing is as simple as it seems," Hawkins said with an air of unexpected kindness. "Instead of blaming others, perhaps we should examine ourselves with more care."

"Are you insinuating Westminster has been compromised?" the young gentleman asked.

"It's a possibility."

"By whom?" The man made a throaty huffing sound. "Surely you don't suspect me? I'm honorable."

"Every man has a price. Even the honorable ones. But no, I

don't suspect you're our rat. This time." The last two words were said on a whisper but with a heavy portent.

The young man mumbled something intelligible.

Hawkins continued. "If you want to be of help, look into Lord W's most recent whereabouts."

"Why don't you just ask him your— Oh!" The man tugged at his collar. "I can't fathom Lord W would... Are you certain?"

"Of course I'm not certain. This is why I employ men like you, Davies. Ask at White's or Almack's or even here. Discreetly, if you please, and remain on guard."

"Yes, sir." Davies didn't salute, but it was clear he had his marching orders.

After Davies moved back to the house, Hawkins spun around. Marcus dropped behind the stall, holding his breath, waiting to be exposed. Hawkins muttered, "I'm seeing devils in shadows these days," and returned to the party.

Marcus remained in the stall, absently stroking the horse's forelock. It was apparent that Lord W didn't refer to him, so who was he, and what had he done to earn Hawkins's suspicions? Did "lord" denote peerage, or was it a code name? And most pertinently, was Lord W the mystery man who had killed Quinton?

Every door that opened sent him further into a maze of suspicions and suspects. A voice of doubt niggled. Was he putting himself in danger for naught? What if the book didn't prove his father's innocence and rather verified his guilt? And if it was in code, as Hawkins had insinuated, would he even be able to decipher it?

It was a sobering, depressing thought and one he refused to dwell on. Besides the personal vindication of his honor, he needed a good name in order to sell quality stock to the upper echelons of Society.

Another compelling reason had presented itself in stark focus over the past few days. If he wanted to properly court

Delilah and marry her, he needed status and honor. Two traits he was currently lacking in Society's eyes. She deserved that much at least.

The race was on to clear his family's name before Delilah accepted—or was forced to accept—Sir Wallace Wainscott's offer of marriage.

CHAPTER 8

*S*itting along the wall of the dance floor, Delilah stifled a yawn against the back of her hand. Lady Casterly had insisted they attend Lord and Lady Danforth's annual ball. Delilah had attempted to make an excuse, but her mother had insisted they go, especially as Sir Wallace had not graced them with a morning call. Delilah had been relieved not to have to receive him, but her mother was a knot of anxiety.

Her mother had spent the carriage ride encouraging Delilah to simper, flutter her eyes, and hang on Sir Wallace's every word. Delilah, however, had other plans. She would nurture the awkwardness that had sprung between her and Sir Wallace. Perhaps she could even put Sir Wallace off her entirely—despite her enormous dowry. As Sir Wallace had yet to make an appearance, it seemed neither her mother's nor Delilah's contrary plans would be put into motion.

Delilah's dance card was sparsely filled, which suited her fine. She had slept poorly the night before, her thoughts circling a future that was looking more and more bleak. She blamed Marcus and the kiss. Imaging such intimacy with another man set her stomach to squirming like an earthworm on a hot stone.

A footman approached holding a salver. "Miss Bancroft?"

"Yes." She straightened.

"A note, miss."

Taking the folded missive, Delilah waited until the footman retreated and stole a surreptitious glance around her. Her mother and Lady Casterly were some feet away in conversation with a group of matrons and paying her no mind.

The intricately folded parchment revealed a message written in a masculine hand. *"Meet me in the servants' hallway. W."*

W could be Lord Wyndam or Sir Wallace Wainscott. She refolded the note and tapped it on her chin, trying to imagine prim and proper Sir Wallace inviting her for an assignation. On the other hand, it would be just like Marcus to sneak into the ball through the servants' entrance and bribe a footman to bring her a note.

Her conscience barely put up a fight. Of course she would meet Marcus in a hopefully deserted hallway without a chaperone. Her common sense where he was concerned approached naught. Had he discovered something important that required her help? Would he ask her to accompany him to Fieldstones?

She rose, shook out her skirts, and sidled along the edge of the crowd toward the door. Her mother and Lady Casterly hadn't noticed her departure, and if they did, they would assume she was either on the dance floor or in the retiring room.

Linking her hands demurely around her fan, she smiled and nodded her way out of the ballroom and into the entryway. One hallway was crowded and led to the refreshments and card rooms. She swiveled her gaze toward the other hallway without yet making a move. Narrow and dim.

When she was a child, she'd learned the easiest way to sneak was not to sneak at all, but to walk purposefully toward her destination. Confidence was rarely questioned. With the lesson in mind, she strolled toward the narrow hallway, her pace even, and didn't cast furtive glances over her shoulder no matter how she was tempted.

No one stopped her. As soon as she entered the shadows of the hallway, she slowed, taking her bearings and reassembling her nerves. A man-shaped shadow drew her attention.

"Marcus?" she whispered.

The shadow made a follow-me gesture and disappeared. She crept closer, anticipation warring with a clang of alarm.

She rounded a corner and was roughly spun around. An arm clamped her torso, and a hand covered her mouth and nose. Panic swamped her, and she grabbed at the hand over her mouth, unable to draw in a breath. The man's grip was implacable. Her lungs grew tight and panic roared in her ears. She knew she should scream for help, but all her body could focus on was a breath. She needed air.

The man dragged her backward. Her feet scrabbled against the floor, searching for purchase to dislodge her attacker. Her efforts only tipped her weight onto him, making it easier for him to control her. She could hear nothing but her own heartbeat, banging like a fist against a door in her chest.

"Now, now, Miss Bancroft, calm yourself. I only wish to speak with you." While his hand remained covering her mouth, it had loosened enough to allow her to breathe through her nose.

She took several deep breaths, the scent of root vegetables strong. He had dragged her into a storage room. As she calmed, another scent—musky and dangerous—cut through her senses. One that matched the icy, malevolent whisper in her ear. Quinton's killer had laid a trap, and she'd waltzed into it like a ninny.

"I won't hurt you. I promise." How easily the lies tripped from his lips.

If he knew she'd witnessed Quinton's murder, he would kill her and leave her to bleed out on the potatoes and turnips. Her only chance was to convince him she was but an innocent, ignorant debutante who knew nothing of him or what he'd done. Or he might kill her no matter what she said.

"I'll drop my hand if you swear not to scream," he said smoothly.

"I-I promise," she mumbled against his skin, unfortunately not needing to fake the fearful tremble in her voice.

He dropped his hand but kept her back to his front so she couldn't see his face. "Now we can have a polite conversation."

"This is most improper, sir. Lady Casterly will be hearing about this affront to my innocence."

"I have no interest in ravishing you, my dear." The humor in his voice was of the darkest variety. "You're pretty, but not sophisticated or experienced enough for my tastes."

A shiver skated through her at the thought of him watching her while she was unaware. "What do you want with me then?"

"I wish to return something that I believe belongs to you." His hand pressed against her back as he rummaged through a pocket in his jacket.

"I can't imagine what." It was her turn to lie. She knew exactly what he would pull out. Her blasted fan.

Sure enough, he opened it and stirred the air in front of her. "Your fan, is it not?"

"I am missing no fan, sir. If you'll kindly let me go, I'll—" She yelped when his grip tightened around her upper arm.

"Do not lie to me." Anger sharpened his voice. He shook her so hard her teeth clicked together.

"I-I'm not lying. I don't know whom this fan belongs to." She wished she were only pretending to cower. The darkness added to the menace building around her. How far away was the door? Was it locked? It wouldn't matter unless she could free herself from his implacable grip.

His voice cooled like fire-hot iron doused. "This fan turned up in a most unusual place."

"I can't imagine where," Delilah said.

"You know exactly where you left it, don't you?"

"The ladies' retiring room? That would be a most unusual place for a gentleman such as yourself to find a lady's fan. What were you doing there?" She infused as much horror at his impropriety as possible into her words.

He tutted. "I'm excessively tired of games, Miss Bancroft. Either you work for Hawkins and are very good at your job. Or... you are an innocent caught up in something you don't understand. How much did you see?"

She calculated her odds at surviving. Not promising, in whatever direction she headed. "Who is Hawkins, sir?"

"So you're an innocent who knows nothing? We'll see about that." He held up the fan, its shadow muted but visible. The percussive snap of the wooden spines in his fist stole her breath as effectively as his clamping fingers had earlier. She imagined her neck under his hands. Hands that had more than a passing acquaintance with murder.

"I know nothing of who you are," she whispered on a wisp of air.

"But you know what I did." It wasn't a question to be answered, so she said nothing. "I'm terribly sorry it's come to this."

She had played her hand wrong. She could have claimed to have left the fan in the study much earlier. Instead, by claiming total ignorance, she had signed her own death warrant. There was no time for regrets.

She could either stand here while he led her off a cliff's edge like a sheep or take action. Shifting, she reached out with her foot and bumped a sack piled high with some sort of vegetable.

"What is your plan? To strangle me and leave me here? Or stab me through the heart like Quinton? Think of the mess and the fuss my family will make." Her bravado was merely to keep him talking and buy her time.

"And here I heard you were a missish lady."

"You were misinformed." Her only option was to go on the offensive. A flood of cold steadied her nerves. She had survived a night in the bogs when she could have given up. She would survive this man.

"I know old Wyndam's son has been sniffing around you. And I know your parents don't approve. It would be understandable if a traitor's son lost his temper and murdered the lady he was denied. An age-old tale. And one that would dispose of two headaches for me."

Damn and blast, with the rumors circulating already, the lie would catch like wildfire, and Marcus would be in Newgate by dawn.

Unless she acted. His arm around her torso loosened, and his hands shifted toward her neck, leaving her momentarily free. She struck. Quick as an adder, she lunged forward, grabbed whatever was in the closest sack, and threw it behind her at the man's face. He grunted, his balance upset.

She screamed like a banshee and grabbed what turned out to be turnips, turning with the throw and knocking him square in the chest. She lobbed another, but having lost the element of surprise, the vegetables did little to slow his pursuit. He caught her wrists in a grasp that might as well have been manacles, tight and unescapable. He transferred her wrists to one hand as he grappled for something in his boot. A knife?

The meager light didn't reveal the details of his face, but she could make out a strong jaw, the blade of a nose, and light-colored hair.

"Be still, you hellion." His voice had lost a portion of its austere control and took on a new feeling of discomfiture.

"Never, you… you…" Her mind blanked on an appropriate insult, so instead she did what Alastair had taught her to do if accosted. She butted her head up against his chin and lifted her knee to jab him between his legs.

His teeth clacked together, and he groaned, shifting his

hands to where she'd kneed him. Stumbling over the stores of food, she made for the door, yanked it open, and ran into the hallway. She glanced over her shoulder, fearing the man was inches away from grabbing her and dragging her back into the darkness.

As she rounded the corner, she bumped into a hard, warm body. How had he circled around her? A yelping scream escaped her, and she backpeddled, bumping into the wall.

"Where have you been?" Marcus's voice bordered on frantic, and it was the most beautiful thing she'd ever heard.

She launched herself at him, winding her arms around his neck like a clinging vine. He held her, his solidness a port in the chaos. She buried her face between his cravat and hair and took a deep breath, her numb lips against warm skin. His scent was rain and hay and summer wind. She tightened her hold.

Music wound its way to them. Marcus led her into the shadows of a shallow alcove at the edge of the servants' hallway. "Are you injured?"

"No. I'm well." Or at least she would be.

"What happened?"

"I received a note. I assumed it was from you."

"What did it say?" Marcus asked.

She fished the note out of her reticule and handed it to him. He stared at it and murmured, "W."

"For Wyndam, I assumed. Who else?"

"A man called Lord W, I presume, and Quinton's killer." He didn't wait for the questions forming sluggishly in her head to emerge. "I overheard Hawkins and an underling speak of a Lord W in connection with Quinton's murder. Could it have been him?"

"Yes, it was him, although he didn't introduce himself."

Fury rampaged across his face as he pulled away and took a step back toward the narrow hallway. "I need to—"

"No. Don't leave me." She held him fast, unable to bear being left alone and vulnerable to another attack. "He knew I witnessed Quinton's murder."

"How the devil did he know that?"

"I neglected to tell you something about the night in the study. Something I only remembered later that tied me to the scene," she said with reluctance.

"What?" He searched her face, strain and worry tightening his expression.

"I left my dance fan on the settee before I hid behind the draperies. He found it. I never dreamed he could tie the fan back to me."

Marcus briefly closed his eyes. "It would take but a few subtle questions to reveal you as the fan's owner and possible witness to his crime. I wish you had confided in me."

"I didn't remember at first, and when I did, I felt like a fool. Anyway, what could you have done?"

"I would have dogged your heels to protect you. Damn your mother and Lady Casterly's poor opinion of me."

She found a smile, although it trembled around the edges. "How did you find me tonight?"

"Luck and persistence. I regretted our last parting and bribed your cook to tell me which ball you were attending. After searching the ballroom and the gardens without any sign of you, I was beginning to panic." He shrugged. "Honestly, I was standing here at a loss when you bumped into me."

Delilah looked down the dark hallway. Might-have-beens stacked terror upon terror in her imagination. If things had gone differently, she could now be lying in the deserted store room strangled or stabbed to death. The shivers passing through her weren't from cold; nevertheless, Marcus drew her close and stroked her hair as one might comfort a child or a favorite pet.

"It was a near thing, Marcus. He was ready to strangle me and pin the murder on you." She took a deep breath of his unique scent and latched herself even closer to him. "He assumed I was docile and weak and wouldn't fight him."

A slight rumble in his chest helped abate a portion of her anxiety. "He was sorely mistaken."

Somewhere, somehow, she found a small smile. "I threw a turnip at his head."

"A spy and murderer done in by a turnip-wielding debutante. I wish I had been there."

"Me too." Her smile turned into a little sob.

A madman was on the loose and wanted her silenced. The only way to accomplish that was to kill her. She wasn't naive enough to think he would give up now.

"What am I to do?" Her words emerged on the hitch of her tears.

He cupped her face and tilted it to his. "You mean what are *we* to do?"

"Mother won't even allow you to call on me. You can't protect me."

"That's all true." His voice was exceedingly calm. "I know of only one solution."

With her face still cradled in his hands, he leaned down and kissed her. Unlike the scorching wildfire of their last kisses, this one kindled a warmth that inched through her until she needed to shed a layer of clothes. She shuffled closer, craving the comfort and distraction he offered. She closed her eyes, and the world and her worries fell away, if only for a moment.

"I apologize, Delilah," he whispered against her lips.

"For what?"

A gasp and spate of laughter registered like the echo of a call, distant and muted. She blinked her eyes open and looked to the left. At least five matrons gathered in the mouth of the hallway. If she was lucky, none would recognize her.

Lady Casterly elbowed her way through the group to stand like a general at the head of an advancing army, her cane planted in front of her. Delilah's only saving grace was that there was no sign of her mother. Delilah took a step away from Marcus, even as her body tingled from his touch, and braced herself for a blistering set down from Lady Casterly.

Lady Casterly didn't even look at Delilah. She rapped her cane once on the floor, the noise quieting the titter of the ladies behind her. "Mr. Bancroft will expect a visit from you on the morrow, Lord Wyndam."

"Yes, ma'am." He executed a small bow.

"Very good, my lord." Only now did Lady Casterly direct her gaze toward Delilah, holding out her hand. "Time to find your mother, my dear."

As they walked side by side toward the ballroom, Delilah's blush intensified with the number of eyes and whispers following in their wake.

"I'm sorry," Delilah whispered through her forced smile.

"I can't say I'm surprised. Lord Wyndam is a handsome, charming devil, and you've been enamored since the beginning. A match with Sir Wallace would have been more advantageous for you and your family, no matter that Wyndam holds an earl-dom. Dear Edward left a shambles for the poor boy."

The events in motion made her feel like the earth was spinning out of control. "It was only a kiss."

"A kiss in a dim, secluded alcove with a man whose reputation is tarnished will blacken yours. The only way to repair the damage is to marry him. At least it wasn't a footman. You will be a countess, after all."

"Marry Marcus?" Her feet stuttered to a halt. "But… but…"

Lady Casterly raised an eyebrow. "If you choose not to marry Lord Wyndam, the rumors will leave you ruined and your family as well, to a lesser extent. Not even my protection could save you then."

Protection. Was this Marcus's plan to protect her? Ruin her so she was not welcome in Society? Perhaps he expected her parents to ship her off to the country. Would she be safe in Stoney Pudholme? A retreat from town wasn't the worst idea, but she would have strong words for Marcus on his methods.

Lady Casterly took her elbow and steered her through the crowd to the front door. Her mother waited in the entry, the brittle smile on her face reflecting pain and disappointment.

Delilah couldn't meet her eyes. "Mother, I'm—"

"We'll discuss matters with your father once we arrive home," her mother said through clenched teeth.

Once the three of them were cloistered in the carriage, her mother's voice came from the corner, low and furious. "You've thrown your life away tonight. I hope you understand that, Delilah. The future I dreamed for you is no more."

"It was merely a kiss." Delilah tucked her trembling hands under her legs. If her mother knew how close Delilah had come to losing her life tonight, would she be so upset? "My life isn't forfeit. I'm alive and well."

"And ruined."

Delilah didn't feel ruined. In fact, she felt more aware of her heartbeat and strength and fortitude than ever. "What will happen now?"

Lady Casterly's voice was calmer and more measured. "Wyndam will meet with your father in the morning to decide your fate."

Would Marcus offer for her? Would he even make an appearance? Delilah wasn't so sure. "It's my life. My future. Don't I get to voice an opinion?"

"You gave up that right when you succumbed to a rake's advances." Disgust had crept in to color her mother's disappointment.

"Marcus is—" A thump from Lady Casterly's cane hastened a correction. "I mean Lord Wyndam is not a rake, Mother."

Or was he? Perhaps Marcus made a habit of seducing

women he met over dead bodies. A hysterical, desperate laugh threatened to pop out. She stifled it. Barely.

"If not a rake, then a fortune hunter. All he could possibly want from you is your dowry." Her mother's assessment made Delilah's shoulders slump.

A heavy silence accompanied them the rest of the way to their elegant town house. Lady Casterly led the way inside, the clack of her cane like the striking of a clock heralding a hanging. Was Lady Casterly to be a witness in her defense or prosecution?

Delilah's father lay his book over his lap and removed his spectacles when her mother swept over the threshold of his study. When Delilah tried to follow, her mother blocked her. "Go to bed," she said and slammed the door.

Delilah stood for a long moment, staring at the closed door. How could a mere kiss cause such an uproar? And why did Society deem a woman tainted afterward? She was the same person she'd been before the kiss. Nothing she could say would convince her parents, Lady Casterly, or Society in general of her innocence. Finally, she understood Marcus's frustration.

The unfairness of it all made her want to kick something, but that too would be unladylike. She stomped across the marble entryway, her slippers making it less than satisfying, and ran up the stairs to her room. A timid scratch on the door signaled her maid. "Come in."

Millie entered, her eyes wide and curious. "Quite an uproar downstairs."

While Delilah wished she had someone to confide her trouble to, she wouldn't put the girl in danger. As Millie worked to help Delilah undress, she asked the maid how old she was.

"Eighteen, I believe, miss."

"You believe?"

"I was raised up in an orphanage."

Delilah half turned and lay her hand over Millie's. "I'm sorry."

Millie seemed taken aback at her sympathy. "It was a fine home, miss. Run by a church, it was. They were good to me. Taught me my letters and got me this job. I'm right grateful for it, I am."

"Is this what you want to do with your life?"

"There's worse things. Walking the streets, for one. That's a hard life for a woman." Millie shrugged, speaking with a matter-of-factness earned through facing challenges. "I reckon a warm bed, plenty of hot food, and waking up alive every morning is all I need."

Millie smiled and slipped out with no inkling she had left her mistress feeling off-balance. Delilah climbed between the sheets and let her mind wander. Waking up alive wasn't even a given now she'd been identified by the killer.

For a few hours, she dreamed of a simpler world. The one before she'd found Quinton dead on the library floor and had never met Marcus. She woke with a bittersweet feeling in her heart.

CHAPTER 9

arcus hopped out of the hack in front of the Bancrofts' town house, straightened his collar, and smoothed a hand over his best frock coat, which wasn't saying much. He would be judged on his clothes as much as his character, and neither were in the best shape.

O'Connell poked his head out of the window. "Ach, laddie, are you certain this is what you want?"

"My honor demands it," Marcus said.

O'Connell had stood by him throughout the tribulations of the past year and had lent Marcus confidence when he was bereft. Marcus trusted him. He looked over his shoulder at the old man. "Do you think I'm making a mistake?"

"She's got grit, I'll give her that." O'Connell's assessment made Marcus smile. "But your future is far from settled, lad. A wife will only make things more difficult."

The understatements made him wonder at his recklessness the evening before, but while he wasn't looking forward to what was sure to be a well-deserved dressing-down by Mr. Bancroft, the thought of marriage to Delilah didn't fill him with dread. In fact, something akin to the excitement of acquiring a quality horse lightened his step up the stoop.

Not that he planned to admit such to Delilah. Likening a woman to a horse had never worked out well for him, even when he considered it the highest of compliments.

It was unforgivably early for a social call in normal circumstances, but he would be expected. He patted his pocket and felt the crinkle of the special license tucked inside his jacket. Rousing the archbishop at dawn to provide it had presented its own challenges. Luckily, the archbishop and his father had been friends, and he had provided the license with minimal grumbling. The outlay of coin had cut deeply into his meager savings, yet he could summon no regret.

He rapped on the front door and was greeted by the sour-faced butler who hadn't allowed him entrance the last time he'd called on the Bancrofts. This time, the man had no choice and led Marcus into a narrow study. A set of windows provided murky light from the gray day outside.

The bespectacled man behind the desk rose and leaned onto his fists. While Mr. Bancroft wasn't a large man, Marcus was suitably intimidated by his flinty expression.

"Lord Wyndam, I presume?" His voice was spare and unwelcoming.

"At your service, sir." Marcus dipped his head in deference. "May I say—"

"No, you may not. I will speak first." Mr. Bancroft gestured to the chair across the desk. Once Marcus was seated, he continued. "No doubt, you are aware Delilah is in possession of a considerable dowry and made it your mission to ruin her."

"No, sir, that's not at all what happened."

"Then enlighten me, I beg you." Mr. Bancroft chopped his hand down to bang his desk.

Marcus opened his mouth, then closed it and cleared his throat. The truth of what brought them together could not be shared, but he didn't want to outright lie, either. "Your daughter is a remarkable woman, sir. She is brave, headstrong, intelligent, and I'll be a better man with her by my side."

His answer flummoxed Mr. Bancroft, who cleared his throat and shifted before crossing his arms and sitting back in his chair. "Be that as it may, Delilah will bring no money to your union."

Marcus hadn't considered marrying Delilah would bring him much-needed coin—he'd been more concerned with keeping her alive—but he also hadn't considered how Delilah would feel about living in reduced circumstances. "And if we don't wed, what will happen?"

"Sir Wallace is willing to take her as wife by special license." Mr. Bancroft's gaze slid away from Marcus's.

"For an additional bride price, I assume?"

A brusque nod was his answer. "Or she can retreat to our house in Suffolk for a time until the scandal is forgotten. Perhaps I can find her a vicar to marry."

A vicar? Never. "Or she can marry me," Marcus said.

"From the tittle-tattle I've managed to gather, your father was a traitor, and to say your circumstances are reduced is being kind."

Marcus stood. "My father was not a traitor, as I will prove."

"And your circumstances?"

The back of Marcus's neck heated. "Will improve. I have a plan."

"There is no guarantee your plan will ever bear fruit. My daughter deserves more."

What Delilah deserved was to not have her future hashed out without a say. "I propose you allow Delilah to decide her fate. It's the only way she'll be happy, and isn't that both our goals?"

Bancroft regarded him, his forefinger stroking his bottom lip. This was a man who did not make rash decisions, and whose mind was not easily swayed once on course. Marcus let him mull over the wisdom of his proposal.

"Ever since Delilah almost died two years ago, she has been weak in body and spirit. I'm not confident her nerves can handle such a serious decision," Mr. Bancroft said.

Now it was Marcus's turn to be flummoxed. Weak in body and spirit? The woman had scaled a town house, faced a series of dangers that would have left most men in vapors, and fought off a man twice her size with a few turnips. He couldn't help but smile quizzically. "Are we discussing the same lady?"

Bancroft's face was a blank slate. Finally, he nodded, rose, and pulled a bell cord. The butler popped his head in the door.

"Kirby, fetch my wife and daughter to the study."

Marcus and Bancroft waited in a tense silence. Delilah entered at a skipping run, a pretty blue dress swirling around her ankles and a barely suppressed energy vibrating the air around her. Mrs. Bancroft followed as if walking a funeral dirge.

Delilah's wide brown eyes met his with questions only she could answer.

Mrs. Bancroft did her best to ignore Marcus's existence. "Is everything settled satisfactorily?"

"Wyndam believes Delilah should have a say in her future," Mr. Bancroft said.

"No! He must depart and never return." Mrs. Bancroft still didn't favor him with so much as a glance.

"As it happens, I tend to agree with Wyndam on the matter." Mr. Bancroft gestured Delilah over and took her hand. "First, let me say your mother and I only want the best for you, my dear."

Delilah shot a look toward Marcus but nodded at her father. "I know."

"I heard from Sir Wallace this morning." Bancroft turned

and picked up a missive from his desk. "He is willing to wed you by special license this very afternoon."

Delilah's shoulders squared. "What enticement did you offer him?"

Mrs. Bancroft wedged herself between Marcus and Delilah, touching her daughter's arm. "Sir Wallace loves you, darling."

Delilah barked a laugh. "No, he doesn't. Did you have to double my dowry? Triple it?"

Red burnished Bancroft's cheeks, and he stared at the letter. "It matters not. He offers an honorable union."

"It matters to me," Delilah said, lifting her chin. "What are my other options?"

"You can leave for Suffolk and live quietly until this incident is forgotten," Bancroft said.

"And how long would that be, do you think?" Delilah asked.

"Lady Casterly thinks you could perhaps reenter Society in a few seasons," Mrs. Bancroft said.

"*Years?* Years of exile because of a kiss?" Delilah sounded aghast. "What else?"

When her parents remained silent, Delilah shifted to Marcus, bitterness flavoring her snapping brown eyes. "Are you presenting an option for my future as well?"

"I most humbly offer myself in marriage as an alternative to banishment and Sir Wallace." Marcus held up a hand when Delilah opened her mouth to speak. "However, your father has made clear that if you choose me, you will not come with a dowry."

Delilah's gaze never left his as she murmured, "May I have a moment alone with Lord Wyndam, please?"

Her mother sputtered out a nonsensical protest.

"The damage has been done, has it not?" Delilah asked sharply. "I need to speak with Marcus. Alone."

Mrs. Bancroft called out as her husband herded her out the door. "We'll be right outside if you need us, dear."

Once the door closed, Delilah went from quietly still to a whirling dervish in a blink, slapping him on the arm. "How could you?"

He rubbed his stinging biceps. "I'm doing the honorable thing by offering marriage."

"Why didn't you do the honorable thing last evening and not kiss me in front of half the ball?"

Dammit. He hadn't let himself examine the whys and wherefores of his behavior. Unlike Delilah, he had been more than aware of the danger of being caught. In fact, he'd counted on it. This was the only way he could protect her. The only way he could be by her side day and night.

"I apologize profusely, but a killer is on your trail, and heaven knows who else is part of this terrible business." Hesitantly, he took her hand and was gratified she didn't pull away. "I couldn't bear to see you hurt on my account."

"You had nothing to do with me stumbling upon a murder or leaving my fan behind. I've brought this on myself, and there's no need for you to sacrifice yourself."

He squeezed her hand until she glanced up through her lashes at him in an unconsciously alluring way. "Marrying you would require no sacrifice on my part, Delilah. In fact, we are quite compatible in many ways."

"How do you suppose?"

"Unless I'm gravely mistaken, you enjoy kissing me."

Her face turned pink, but her gaze held steady on his, and he almost smiled. "You enjoy kissing me as well," she said accusingly.

"Indeed, I do. Which leads me to believe our marriage bed will bring pleasure to us both. Unless you'd prefer Wainscott in your—"

"No!" She pulled her hand from his and stalked to the fireplace, staring into the empty grate. "I suppose it was always my fate to have my future decided for me by my parents, by my future husband, and by Society itself."

His heart ripped in two. One-half lifting at the words "future husband," the other crashing to the floor at the dejection in her voice.

"I have an estate, such as it is, and an earldom. I also have plans ready to be put into motion. You'll have freedom, and I hope we'll come to—" Love seemed too much of a presumption considering their circumstances, "—care for one another."

"You would take me without a dowry?" she asked.

"Yes, but you should be aware, if you accept my suit, I won't be able to provide you with a cadre of new dresses. Not yet, at any rate. The estate needs attention." Marcus tensed at the understatement.

The silence stretched, broken by the tick of the clock as it wound toward his fate.

"Fine. I choose you." She whirled, her face reflecting determination but no happiness. "Mother. Father," she called. "You may come in now."

"Shall I send for Sir Wallace?" Her mother bustled in and took Delilah's hands.

"I will never wed Sir Wallace, and if I accept banishment, how can I be sure you and Father will not force a match with someone equally odious in the future?" As if she knew how much her decision would hurt her parents, she said gently, "I have accepted Marcus."

Bancroft's face turned stony. "You'll not get a farthing from me, Wyndam."

"Delilah is prize enough." Marcus turned to her. "How long will it take you to pack? I have a special license and a rector ready to marry us."

"Now?" The reality of her decision was writ as trepidation across her face.

"Now. Pack a valise with only the necessities. Your parents

can send your trunk on to the estate." He didn't want to give the killer time to track her to her town house or give the Bancrofts time to lock her away from him. Their gazes held, and he wished he could interpret the myriad of emotions.

"I'll be but a few moments." She left him to face the lions alone.

The silence was dark and distrustful. If a sword had been at hand, Mrs. Bancroft would have attempted to run him through. Mr. Bancroft regarded him with only slightly less violence in his eyes.

He took a step backward, putting himself closer to the door and farther from the Bancrofts. "I realize this situation isn't ideal, but I'll care for Delilah. I'll protect her."

"With what?" Mr. Bancroft leaned over his desk, his fists driving into the wood. "Your father left you with nothing. Not even a scrap of honor."

"That is a lie." Was it though? Through the lens of Society, he had nothing, and by taking his name, Delilah would have nothing as well. Had he done the right thing in offering her marriage?

The time to wrestle with his scruples had passed. Delilah returned clutching the handles of a fine leather valise. A matching blue spencer covered her blue dress—her wedding dress—and a reticule hung from her wrist.

"I'm ready." Her shoulders were back and her chin up, but the waver in her voice betrayed her nerves.

Marcus forgot about her parents and went to her, taking the valise. "I may not be the richest of husbands, but I promise to do my best for you, Delilah. Do you trust me?"

"I followed you out a window, didn't I?" she whispered only for him. One corner of her mouth turned up in the meagerest of smiles. "How hard can it be to follow you out a door?"

Kirby opened the door and watched Marcus leave as if he were a rodent. Delilah hesitated with one foot on the stoop and one in her home—her former home. Her parents stood in the entry, her mother sobbing on her father's shoulder as if they were grieving for a child lost to them forever.

"Goodbye." Her soft voice echoed against the marble as she turned and held her hand out to him.

Delilah had chosen him, and he promised himself he would keep her safe.

CHAPTER 10

*W*ith tears blurring her vision, she allowed Marcus to lead her to the black hackney waiting in front of the town house and hand her inside. O'Connell tipped his hat to her from the opposite squab and smiled, his eyes scrunching under his fuzzy eyebrows. "M'lady."

"Not yet, but I suppose I will be soon enough. How are you this morning, O'Connell?" She did her best to beat back the threatening tears. This was her wedding day, after all.

"Right enough. I wasn't sure the laddie would talk you away from your family." The man's smile didn't disappear, but worry stole his twinkle.

The parting with her parents had been more painful than she'd imagined. The finality of it had been funereal. "You're my family now."

O'Connell patted her knee in a paternal fashion. His hand was large and worn with deep grooves and calluses. She grabbed hold and gave it a squeeze. It was a small comfort, but a comfort nonetheless.

Marcus swung inside, sitting close to her, his thigh touching hers. The hack jolted forward. Dust motes danced in the early morning light.

"Where are we going?" Her life had shifted course, and she was blind to the coming twists and turns.

"Chelsea Old Church. A childhood friend took the orders and will marry us."

The speed with which everything was happening disoriented her. She would be a married woman by teatime, and no longer a maiden by morning. Stealing a glance at Marcus, she let her gaze linger on his bare, broad hands. A flutter of excitement broke free from her nerves like a butterfly from a cocoon.

Silence settled over the three of them. The journey seemed to take forever, yet at the same time, she wasn't ready when the hack pulled to a stop in front of the redbrick church. It wasn't as large or intimidating as the grander cathedrals around London.

Marcus helped her out of the carriage and tucked her hand in the crook of his arm. O'Connell followed with her satchel. When Delilah cast her gaze toward the old man, then up at Marcus, he answered her unasked question. "O'Connell will act as witness and stand as my friend. I hope you don't mind."

"Not at all." Delilah turned away to hide a sudden spate of emotion. She had no one to stand with her.

Marcus sent O'Connell ahead of them and pulled her to a stop before entering. She looked at their feet, but he tilted her face up with a gentle finger under her chin. She blinked until he came into focus through her stinging eyes.

"I realize this is not ideal. I would have liked to have properly courted you, but outside forces forced my hand. Do you want me to take you back home?" he asked in a low rumble.

"I have no home." Her voice was thick.

"Of course, you do. Your home is with me, but only if that's what you truly want."

He looked so worried. She leaned into him and laid her forehead against his neck, not sure if she was seeking or giving comfort. A deep breath calmed her. She had no idea if she would come to regret her choice, but hope broke ground. Life with Marcus would be an adventure.

"This is what I want." Weak sunlight shimmered through the gray sky, illuminating spring's new growth before being swallowed by a cloud. A brief shining moment of clarity. "I want you."

The kiss he gave her wasn't marked with passion, but a promise. One she returned in equal measure.

After being introduced to Vicar Allenby, the ceremony was over before the quarter hour chimed. She and Marcus signed the registry. A steady drizzle greeted them outside, and O'Connell trotted off on his bandy legs to hail a hackney.

"What now?" she asked.

"I'll secure us a room at an inn. Gilmore's assignation at Fieldstones is this evening. Depending on what I discover, we will retreat to the country as soon as we can."

While Delilah didn't miss his use of the singular pronoun, her thoughts took a more practical bent. "Can't we stay in your rooms?"

"While it's not as exclusive and strict as the Albany, women are not allowed." Even Delilah had heard of the Albany's ban of the female sex. "I'll need to gather my personal items and direct O'Connell to begin packing for our move to the castle."

The castle. It sounded like something out of one of her novels.

A hackney being pulled by a swaybacked chestnut horse rolled toward them. O'Connell pushed the door open, and she and Marcus joined the old Irishman. Exhaustion crept up and weighed on Delilah. A sleepless night hadn't prepared her to face the upheaval of her entire life. She listened with half an ear to Marcus and O'Connell discussing their immediate plans.

Once they reached his building, the three of them climbed the staircase. Marcus stopped three feet short of his door, dropping into a slight crouch. He glanced over his shoulder and held a finger to his lips.

The wood frame was cracked, and the door stood ajar. Marcus toed the door open. The creak of the hinges was the only sound. No knife-wielding intruder came bounding out.

Marcus peeked inside, straightened, and cursed. "We've been tossed."

Delilah covered her mouth at the sight of the carnage. Cushions were ripped open, and books were strewn about. The contents of his wardrobe lay crumpled on the floor. The bed was upturned, a gash cutting through the mattress.

She picked through the debris to pluck a splayed leather-bound book with a cracked spine off a ripped cushion.

"It doesn't appear anything of value is missing. Not that I have much worth stealing," he added with a twist of sarcasm. "My guess is whoever did this either thought I had the book or simply meant to intimidate me. Salvage what you can, O'Connell. My concern now is for Delilah. And Starlight."

"I'll bed down in the stables tonight with Starlight, lad," O'Connell said.

"I can't ask you to—"

"Ye're not asking. I'm telling. You take your new wife and find an out-of-the-way inn. Somewhere safe. It is your wedding night, after all." O'Connell didn't know how to speak quietly, and his words rushed heat to her face.

She opened the book she was holding and pretended to read. Marcus plucked the book from her hand. "Are you enjoying learning about breeding habits of sheep?"

Of course it would have to be a book on breeding. "I'm looking for some tips."

His eyebrows popped up, and a laugh jolted out of him. Laughter was his natural state. She could tell by the way his eyes crinkled and his lips turned up. He winked. "I wager we'll muddle through without the need of a book."

Muddle through?

"Let me gather what I require, and we'll be gone in a trice," he said.

Still holding the book, she waited next to the door, impatient to leave. Malevolence trailed through the rooms like the vestiges of a slug. O'Connell kicked the stuffing from the settee to a corner. Marcus returned, clasped O'Connell's arm in farewell, then herded her down the stairs, carrying both their bags.

"Where are we going?" she asked.

"I spent my first nights in town at the Dog and Thistle. The innkeeper will keep quiet as long as I sufficiently grease his palm. His wife cooks a hearty stew and keeps a clean house."

Delilah wasn't sure how process the description. Marcus hailed a hack and handed Delilah inside. They were alone. Granted, she'd been alone with Marcus before, but now they were married. They would be spending their days—and nights—together.

Had she made the right decision wedding him? She could have retreated to the country, where there would have been walks, reading, and comfort. And loneliness. With Marcus lurked the unknown, but also the potential of adventure and... love.

"I realize this is not ideal," Marcus said, as if reading her mind. "I'm not what you dreamed of in a suitor or a husband, I imagine."

What had she imagined when picturing a husband? For some reason, she couldn't remember. All she could see now was the man sitting across from her.

"Will we be happy, do you think?" It was too late now, of course, but his answer seemed of vital importance in this moment.

"I don't know." It was an honest answer, not that it offered much in the way of comfort. "But I do know you are not meant for a disgraced spinsterhood or marriage to a clodpoll like Sir Wallace."

"What am I meant for?"

"Passion." Marcus didn't dodge her gaze. Softer now, he said, "You were meant for passion."

Her childish thirst for adventure had never truly abated. Living through her novels had only satisfied her for so long. Perhaps it was fitting she was marrying a man she'd met over a dead body.

The carriage pulled to a stop. The Dog and Thistle was located off the main road in a narrow alley with stone underfoot. Paint flecked off the sign, and coarse men gathered outside in a loud group, already drinking when they should have been hard at work. Delilah felt her sheltered country upbringing keenly.

She gripped Marcus's arm tightly and pulled her bonnet closer to hide her face. Marcus ducked inside the low-timbered door, and she followed him into the darkened maw of the inn. The scent registered first. Ale and smoke and unwashed bodies.

The bottom floor served as a common room, and clumps of working-class men gathered with dark-colored ales. Two women in dresses with low-cut bodices sashayed through the room, serving drinks, exchanging laughter, and occasionally slapping away a wandering hand. Wide-eyed, Delilah wasn't sure whether she was scandalized or fascinated, and she shuffled closer to the action.

"You're a pretty thing," said a bullish man leaning against a wooden pillar. The rough-hewn voice matched the visage of the man, who grinned at her with several missing teeth and a nose that had been squashed flat by misfortune.

"Thank you." The polite response popped out unthinkingly. It had been the wrong thing to say. She realized it as soon as the opportunistic light came into the man's expression. Politesse was not a language he understood.

The man stepped forward and made to wrap his arm around her waist. Before his fingers could do more than brush her skirts, she was picked up and deposited an arm's length away by Marcus. He stepped between her and the brute.

"Hands off, or I'll plant your nose in the back of your skull." Marcus's voice had roughened, his accent thickening with aggression. While Marcus was leaner, he was just as tall as the bullish man and looked fitter by far.

"The bird was giving me the eye. I didn't know she were yours."

"Well, now you do. The bird is mine."

While she wasn't keen on being referred to as a bird and treated like a possession, she also wasn't an idiot. Now was not the time to assert her independence. In fact, in the spirit of self-preservation, she scooted farther behind Marcus and tried to look as sparrowlike as possible. Not what one of the heroines in her novels would do, but then again, they were often reckless and rather foolish.

The moment tensed with the expectation of a brawl. The men around them quieted and waited. The bullish man touched his forelock and retreated but only after casting a dress-stripping gaze in her direction.

With a hand branding her back, Marcus maneuvered her to the staircase. The treads were worn, but the banister was polished to a shine. The second-floor hallway smelled of cooked onions and beef, but based on the common room below, it could be worse.

She had never stayed at a public inn. Their trip from their country house had included a short stay with Lady Casterly for refinement lessons. The stately manor had been less a home and more a museum or perhaps mausoleum. She had been afraid to touch anything, and the quiet had been deafening. What was Marcus's home like? Her home now, although it was difficult to imagine being in charge of a household.

Marcus unlocked the door at the end of the hall and entered their room. She shuffled over the threshold, her wonderings screeching to a halt when she surveyed the clean, cozy room. A bed dominated the space. Piled high with pillows and quilts, it looked inviting after her sleepless night. Delilah glanced in Marcus's direction.

A convenient bed plus a new husband was a tricky equation. She had no idea what he expected of her. Would he strip her naked and throw her on the quilt for a ravishing? An unladylike thrill zipped through her. She should be horrified, shouldn't she?

Marcus deposited their bags on the chest at the foot of the bed and collapsed in an armchair in front of an empty grate. As there was the only one chair, Delilah perched on the edge of the bed, her feet dangling off the floor. She removed her bonnet and patted her hair into place self-consciously.

Marcus extended his legs, crossing his booted feet at the ankles, and leaned his head back, his eyes closing. The silence grew taut until she couldn't stop her words from breaking it. "What are your expectations?"

He opened one bleary eye and twisted his neck to see her. "I expect us to stay alive. Or maybe it's less an expectation and closer to a hope."

A huffing nervous laugh escaped her. "Not that. Of course, I hope we remain in the land of the living as well, but I'm talking about this." She gestured over the breadth of the bed.

"Ah. *That.*" The single word had the heft of twenty stones.

She sat mute, even as fears and hopes, pleas and commands battled to escape.

He looked to the empty grate and rubbed his bottom lip. "I'm not a brute. I'll not force myself on you, if that's what worries you."

It wasn't, actually. He'd had ample opportunity to be cruel, yet he'd done what was in his power to protect her. Ice shot through her. What if he'd only wed her to protect her? Although she was afraid of his answer, she refused to turn into a coward now. "Will we have a real marriage? You need an heir, after all."

He jerked his head around, his eyes no longer bleary but intense. He rose and moved with an animalistic grace to stand in front of her. She tilted her head back, her gaze holding his as if she could discern his intentions in the dense forest of his eyes.

"Delilah." He spoke her name with a soft reverence she'd never heard, but then again, she'd never had a husband before. "I will take great pleasure in the consummation of our marriage, and I hope to bring you great pleasure as well."

Her lips parted to speak, but her words garbled somewhere between her lungs and voice box. He cupped her cheek, his bare fingers sending tendrils of sensation through her scalp and down her neck, as if his reach was far greater than a few inches of skin.

He brushed his lips over hers. Her heart kicked against her ribs. She reached for him, her hands fisting around the lapels of his jacket. His hands covered hers. Then… he ended the kiss.

She blinked her eyes open to find him watching her with an expression that veered closer to worry than arousal.

"What now?" She wasn't sure what she was asking, but if he stripped her bare, she wouldn't protest.

"Now we rest. Tonight is Gilmore's assignation at Fieldstones, and what has become clear is that I can't leave you here. The danger is too great. The lummox downstairs looked as if he wanted to eat you up." Marcus chuckled. "Not that I can blame him."

A bolt of shock had her straightening. "You are asking me to accompany you? I thought Fieldstones was inappropriate."

A puckish tilt of his lips banished a portion of his worry. "For an unmarried debutante, Fieldstones would be ruinous. For a married lady in masquerade, not so much."

"We'll be masked?"

"Yes, and only there to find Gilmore. Not to… partake."

"We shan't partake of the refreshments?" She had never been warned off cake and lemonade.

Marcus shook his head. "I fear you'll be scandalized and swoon before we can complete the mission."

She harrumphed and settled back against the pillows, feeling more than a little put out with his assessment. "If I didn't swoon after discovering a dead body, I doubt observing the ton carousing will send me over the edge."

He hummed and murmured, "We'll see. Get some rest."

Marcus retook his position on the chair, his focus inward now. She lost the battle to keep her eyes open within minutes.

CHAPTER 11

*M*arcus transferred his gaze from the grimy window of the hack to Delilah. She shifted on the squab across from him and tugged at the bodice of the scandalous green dress, but there wasn't another inch to be had. The landlady of the inn had braided and pinned Delilah's hair into a coronet on top of her head, and her face was covered from the tip of her nose to her hairline by a black silk mask. She was unrecognizable as the innocent debutante in white of the week before.

The sway of the carriage only made him more aware of the delectable amount of creamy skin exposed from neck to bosom. Marcus did his best not to stare even though he was entitled to the liberty of looking at his wife. And more.

Wife. He'd had to remind himself of his current reality a half dozen times. Marriage hadn't been on the horizon a scant fortnight ago, and now he was bound to Delilah forever. Performing his husbandly duties would be no hardship, but he didn't want their first coupling to be in a rented room on worn sheets.

She deserved more. Better. Better than him. But now that

she'd chosen him, he would do his best to keep her safe and make sure she didn't regret the decision.

Marcus cleared his throat and rubbed his fist over the smudgy window, his foot tapping with a combination of nerves and anticipation. Was the conclusion to the drama within sight?

Marcus patted his jacket. The book, *The Fair Breeding of Cattle,* Delilah had salvaged from his apartment was tucked inside his pocket. It was only supposition that the book's leather binding and size would fool their quarry into believing it was valuable to anyone but a cattle breeder. "I don't think the book will be necessary."

Using the book as a possible decoy had been Delilah's idea. She'd read a novel that featured a cursed book and a heroine who had been tasked with its destruction without angering the ghosts protecting it. The heroine had replaced the cursed book with a copy in order to burn it, thereby saving not only her life, but the handsome, eligible baron who lived in the haunted castle. Marcus hoped he and Delilah would get a chance at a happily ever after.

"Preparation is the better part of valor," Delilah said haughtily.

Marcus couldn't help but smile. "I believe the quote is, 'discretion is the better part of valor.'"

"Oh yes, you're right." Delilah deflated slightly against the seat. "I have the feeling we'll require both this evening."

Marcus anticipated less discretion and more violence. He fully expected to come to blows in order to retrieve the book from Gilmore, who understood the coded book represented life and death. The presence of the murderous Lord W complicated matters even more. If he couldn't retrieve the book before the handoff was made, the danger increased exponentially.

"Let's go over the plan once more," he said in a calm voice that didn't reflect his inner turmoil.

"I'm not to talk to anyone. I'm not to look at anyone. I'm to stay by your side and keep my eyes on the floor at all times." She ticked off his instructions on her glove-clad fingers. "Although it's too late to protect my delicate sensibilities."

"This is not like stumbling across a dead body," he said primly.

She harrumphed and cast him a disbelieving glare. "Are you quite mad? Nothing we encounter in Fieldstones will shock me. I can promise you that."

All Marcus could do was shake his head. From what he'd gleaned of the club, it made the usual dens of inequities look chaste. But if his plan held, they would be in and out without encountering any serious debauchery. Although, just in case, they had to look the part, hence Delilah's dress and their masks.

The hack passed a set of gleaming black doors and pulled to a stop at the alleyway as instructed. Marcus hopped out and looked up and down the street, seeing nothing out of sorts before turning to help Delilah out. When she would have stepped toward the front entrance, Marcus took her elbow and led her into the darkened alley.

"Where are we going, and what's that smell?" She held her gloved fingers under her nose.

"It's best we don't investigate the origin of such scents. Let's hope my contact managed to leave the door cracked for us."

"Who is this mysterious contact?"

"A serving girl I happened across on purpose in Covent Gardens."

"How did you convince her to help you?" The tartness in Delilah's voice was new and tainted green.

"Using only my Irish charm." He exaggerated his Irish lilt and gave her a crooked grin. "Let's hope I left a favorable impression. If I didn't, the coin I slipped her should help."

The door had indeed been left cracked open, and they found themselves in a utilitarian hallway lined with closed doors. Music, the low hum of conversation, and the occasional bark of laughter drifted from behind a black velvet curtain at the end of the hall.

"What happens now?" she whispered.

"We find somewhere to wait and keep watch for our quarry." Marcus took her hand and led her toward the curtain that separated the hallway from the revelry in full swing beyond. They were too conspicuous in the deserted hall, yet as he gripped the edge of the heavy velvet, he hesitated. Once they were beyond the veil, so to speak, could he protect Delilah from what she might see? Did she even need protection?

"We're awfully exposed here," she whispered.

Not sure what they'd find on the other side, he pushed through the curtain. He blinked and looked around with astonishment. The space had the scope of a ballroom, and there was a four-piece ensemble playing a lilting piece in the corner, but that's where the similarities ended. Instead of couples gathered for dancing, they milled about flirting or sprawled on settees scattered throughout the room.

The scent and excitement of sex permeated the room. It was heady. The couple on the nearest settee were kissing. No, not just kissing. They were in a preamble to sex. The woman sat between the man's spread legs. While he fumbled to loosen the tapes of his partner's dress, she tucked her hand into his breeches, the stroking movements quite familiar to Marcus.

"What is she doing to him?" While she kept her voice low, Delilah stared and took a step closer to the couple.

Marcus took her by the arm and drew her into his side. "She's taking him in hand." At Delilah's blank look, he added, "Giving him pleasure by touching him."

Delilah cast a speculative look up at him. "Interesting."

"We can't let ourselves be distracted. We must find Gilmore." Marcus tried to tamp down the arousal incited by the scene. "Stay focused."

Marcus guided Delilah away from the man and woman on

the settee, but the waters only grew more dangerous to his sanity. On their right were alcoves with the same velvet curtains at the doorway drawn for privacy, but the grunts and moans emanating left little to the imagination. He could only hope Delilah didn't recognize what they implied.

"I see him," Delilah whispered close to his ear. "On a chaise with a woman. And a man?"

Marcus spotted him. It seemed the man's degenerate reputation was well earned. How long would the man be? They couldn't stand in the middle of the room and gawp at Gilmore like simpletons.

"Let's retreat to watch." Marcus wrapped an arm around her waist and drew her into an embrace in the shadows next to the curtained off hallway. He wanted to keep his eye on both Gilmore and anyone who might enter through the back door.

To keep up the pretense, Marcus pressed kisses along Delilah's temple and let his hand roam her curves, all the while staying focused on why they were at Fieldstones.

At least, his mind stayed focused. His body, and more specifically, his cock, had gained a new sense of purpose. The blasted organ had one mission—escape his breeches and find satisfaction with Delilah. It wasn't even picky as to how at this point.

She circled her arms around his torso and grabbed the back of his jacket, drawing them ever closer. He took a deep breath and rocked his hips against her.

"Gilmore is heading this way," Delilah said on a ragged breath.

Marcus cursed himself under his breath. He wouldn't get them out of Fieldstones alive, much less with the information he sought if he allowed himself to be distracted.

With his mouth pressing kisses along Delilah's jaw, he watched Gilmore. Disheveled, with sweat glistening on his forehead, the man shuffled toward them but not in a straight line. Not a half dozen feet away, he stopped, swaying, to stick a hand in the pocket on the inside of his jacket. He pulled a hand-sized book partway out before tucking it away again and continuing, his destination the hallway.

Marcus's mouth dried with nerves and anticipation. Gilmore had the book and was foxed. The opportunity was ripe but brief. Marcus had to act. He shifted Delilah under his arm and stumbled from the shadows to intercept Gilmore before he reached the curtains.

He misjudged the distance slightly and caught up with Gilmore as he was fiddling with the curtains to locate the edge. Letting go of Delilah's hand, Marcus tipped his head and feigned drunkenness himself, stumbling into Gilmore. They twisted in a clumsy waltz in time to the music and found themselves tangled in the curtain, halfway into the hallway.

"I say, who the devil are you?" Lord Gilmore's words slurred, and the fumes of his breath could have been lit on fire, but Marcus sensed something else. Fear. Suspicion.

"No one of import," Marcus answered in a hopefully convincing slur. "I'm terribly sorry. I'm a trifle disguised."

The book and perhaps the truth was within his grasp. His heart tapped faster against his ribs. Timing was everything, and it seemed the gods were smiling on him this night.

He faked a trip and fell into Gilmore. It was the work of a few seconds of grappling to retrieve the book from the pocket of Gilmore's jacket and replace it with his decoy copy of cattle breeding. Marcus palmed the stolen book behind his back.

"Apologies, my good man. The blue ruin will be the death me. Probably best we take our leave." Marcus took a stumbling sidestep toward the exit to the alley.

The alley door rattled, and a man stepped inside. Gilmore stared, slack-jawed, as if Beelzebub had appeared to claim his soul. Between the dim light and the man's concealing cloak and hat, his identity remained a mystery.

Not to Lord Gilmore, however. "Lord W," the man said on a

soft quiver. He was already a mass of nerves and trepidation, and he hadn't yet realized he had a fake book.

Marcus felt a moment's hesitation. Were they dooming Gilmore to the same fate as Quinton? Marcus stared into the shadow of Lord W's face and could feel the man's cold regard. It was almost as if the man were indeed a devil and did not possess a beating heart. His hand had done evil and would again given the provocation. Or even without.

While a fundamental part of Marcus wanted to unmask Lord W and seek retribution, until he could examine the book himself, it was neither the time nor place for such a confrontation. Gilmore, on the other hand, had made his bargain with the devil and was obliged to pay the price. Hopefully, Hawkins would make his move soon. Marcus's only concern now was protecting Delilah.

Marcus pulled her back through the curtain.

"Marcus, what—"

Tucking the book into his own jacket, he shushed her and scanned the room. The bacchanalian atmosphere was growing wilder by the minute. He spotted a staircase beyond the semi-private alcoves. Moving deeper into the heart of the house was a risk but one that seemed safer than waiting to be discovered. They swiftly climbed the stairs side by side. Couples milled up and down the corridor at the top. Some were well-dressed; others were barely dressed at all.

Marcus moderated his pace, chose a door halfway down the right side of the corridor, and entered. It was a narrow, dimly lit room portioned off by yet more curtains. At the moment, it was empty, as was the larger room it overlooked through a series of viewing windows. Marcus led Delilah to the farthest corner and concealed them behind the heavy velvet.

"Did you recognize him?" Marcus whispered.

Delilah's eyes were as round as saucers. "The man in the

state of undress on the pedestal? I don't know who he was. His mask was quite elaborate, but to be honest, I was rather distracted by… Well, I wasn't making a close examination of his face." Pink rushed up her cheeks to the edge of her mask.

"I meant did you recognize the man in the hallway?" he asked dryly.

"Oh him. He had a cold air about him, didn't you think? Surely there can't be two such men wandering London."

Based on Marcus's last few weeks, his count of evil men was reaching a half dozen, at least.

"Do you think he recognized me?" For the first time, fear splintered in her voice.

There was only one answer to give even if he wasn't sure it was true. "Not with your mask. We'll be safe enough."

"What now?"

"Now we bide our time until we can slip out with no one the wiser."

"What about Gilmore and the killer and the book?"

"We must leave Gilmore and Lord W to Hawkins." He opened his jacket and patted the inside pocket. "I pilfered the book when I stumbled into Gilmore and replaced it with our decoy. Although that was a deuced useful book on cattle. I'll miss it."

She blinked, her mouth in an O. "I didn't even notice. Well done. Should we examine it?"

He traced the outline of the book in his pocket like a talisman, much the way Gilmore had done. It was smaller and thinner than the book he'd slipped into Gilmore's pocket. "Later. When we're alone and safe."

"What are we waiting for? Let's depart." She moved toward the heavy velvet curtain but paused before drawing it aside when the sound of voices grew closer.

Her gaze shot to his with a question. He covered her hand

and shook his head. How long would it take for Gilmore and Lord W to discover the real book had been lifted? Would they tear Fieldstones apart or assume the thief had absconded into the night after obtaining the book?

Marcus was betting on the latter. They would hide for now and scurry back to the inn after the drama played out between Gilmore, Lord W, and Hawkins. He drew Delilah toward the shadowy corner of the small space. Movement drew their attention to the larger room on the other side of the windows. With a jolt, Marcus understood the odd configuration. They were in a viewing gallery, and the man and woman on the other side were their entertainment.

The couple's desperation and arousal were palpable, and it was impossible not to be affected by the shift in atmosphere. A storm was coming.

The woman wore no mask, while the man's mask was plain and black. It seemed almost an afterthought, or more likely, a reminder his name or title wasn't to be used within the confines of the club. The woman's hair was black and waved around her shoulders, her skin alabaster, and her lips full and very red.

She pushed the man onto a green velvet chair with a curved back but no arms. He spread his legs, leaned back, and laced his hands behind his head. The woman gave a throaty laugh. "My, you are eager, my lord."

"Eager for your mouth, my dear. Now, get to work on my cock." His voice was cultured and teasing.

The woman dropped to her knees and opened the man's trousers. He wore no smallclothes, and his cock sprang free, already hard. The woman wrapped her hand around the base and twirled her tongue around the tip of his erection. The contrast between the woman's pale fingers gripping the ruddy cock and her red lips at the head was decadent and primal.

Marcus peeled his gaze away from the scene in the other

room to gauge Delilah's reaction. She was an innocent. While she might not swoon, he could imagine her filled with shock and disgust.

Neither were reflected on her face. She stared at the couple in utter concentration. Her tongue darted across her lips in a reflection of the woman who was wetting hers before engulfing the man's cock in her mouth.

"Oh my." Delilah touched her own mouth, her flushed chest rising and falling with her quickened breaths.

Marcus swallowed hard. If he had to guess at her state of mind, he would say she was… aroused.

"Delilah? I can whisk you away and—"

"No." While her voice was soft, it was emphatic. She stepped into his body, her back to his front. "Is this normal?"

He wasn't sure whether she was asking about the sexual act taking place or her reaction to it. "Between a man and woman who are attracted to one another, yes."

"Even between a gentleman and a lady?" She glanced over her shoulder and looked up at him through her lashes. Her innocence veiled a sensuality he longed to unleash. His blood roared through his body, and his own cock hardened.

Shifting closer, he grasped her hips and pressed himself against her bottom. She gasped but didn't pull away. In fact, she arched her back and let her head fall to his shoulder. He nuzzled her cheek and temple.

"Even between a gentleman and a lady. When we're in bed together, we will be merely a man and woman."

"Would you like me to do to you what she's doing to him?"

He did his best to modulate his enthusiasm. "Yes, but only if you want to."

"I think I do." She squirmed against him. "Watching them is making me feel strange. Restless."

"I can ease you. Satisfy the ache."

"Now?"

His mouth dried. He didn't want her first time to be pressed up against a wall in a depraved club. "As soon as we make our escape from this place."

Delilah took his hand and shuffled toward the curtains. A chesty groan from the man in the other room stopped her short. He pumped his cock and spent into the woman's open mouth. With a saucy smile aimed over her shoulder at the onlookers, the woman rose, scooped up the mess on her chin, and sucked her finger clean.

"Turnaround is fair play, isn't it, my lord?"

"Indeed, it is." The man slipped from the chair to his knees, not bothering to refasten his trousers. The woman sat with her bottom at the edge of the chair and propped one foot on the man's shoulder, leaving the other on the floor, her knees spread wide.

The secret place between her legs was shadowed, but Marcus could tell she wore no underthings. The man's first lick between her legs sent a quiver to his knees. True pleasure flitted across the woman's face. She might be a whore, but she was truly enjoying herself.

Delilah shot him a questioning look. Marcus smiled. "Yes, love. I'll pleasure you like that too."

Marcus was anxious to make their escape for a sundry of reasons. The longer they remained at Fieldstones, the more vulnerable they were. Marcus wanted to examine the book in private, but even more than that, he needed Delilah. Base instincts overrode even his burning desire for the truth.

It was their wedding night, after all. He'd planned to wait until the tangled web of deceit surrounding his father was unraveled. He wanted to woo her and give her a chance to get to know him better. The inn wasn't the ideal location. None of his good intentions or plans mattered. The way she clutched at his lapels told him she wasn't going to allow him to play the gentleman.

He took her hand, brushed the curtains aside, and tugged her toward the main hall. Paying them no mind, the couple in the space next to them kissed and fondled one another, flashing scandalous amounts of bare skin.

Delilah stumbled into him when he stopped to decide on their exit route at the top of the stairs. Her eyes were huge, taking in everything and everyone around them. The corridor was more crowded than when they'd entered the viewing gallery, and the buzz of conversation coming from downstairs was louder. Good. It would make slipping out unnoticed easier.

He and Delilah descended the staircase, but when she would have taken a step toward the curtained off hallway they'd entered through, he pulled her flush against him and whispered, "Too dangerous to retrace our steps. Better to take our leave through the front door as if we have nothing to hide."

She nodded. He tamped down the instinct to hurry, keeping his steps slow and measured as they weaved their way through the crowd. It was as if Bacchus himself had arrived to oversee the gathering. No sense of modesty or decorum afflicted the couples and threesomes frolicking on the chaises scattered throughout the room.

Finally, they stepped into the chilly night. The afternoon drizzle had cleared, leaving the world outside damp and foggy. A wigged footman stood at the top of the stairs.

"Can you summon us a hack?" Marcus asked.

"Aye, sir. Right away, sir." The footman's accent was broad and country-fed. Marcus wondered what the young man thought of the revelries inside, or perhaps he didn't understand the depravities taking place behind the elegant facade.

With an efficiency that would do any household proud, the footman had a hack at the curb in moments. While Marcus gave the jarvey their direction, the footman handed Delilah into the carriage. Marcus pressed a coin into his hand.

"Blessings to you and your lady, my lord."

"Thank you. We need them." Marcus rapped on the door and the hack lurched into motion.

Delilah turned to him, her knees bumping his. "I had no idea."

"I had no idea such a place existed, either," Marcus said.

"No. I mean, yes, that is quite shocking as well. In fact, I think I recognized a few of the patrons, but I'm speaking of the sorts of things that take place in the marriage bed. Mother led me to believe it was something to be endured. I already knew, of course, that I enjoyed kissing you, but—"

With an unexpected hesitancy, she reached out and lay her hand on his thigh, then slid it upward until her fingertips grazed his still-hard cock. He let out a growl and wrapped his arm around her, pulling her close enough to kiss.

All his good intentions had been burned to ash by desire. Wooing would have to wait. He was an animal, plundering her mouth and nipping at her lips. She was equally crazed, her fingernails driving into the muscle of his shoulder while her other hand moved to fully press against his erection. Her curiosity outpaced her innocence.

He should have guessed Delilah would be as adventurous and brave when it came to sexual intimacies as she was in life. He slid a hand up the slick fabric of her gown to her breast, barely contained by the bodice. Her nipple was budded against his palm. He could stand it no longer and tugged the fabric lower.

Her breast was pushed high, full, ripe, and begging for his mouth. He lowered his head, his gaze cast upward to watch the wonder and shock flicker over her face as he teased his tongue across the tight peak. When he sucked her nipple into his mouth, her eyes closed, and her hand curved around his cock, making him groan.

The hack jerked to a stop. He lifted his head and stared into her half-lidded eyes. Her lips were red and puffy from his earlier kisses. With her breast exposed, she already looked well-tumbled. He lifted the edge of her bodice but could still see the outline of her nipple.

"Wait here a moment." He took a deep breath and refocused his attention from his cock to the possibility of lurking danger. He couldn't afford to take chances now that he had acquired the book and had Delilah to protect.

Hopping to the pavers, he got his bearings and scanned the small courtyard and the alley running to the side of the inn. Nothing struck him as out of the ordinary. After paying the jarvey, he gestured for Delilah to descend. He tried—and failed—not to stare at her décolletage as she leaned forward to take his hand.

He whisked her into the common room and toward the stairs to their chambers. The man who had accosted Delilah earlier was still there and followed them with his hooded gaze. The hairs on the back of Marcus's neck wavered. He stopped midway up the stairs and glanced over at the man once more, but his gaze had fallen to his ale.

Marcus locked the door of their chambers, pulled the book he'd pilfered from Gilmore out of his pocket, took a breath, and opened it. Hawkins had mentioned the book was in a cipher, so he didn't expect to see a declaration in ink of his father's innocence, although it would have been nice. The book held page after page of gibberish. Letters that spelled nothing were interspersed with random numbers.

Delilah looked over his shoulder. "It's likely more complicated than a Caesar's cipher. Perhaps a Vigenère's cipher which means we need the key word."

The book merely posed other unanswerable questions. He

closed it and fought the urge to break something. The book held great value, or Quinton would not be dead and Gilmore so terrified, but there was nothing to be done at the moment. With the book in Marcus's possession, they could retreat to his country estate forthwith to study it at their leisure.

He shrugged out of his jacket after tucking the book back in the pocket. "How do you know about ciphers and keys, wife?"

"Wife," she repeated with a whimsical smile. "That will take some getting used to. But to answer your question, I recently read a novel about an antiquities hunter trying to enter an Egyptian tomb."

"You do realize your novels aren't real."

"Where would we be if I hadn't suggested bringing along a decoy book? Hmm?"

"It was a stroke of genius." He was rewarded with a saucy smile that made him want to strip that garish gown off her where she stood.

"The heroine in this particular novel had to decipher a series of hieroglyphs using a key she found in a different tomb. It was quite exciting." She leaned against a poster at the foot of the bed. "As was tonight."

Marcus picked her up and set her on the edge of the mattress. She yelped, grabbed hold of his arms for balance, and didn't let go. Leaning forward, he kissed her. The primal intensity from the club and hack ride home had banked like coals, flaring with the addition of a bed.

"I had intended to wait," he murmured, his fingers tugging impatiently at the tapes of her gown.

"Until when?"

"Until I could woo you properly. Until you were comfortable with the thought of me in your bed. Until you wanted me."

"I do want you." Her declaration sent satisfaction whizzing through him, even though he knew she didn't understand what she wanted yet. But she would very shortly. The bodice slipped lower an inch at a time. She caught the fabric to her chest before her breasts were exposed to his hungry gaze.

"Should we put the candles out?" Nerves had stamped out the bravado in her voice.

While she might indeed want him—and he was desperate for her—she was a virgin, and this was her wedding night. He would make sure she enjoyed the night, even if it killed him.

CHAPTER 12

*C*ool fingers of air swirled over the scandalous amount of exposed skin along her bosom. Another inch, and she would be completely exposed to his gaze. And his *mouth*. Dear God, his mouth had performed a wondrous act in the carriage.

Her mother hadn't been given the opportunity to share the customary pre-wedding night talk with Delilah, but from what she'd gleaned, husbands visited wives in the darkness to avoid any embarrassment. Delilah was expected to close her eyes and endure.

"The candles, Marcus, please." She splayed her hand over her chest, the slippery fabric shifting against the skin of her breasts erotically.

"You are entirely too lovely to make love to in the dark." He leaned in to lay a kiss on the top curve of her breast. "Allow me see you. Let me touch you."

The command in his voice was strangely alluring. If she hadn't observed the couples frolicking in various states of undress and intimacy at Fieldstones, the request might have left her nonplussed. But it was easier to envision now.

And then she forgot the existence of modesty when he nudged the top of the bodice aside and flicked her nipple through her white shift with his tongue, rendering the fabric nearly transparent. Oddly enough, the heat rushing to her face caused shivers to course through her body.

Her dress puddled at her waist, leaving her in only the thin, low-cut shift. He worked the fabric over her hips and dropped it on the floor. Her slippers and stockings followed. He pushed her shift up her thighs.

The disparity in their states of undress struck her as unfair. She pulled his shirt free at the waist while he unwound his cravat. His shirt joined her dress, and she was now thankful for the candles, because his chest was a marvel.

Light brown hair peppered the taut, lean planes. She ran her hands from his waist up his chest and over his shoulders, reveling in the feel of his skin under her fingertips. The ridges and dips of muscle and rough hair were a contrast to the curves and smoothness of her body.

He seemed as thrilled and enchanted by her form as she was by his. Tugging the straps of her shift over her shoulders, he didn't stop until the garment was at her waist. She didn't have time to be embarrassed or cover herself. He cupped her breast and sucked her peaked nipple into his mouth. The pleasure drove the restless feeling between her legs to new heights.

Using the weight of his body, he pushed her to lie on her back, her legs still dangling over the edge of the bed. Somewhere in the maneuvering, her shift disappeared, as did her drawers. She was naked.

His body covered hers, and she spread her knees to accommodate his hips. He brushed his lips across hers. While she appreciated his show of restraint, she wanted him to lose control with her. She flicked her tongue along the seam of his mouth. With a groan, he deepened the kiss.

Yes. She wrapped her arms around his neck, spearing her

fingers in his hair. The friction of his chest against hers made her hips undulate against him.

He raised slightly and whispered, "Are you ready for another adventure into the unknown?"

"At your side? Always."

"I was thinking more between your legs." His smile was so puckish and naughty, she couldn't stop from smiling back.

But her smile transformed into gasping shock when he slid down her body, grasped her ankles in his strong, callused hands, and spread her legs, pushing her knees close to her chest. At first, she tensed at the position, but as his intent became clear, she let her head drop back and closed her eyes, gloriously at his mercy.

Before tonight, she would have never been able to imagine such a thing, but now her body longed for his scandalous kiss. As she teetered on the cusp of begging him, his hot breath skated over her core, followed by the stroke of his tongue across the most sensitive part of her. Words became impossible.

She spoke in breathy moans and ceased to worry about her nakedness or her vulnerable position. In fact, she moved her feet to the mattress and lifted her hips. His tongue and lips worked an alchemy, and the feeling of a fraying rope ready to snap had her back arching and her muscles quivering.

The tension bordered on pain, and a sob escaped her throat. She needed something else—something more—but she was unable to articulate what, because she didn't understand it herself. She fisted her hand in his hair and moved her hips.

As if he was fluent in her body's language, he slipped a finger along her core as his tongue daubed at the knot of sensation between her legs. He filled her with two of his fingers, easing an emptiness she hadn't recognized until that moment.

The tension broke, and pleasure washed over her. Her body clenched his fingers as he pumped them in and out of her in a rhythm her hips recognized and matched. A languid satisfaction came over her, and she stretched her arms over her head like a cat finishing its cream.

Marcus stood, his jaw slack and his eyes hooded. While his one hand loosened the disks at the fall of his breeches, he sucked the fingers of his other hand in his mouth. The sight made her body clench once more.

"You are lovely in every way, Delilah." His breeches fell to his knees, and he gripped his cock. It was thick and long, the head flanged and dusky.

She said the first thing that popped into her head, "Your cock is lovely too, my lord."

The chesty sound he made was a cross between a growl and a laugh, but she was too enamored of the length jutting from between his legs to pay his amusement at her expense any mind.

The woman at Fieldstones had taken the man's cock into her mouth. After what Marcus had done for her, she wanted him to experience the same pleasure. Scrambling to her belly, she turned so she faced him.

"Would you like me to work your cock?" she asked hesitantly, mimicking the woman at the club. Could she fit it in her mouth? When he didn't answer, she cast her gaze upward, wondering if he hadn't heard her or if she hadn't been clear. She moistened her lips. "With my mouth, I mean."

Another grunt-laugh emerged from him, but a grimace tightened his mouth, not a smile. He wrapped a hand around her nape, his thumb caressing her jaw. "Desperately, but only if you wish to, Delilah."

She returned her attention to his cock, wrapping her hand around the base and skating her lips across the tip. The skin was softer than she'd imagined, even as the length was like holding an iron rod. Twirling her tongue around the flanged end, she savored the slightly musky, very manly scent and taste of him.

She took him inside her mouth, only managing half his length before gagging and retreating to catch her breath. His hands threaded through her hair as she sucked him inside her mouth once more. His hips pumped, setting a rhythm she recognized from the fingers he'd thrust in and out of her during her wash of pleasure earlier.

She squirmed on the bed, the emptiness of her body making itself known once more. What would it take to satisfy her?

Marcus stepped back, stripped off his boots and breaches, and joined her on the bed, flipping her to her back.

"You didn't finish, did you?" She was confused. Marcus hadn't shot any fluid from the end of his cock like the man at Fieldstones.

"I shall finish inside you." He pushed her legs apart and settled his cock against her core.

Finally, she understood what it would take to satisfy her need. Her body clamored for his cock even as her head wondered how he would fit. The tip of his cock prodded for entrance.

"Will it hurt?" She gasped the question out.

"As it's your first time, I expect it might be uncomfortable." He dropped to press a quick apologetic kiss on her mouth. "But you're slick with wanting me."

It was true. She wanted him and tilted her hips in invitation. He pushed farther inside her, and her body clenched with pleasure. The pleasure became a pinching pain, but he didn't stop until his hips were seated between her legs. He held himself still over her with arms that trembled.

"I need to move, love. Are you ready?" His voice was strained and harsh.

The feel of him impaling her and his weight pinning her hips to the bed was foreign. She was at his mercy and wasn't sure if she was ready or not, yet she nodded, not wanting to disappoint him.

He pulled almost all the way out of her and then buried himself once more. The primal rhythm of his thrusts banished her trepidation, and an unexpected pleasure built in her belly, the same tightrope of tension from earlier, but with a new urgency as they both chased the same goal.

His hips moved faster and harder, and his breathing turning ragged. She clutched at his shoulders, scoring him with her nails as she went over the cliff and crashed into the waves of pleasure.

Dimly, she was aware he had stilled above her, his entire body strung as tightly as a bow. A flooding warmth filled her. He had spilled inside her. A satisfaction that went beyond the physical brought tears to her eyes.

They were truly husband and wife.

After blowing out the candles, he gathered her close to him and tucked them under the coverlet. The darkness provided a different sort of concealment. Even her wild and wandering imagination couldn't have envisioned the night's events. From their foray to Fieldstones to the consummation of their marriage, revelations had revealed themselves one after another.

She closed her eyes and gave thanks to whatever mischievous spirit was watching over her. What if she'd been forced to marry Sir Wallace by special license that day? She would be in his house, in his bed.

She clutched Marcus tighter and buried her face in his neck. How had Marcus come to mean so much to her in such a short amount of time? The sweeping emotions scared her. While the murderer on their trail was dangerous, Marcus possessed the power to devastate her. Power she'd freely given him.

His hand played in her hair. "What is going on in that active mind of yours, wife?"

Unable to reveal her most vulnerable thoughts, she offered a different truth. "I was giving thanks I didn't have to perform my wifely duties with Sir Wallace tonight."

His laugh rumbled his chest against her. "No regrets accepting my offer then?"

She kissed his jaw. He turned his head to capture her lips, the sweetness making her toes curl. When they broke apart, she whispered, "None."

She opened her mouth to ask him the same but remained silent. Her lot in life had always included marriage to some man, but Marcus could have walked away from the complication. Yet he hadn't.

Still the question remained. Had he married her to assuage his bruised family honor, or did he truly care about her?

CHAPTER 13

a noise jolted Delilah awake. The shadows that climbed the walls were in the wrong places, and the usual scent of lavender had been superseded by the smell of bread baking. Where was she? Her heart leaped in panic before she remembered *everything*.

She pulled the quilt to her chin and took stock. She was naked. It was the first time she'd ever slept naked. Of course, last night was the first time she'd done many things. Movement at the window drew her attention.

Wearing his buckskin breeches and nothing else, Marcus peeked around the curtains. For a moment, she was distracted by the sheer beauty of the shifting muscles along his shoulders and back. Then the tautness of his body registered, churning her own anxiety higher.

"What's amiss?" she whispered.

"I'm not sure. Perhaps I'm being overly suspicious."

"But?"

"But it would be best if we departed."

"Right now?" No hint of the dawn gathered outside.

"I'm afraid so. Wear your warmest traveling clothes." Marcus pulled on the rest of his clothes, then helped her fasten her dark blue habit. "Are you an accomplished rider?"

She hadn't grown up with horses. It was only after her father had begun to amass money that he had bought her a pony and she'd learned she had no affinity for riding. Even the pony had understood who was in charge, and it hadn't been the awkward piece of baggage in the saddle.

"I won't fall off." She considered the truth of her statement for a moment and amended her answer. "Probably."

He made a sound that fell between worry and laughter. "We'll remedy that soon, but you'll have to muddle along today."

A bump in the hall had them both staring at the door. It was likely someone returning late or rising early. Still, Delilah's heart drummed in her ears. The door handle swiveled ever so slowly, and the door bowed as if a shoulder were being applied. The bolt held. For now.

Marcus hissed and gestured her toward the window. This was becoming a dangerous habit. He nudged her out the window onto a rickety wooden staircase and handed out their traveling bags before dousing the candles and closing the window behind him. They were on the ground without an issue this time and not a second too soon.

The faint sound of wood splintering carried to them. She froze and stared up at the room. Marcus grabbed her hand and pulled her out of the dim courtyard into a dark alley. The brutish man with the squashed nose pushed the window open and looked around the courtyard, letting out a string of curses before he disappeared.

Marcus led them farther into the maze of alleys and streets until they were out of sight of the inn. His pace quickened until she was nearly trotting at his side. Confused and lost, she held on tightly to Marcus with one hand and her bag with the other, thankful one of them had a sense of direction.

After a quarter hour, he halted in an alley smelling of horse dung. When she would have spoken, he put his finger against her lips, his head cocked. The shuffling of hooves and soft whinnies sounded over a city coming to life. A cart full of vegetables pulled by an old nag rattled by on the main thoroughfare.

Marcus gave a brusque nod and led her into a stable, stopping at a stall near the end. Delilah peeked over the door. Snuffling softly, O'Connell slept upright in the corner on a saddle, his chin on his chest and his arms crossed. The horse gave a chuff and walked toward the hand Marcus held out.

Even knowing little about horses, Delilah recognized the beauty of the mare. This must be Starlight. Her silvery coat and long mane lived up to her name. No wonder Marcus was keen on having O'Connell protect her. He caressed her muzzle, and she moved closer to bump her head against his shoulder, the affection between them obvious.

He let himself into the stall, shook O'Connell awake, and pointed toward the exit. The old man asked no questions, only rose, gathered the saddle, and began the process of saddling Starlight.

Marcus moved into the neighboring stall and saddled a bay who also looked to be of fine quality. It tossed its black mane with impatience to be gone. The third horse to be readied was a round-bodied piebald with white whiskers. Marcus heaved a sidesaddle on the old gray, which answered one question.

O'Connell mounted the bay using a block and held Starlight's reins. Marcus brought Delilah closer to the old piebald and whispered, "His name is Pigeon. He's not much to look at, but he's as steady as they come."

"Will he be able to keep up with Starlight and—" She pointed at the bay.

"Queenie. Pigeon will manage."

As Marcus gave her a leg up, she murmured, "But will I?"

Dawn had come to London, muted by clouds and dampness.

They rode single file, Marcus in front, Delilah in the middle, and O'Connell at the rear. Instead of remaining on the wide main roads, Marcus led them through twists and turns until Delilah had no idea which direction they headed. Pigeon plodded along as if playing follow the leader, and Delilah had little to do but stay atop him.

Only an hour into the ride, and the ache in her backside bordered on painful. The jostle reminded her of their marital activities the night before. Even with her thick habit and cloak, she was chilled by the time the buildings thinned and newly plowed fields outnumbered cottages. How far did they have to travel?

Marcus fell back to ride next to her. "How are you managing?"

"Pigeon seems docile."

"He is, but how are *you?*" His green eyes were full of concern but also worries.

Again she deflected. "How much farther will we ride?"

His wince created a pit in her stomach. "Quite a distance, I'm afraid. I hope to reach the Wyndam estates by nightfall. It's a bit beyond the village of Lipton on the western road."

Four hours later, she was biting the inside of her mouth to distract herself from the pain and cramps in her bottom and legs. A raindrop hit her cheek. She looked up, but a low fog obscured her vision.

Another half hour of pure misery passed before the outline of an inn came into focus like a mirage out of the fog. She nearly wept with gratitude. They veered into the inn yard. Eager to get solid ground under her feet, she kicked out of the stirrup, unhooked her leg, and slid to the ground. Her knees nearly buckled, and she hung on to the saddle until her legs could support her weight. She tramped through two inches of mud toward the shelter of the common room.

Only a handful of patrons filled the smoky, dim room. The

earthiness of the peat fire overlay the scents of men and rich food. The weather had kept most travelers off the road.

She gingerly sat on a bench close to the fire, pulled her sodden gloves and hat off, and warmed her fingers until the pins and needles were gone. Marcus spoke with the innkeeper's wife while O'Connell settled the horses.

Marcus joined her with warm ciders, took her hands in his and chafed them. "The fare is simple but hearty. Stew and bread. I wish we could have waited to travel when the weather cleared."

"Obviously, staying in London was too dangerous," she said.

"You're missing your family's fancy carriage about now, aren't you?" His gaze was on their hands.

She thought fondly of the velvet-covered squabs and warming bricks and lied to alleviate his frown. "Nonsense. I enjoy the brisk country air."

He wasn't fooled. "There's a carriage in storage in the stables at the estate. O'Connell and I will set it to rights for your use, I promise."

"I'm looking forward to seeing the estate." The brightness she forced into her voice did little to lighten his expression.

"You should know that—"

"We have a problem, laddie." O'Connell boomed from the door.

Marcus gestured him over. He sat and removed his hat and gloves, water dripping off both. He took a swig of cider before saying gravely, "Pigeon is favoring his back limb, the poor old boy."

"What do you suggest?" Marcus asked.

"Leave him here, or he'll be lame by the time we get to the castle."

"Do they have a horse for rent?"

"Nay. They have no horses for any price. I already tried."

"We could take a room here," Delilah said hopefully. A fire and warm bath sounded heavenly.

Marcus considered her for a moment before returning his attention to O'Connell. "Go find out how far to Wintermarsh."

"What's Wintermarsh?" Delilah asked.

"Earl Winder's estate. I would prefer to beg hospitality from the earl rather than chance another night in a public inn. I should have paid my respects to the earl before now."

"Will we be welcome?"

"Our families have been neighbors for generations." The lack of confidence in his voice was disquieting.

O'Connell returned. "Two hours' easy ride."

"I'll take Delilah there on Starlight. You continue on to Lipton, take a room for the night, and gather supplies. We'll meet tomorrow at the castle." Marcus passed over a few coins.

A serving girl delivered three bowls of stew and warm, crusty bread. Delilah's stomach rumbled. They'd missed breakfast, and she had been too nervous to eat much the previous night before leaving for Fieldstones. She devoured the stew and used the bread to sop up every morsel.

"Dusk will come early. I want to be off the road well before dark." Marcus stood and tugged his gloves on.

Delilah wished she'd taken more time with the stew. A drizzle still fell, and it felt as if the temperature had followed. She shivered, working on her gloves but shoving her wilted hat into her bag. She placed her foot on top of his, and he hauled her up to sit in front of him. She let out a soft yelp when her bottom made contact with the hard saddle. She squirmed to find a better position.

He tapped her leg. "Bring your leg over."

"But I'm wearing skirts."

"There's not anyone to judge you, lass. It will be more comfortable for you and Starlight if you ride astride." When she still hesitated, he leaned closer to her ear. "Come now, you'll traipse into a club of ill-repute but balk at exposing your ankles?"

The humor in his voice was like little fingers tickling her heart and making it skip. Why was she concerned with her modesty in front of Marcus? It seemed that in spite of their intimacies the night before, they were still strangers in many ways. She hitched her skirts higher and, with his hands steadying her, settled herself astride.

"It was more of a skulk than a traipse, sir," she said with starch.

Now, instead of the hard saddle, she was up against a hard man, which was uncomfortable in an entirely different way. She searched for something innocuous to discuss.

"Starlight is a beautiful mare." Delilah patted the horse's shoulder.

"Aye. Starlight will be the dam to launch my stables. All I need is a worthy sire."

"You don't have one in your stables?"

"I'm flush with mares at the moment, but I have faith I'll find proper studs for them all. One good foaling will turn things around." Equal parts optimism and despair battered his voice. "My dream is to breed the finest horseflesh in England and beyond."

Delilah might not have grown up as part of the ton, but she had learned hard lessons about its insular, unforgiving nature. She shifted in order to see his profile. "This quest to clear your father isn't entirely out of familial love, is it?"

His sigh sent a puff of white into the air. "Not entirely. Who else but my fellow peers will buy my thoroughbreds? Who else could afford them?"

She faced forward and stared at the muddy road framed between Starlight's ears. "Men like my father. Men whose fortunes are rising through shipping or industry."

"Cits?" He sounded astonished.

She jabbed him with her elbow. "Considering you married the daughter of one, I wouldn't have pegged you for a snob, Lord Wyndam."

His good-natured chuckle settled her ire. "Not snobbery. Only surprise at my own nearsightedness. Seeing as how your father is my only connection to that world and would have rather seen me dead than bless our marriage, I doubt he will vouch for me to his friends."

"Father would never have wished you dead. He's not a violent man." She found herself smiling. "In fact, he can be quite jolly. I remember once with Alastair—"

Remembering her brother brought into focus the tangle of fate between her and Marcus.

"Tell me about him." Marcus gripped the reins in one hand and tightened his hold around her waist with his other arm.

"He was smart and handsome and funny. Even more admirable, he didn't treat me as an annoyance. Although there was one time I caught him kissing the baker's daughter behind their shop. I teased him incessantly until he threatened to spank me and chased me up a tree." She laughed. Alastair had pulled her out of the tree, but instead of spanking her, he had tickled her until she begged for mercy.

"He sounds like a good brother."

"He was." She paused to gather her courage. "He wasn't killed performing an act of courage in battle. His rifle misfired due to tainted gunpowder."

The squelch of Starlight's hooves in the mud filled the oppressive silence. Marcus's voice was hoarse. "The whispers against my father accuse him of selling tainted powder to the troops."

"I know. Mother told me of the rumors."

"When?" His body was stiff and unyielding at her back. Starlight shuffled restlessly and tossed her head, picking up on his mood.

"After you called at the house."

"No wonder your parents were willing to sell you to Wainscott to get you away from me." He gathered her damp, snarled hair and pushed it over one shoulder. She shifted around. Her nose brushed his, and his gaze was steady on hers. "And yet you agreed to marry me, knowing my father may have caused your brother's death. Why?"

Starlight halted and stamped her hooves. A raindrop hit Marcus's temple and coasted to his jaw like a tear. Delilah cupped his face and ran her thumb along his damp cheek. "Because you are not your father. Because you believe in his innocence, and I believe in you. Because when you could have left me to the mercy of the wolves, you didn't."

"You might have been better off if I had left you."

"No! No," she repeated softer. "Either they would have killed me as soon as they discovered me with Quinton's body, or Lord W would have finished me off later."

"We're not out of danger yet."

"I trust you to keep me safe."

"I worry I'm not deserving of such trust."

"Then I'll keep you safe." She tried to smile with trembling lips.

He pressed a hard kiss against her mouth before getting Starlight walking again. A chill wind lashed them with a spate of raindrops from the leaves overhead. Delilah tucked her chin down and didn't speak again until Marcus pointed to a long drive emerging in the premature dusk. "The lane to Wintermarsh."

Hundred-year oaks lined the path, stretching their limbs and shielding travelers from the worst of the rain. Through the gloom, a large gray-stoned house stood sentinel at the end of the drive. It was a handsome house, if a little forbidding.

"The earl may not even be in residence," Marcus said thoughtfully.

"If he's not?"

"Then we throw ourselves on the mercy of the housekeeper. Worst case, perhaps the stable master will lend us the use of a dry stall for the night, if not for us, then for Starlight. She needs oats and water and a blanket. I've pushed her hard today."

At the stable door, Marcus dismounted, and without his stalwart bulk and heat behind her, Delilah crumpled into herself, her shoulders hunching. He held up his hands to help her down. Instead of a graceful dismount, she toppled forward, her hem catching on the saddle and pulling her skirts to her knees. A tug freed her and sent her into Marcus's chest, where she burrowed, feeling fragile and perilously close to tears.

Starlight whinnied. A man stood in the doors of the stable, a warm smile on his rough-hewn handsome face. "Looks as if you're nearly drowned. I'm Tom Donahue, the stable master at Wintermarsh, and who is this beauty?"

For a delirious moment, Delilah thought the man referred to her, but Starlight had stolen Tom's attention.

"This is Starlight." Marcus patted the mare's neck. "She's in need of a rubdown and oats, if you have any to spare. I'm Lord Wyndam. My estate abuts Wintermarsh to the west. Although I haven't had the pleasure of making the earl's acquaintance, he and my father were well acquainted since childhood. Is His Lordship in residence?"

Tom's brows drew low and his mouth firmed. "The earl has not been in residence since last summer, I'm afraid. However, his son, Lord Drummond, arrived yesterday from London for a short spell. I'm sure he'll be pleased to receive you."

"We've not been formally invited, I'm afraid."

"You'll find Lord Drummond doesn't stand on formality." While's Tom's words were a comfort, his expression held a veiled warning.

While Marcus and Tom conferred about Starlight, a chuff drew Delilah to a large stall set off from the others. A magnificent black stallion pawed the ground and stared at her with one big dark eye heavily fringed in lashes. As if conferring an honor, the horse stepped closer.

"I'm sorry I don't have a treat, beautiful boy," she said, equally entranced and intimidated.

Tom came up beside her with an apple in hand for her to offer as tribute. "Aries is a gluttonous charmer."

"He's magnificent." Marcus's voice was awed.

"He is that. No one else besides the master dares ride him."

"Has he ever been studded?"

"No, sir."

Delilah wrapped her arms around herself to gather warmth to her chilled body. Somehow Marcus noticed. "Let's throw ourselves on Lord Drummond's goodwill."

They ducked back into the drizzling rain, quickly walked to the front door of the house, and used the iron knocker.

"What if he doesn't let us in?" A shiver invaded her voice.

Marcus rubbed her arms. "He will."

The door opened and revealed a white-haired butler with a perplexed smile on his face. "Good evening, sir. Madam."

"I'm terribly sorry to trouble you. I'm Lord Wyndam, and this is my wife. My estate neighbors Wintermarsh. A lame horse and the weather has driven us to seek sanctuary. We were hoping to warm ourselves and beg a room for the night."

The butler didn't hesitate to draw them inside. "Come in, please. A fire is lit in the drawing room. Let me take your cloaks. Your father was a frequent visitor over the years. I was so sorry to hear of his passing."

"Thank you," Marcus murmured.

Delilah looked up at the unlit chandelier hanging high from the second-story ceiling, dazzled by the size. The marbled floor and sparse appointments of the entry offered a cold welcome. What sort of welcome could she expect from Wyndam Castle?

The drawing room was a lovely surprise. Warmth from a

LAURA TRENTHAM

crackling fire lured her closer. A comfortable-looking settee and two armchairs were arranged to face the hearth. Books were scattered like buckshot around the room, giving it a lived-in appeal.

"I'll let the master know you're here. There's brandy on the side table. I'm Cuthbertson, if you need anything."

Marcus smiled. "Thank you, Cuthbertson."

Delilah turned in front of the fire as if she were a pheasant on a spit and toasted her bottom. "That went well."

As if her assertion was an affront to the fates, the sound of bootheels clashing on the marble floor ratcheted up the tension. The man who appeared did little to settle her nerves. He was as large and intimidating as his stallion. While he wasn't conventionally handsome, he was arresting, with unfashionably long black hair and a dark beard. A scar bisected his cheek and added to the aura of danger around him.

"Wyndam. I'm Drummond." The man approached with an outstretched hand. He and Marcus shook. "I wasn't certain when—or if—you were going to take up residence at your estate. I was terribly sorry to hear about your father."

"As was I. I was in Ireland when I received the unexpected news. I assumed I'd have more time with him."

Drummond smoothed a hand down his beard, matching Marcus's sober tone. "Indeed. Our fathers seem indomitable when we are young. It is only as we mature that we understand human frailties."

"I'm afraid I haven't had the chance to meet your father."

"You won't have the pleasure tonight either. My father is not in residence." The man turned the blast of his intensity on Delilah, and she shivered in spite of the fire. "I wasn't aware there was a Lady Wyndam. A pleasure, madam."

"We are recently wed." Heat spread up her neck and into her cheeks as if she had stuck her head straight into the flames. She

170

cleared her throat and shot Marcus a glance that said "save me," but his attention remained on Lord Drummond.

"How recent?" Drummond's sleek, dark brows rose.

"Very. Yesterday morning, to be exact," Marcus said with more aplomb than Delilah had ever possessed.

"A hasty marriage and a retreat to the country. Will news of a fresh scandal await my return to London?" Drummond asked.

"Scandal? Certainly not." Delilah's laugh sailed high and broke. Lord Drummond's silent stare made words burst forth. "Unless you consider a kiss a scandal."

Drummond's sleek eyebrow rose.

"It just so happened several matrons saw us, including my sponsor, Lady Casterly. Perhaps you're acquainted with her?" Delilah finished with a wan smile.

A middle-aged woman with a chatelaine of keys jangling at her waist saved her. "A room has been readied and a bath drawn for my lady."

Lord Drummond nodded. "Would you escort Lady Wyndam upstairs, Mrs. Devlin?"

Delilah was grateful to escape, but a twinge of guilt had her casting a glance over her shoulder. Marcus sent her a brief smile before turning a guarded expression on Lord Drummond, as if he were trying to decide if he was friend or foe.

CHAPTER 14

*M*arcus didn't like letting Delilah out of his sight and protection but had little choice considering they had thrown themselves on the mercy of Lord Drummond. Trust was a precious commodity these days, and he wasn't sure if the lord of Wintermarsh was deserving.

"Come and sit, Wyndam." Drummond lowered himself into a roomy leather armchair in front of the fire, leaving Marcus to perch on a decorative chair that felt rickety. Was the disparity done on purpose to set visitors at a disadvantage?

Drummond refilled both their glasses with a decanter on the table by his elbow, then he stared into the fire. "I've heard rumblings."

"Of what sort?" Marcus took a sip of the excellent brandy to cover his discomfiture. The direction of Drummond's line of questioning could angle in too many directions.

"Your father's passing…"

"Was tragic." While Marcus hated the rumors and would keep the truth of his death close, it was still safer ground than the true reasons behind his flight from London with Delilah.

"Indeed." Lord Drummond stroked his beard. "Had he many enemies?"

Marcus tensed but tried not to squirm or otherwise give himself away. Drummond's intense stare seemed to miss nothing. "I can't say. I was raised in Ireland with my mother's people. I've heard he counted your own father as a friend, however. You should ask him."

"I would if I could." The edge to Drummond's response had Marcus riffling through what he knew about the earl. Was the man in possession of vital information that could provide Marcus a lead?

"Will your father be returning soon?" Marcus asked.

"One hopes so," Drummond said vaguely. "Strange things are afoot, wouldn't you say?"

The two men were like hunters leaving bait while trying to determine whether the other had left a metal trap.

"Very strange, indeed," Marcus said simply. He forced himself to relax into the uncomfortable chair and take a sip of his brandy. "Are you returning to London soon?"

"As soon as I handle a bit of estate business. My sister, Lily, is in the midst of her first season. Perhaps your paths crossed?"

"Ah, I don't believe so." Marcus didn't want to admit, title or not, he was persona non grata with London's hostesses. Rising, he faked a yawn even as his blood thrummed, keeping him on alert. "It's been a long, trying day, Drummond. I hope you don't mind if I join my wife upstairs."

"How obtuse of me. You are newly wedded, after all." Drummond was slower to his feet, his brows drawn low over his eyes.

The hairs on the back of Marcus's neck quivered. Drummond was a dangerous man who could make a powerful ally or a deadly enemy, but which was it? Marcus couldn't take a risk and be wrong.

"A night in comfort is much appreciated. I'm afraid my

father has let the estate fall into disrepair." Marcus sidled toward the door, keeping Drummond within sight at all times.

"Will you remain at Wyndam Castle or return to Ireland?" Drummond asked.

With the change in subject, the tension between them ebbed as a pang of homesickness reverberated in the heart. "I have nothing left in Ireland. My dream is to breed horses. I have a mare of fine quality. She's boarding in your stables right now. I only need a stallion to breed her. A horse like the one you keep in your stables."

"Aries is a fine horse." Drummond's voice gave nothing away.

"Have you studded him before?" Marcus asked as they made their way into the entry.

"I haven't acquired the right mare. I assume you're offering your mare?" At Marcus's nod, Drummond said, "I would be willing to discuss the matter further after I examine your horse. If you like, we could meet in the stables before you depart."

Marcus had no doubt as soon as Drummond examined Starlight, he would offer Aries for breeding. How Marcus would pay a stud fee was a hurdle he would have to jump.

"Excellent." Marcus put out a hand, and Drummond took it in a firm shake.

"Your room is up the stairs to the right. Third door on the left." Drummond made a small bow and crossed the entry hall to a room opposite the drawing room, giving a brief glimpse of book-lined walls and a large desk.

Marcus climbed the stairs slowly, the ebb of tension blunting the edge of his wariness. He'd taken the concept of safety for granted for most of his life. Now danger was closing in on all sides, and he was left foundering.

He hesitated at the door. Should he knock? While their marriage had been consummated in spectacular fashion the night before, they weren't entirely comfortable with one another yet. After all, Delilah's life had been upended, and he carried a brunt of the blame.

Granted, if she hadn't stumbled into a murder scene, their paths would have veered in opposite directions, never to cross. No one would be chasing her and trying to kill her. She would have married Wainscott and lived an uneventful life.

Relief nearly took him out at the knees knowing she was on the other side of the door waiting for him. He rapped softly and let himself into the room. Candles illuminated a magical scene. The blue hue of the drapes and coverlet shimmered like the sky at dawn. Delilah reclined in a copper tub, her hair piled on top of her head, her bare arms resting along the sides. She didn't move.

Marcus removed his boots and padded toward her on stocking feet, slipping his jacket and waistcoat off and dropping them on a yellow-and-blue brocade chair. She was asleep. He skimmed his fingertips though the water. It had cooled. The ripples he'd created lapped along the curves of her breasts. His hungry gaze took her in, from parted lips to tightened nipples to soft mons shadowed deeper in the water.

His wife. The thought was both thrilling and terrifying.

He knelt by the edge of the tub and stroked her cheek with the back of his hand until her eyelids fluttered open. Confusion knitted her brow.

"You'll catch cold if we don't get you out of the bath and into bed, love," he whispered.

She jerked to full self-consciousness, covering her breasts with an arm. He rose and held up a length of drying linen for her to step into.

With her cheeks pink and her gaze anywhere but on him, she rose, presenting her deliciously round bottom. He wrapped the cloth around her and helped her step from the tub toward the warmth of the fire.

"I didn't mean to fall asleep," she said softly.

"It's been a long, trying day." He let out a huff of laughter. "A long, trying week."

"Indeed." The slightest smile flashed on her face then disappeared. "I need to dress."

"Of course." He sketched a bow and retreated to the window to stare into the darkness. Fabric rustled. The bed creaked. Their intimacy was as fragile as freshly spun glass.

"You can turn around now," she said.

He did as she bade and shuffled toward the tub. "I'm going to wash the day's travel off."

"The water has chilled."

"I'll be quick." He pulled his shirt from his breeches and loosened the ties. He hesitated. "Would you prefer to shield your eyes?"

"What? Of course I would." The covers were up to her chin, and she peeped over like a wide-eyed chick, frozen in either fear or fascination.

He fought a smile. Would she ever cease to surprise him? He dispensed with his shirt, and still felt her heated regard. If he had a scrap of decency, he would turn his back so as not to shock her. Apparently, he was all out of the gentlemanly impulse.

Facing her, he didn't move except to release each disk of his breeches until they grew loose around his hips. He pushed his breeches and his smallclothes to the floor. Blood pulsed between his legs.

Delilah gasped and disappeared under the covers. Marcus glanced down. His cock jutted at full mast. Washing in the tepid water cooled his ardor but didn't extinguish it. Instead of his usual practice of sleeping as God made him, he retrieved a pair of clean smallclothes from his bag.

He snuffed the candles and slipped into bed by the light of the fire. He lay on his back, able to sense Delilah mere inches away but not touching her. She deserved a decent night's sleep in a soft bed. She tossed this way and that, jouncing him.

"Is the bed not to your liking?" he asked with amused exasperation.

"It's not the bed but my bum that's not to my liking." She was on her stomach, her voice muffled in the pillow.

A laugh skittered out of him, and he turned to face her, propping his head in his hand. "What's wrong with your bum? I found it rather fetching as you climbed from the tub."

Her intake of breath was sharp and scandalized which only made him smile wider. "You shouldn't say such things."

"If I can't say such things to my wife, then what's the point of wedding at all?" He lay a hand on her back and traced the line of her spine through the thin fabric of her night rail. "Now, tell your husband what's the matter, so I can help."

"I ache all over. I'm not used to riding so far. Or at all." She looked up at him. "Are you disappointed?"

He skated his hand lower to rest in the dip of her lower back. "Disappointed in what?"

"In me. Your dream is to breed and train horses, and I'm not even a proper rider."

He let his hand wander lower until he was lightly massaging her abused flesh. "I'm not disappointed. You have your fair share of redeeming traits."

"Like what?" She arched her back and pushed more fully into his touch.

He slipped his hand under her night rail and smoothed his palm over her bare bottom. Her skin was silky, the twin globes enticing him to explore further. Delilah's eyes were closed, and she gripped the sheet beneath her, twisting her hips higher and spreading her knees wider. He let out a slow breath and marshaled his self-control.

How could she for one second wonder if she were a disappointment? He lay kisses along her shoulder, easing the fabric over the curve. "Your spirit is strong. You were miserable today, yet you didn't balk."

"You make me sound like a well-bred horse."

He smiled at the hint of tartness in her voice. If she understood how highly he esteemed a well-bred horse, she wouldn't take offense. "You are intelligent. The decoy book was a stroke of absolute genius."

He could deny himself no longer and slipped his fingers between her slightly parted legs. She was velvety soft and wet. At his first touch, she moaned into the pillow and arched her back, surrendering. Her wanton response emboldened him. He scooted closer so the hardened ridge of his cock pressed into her hip. He found the bud of her pleasure and teased her, reveling the silken feel of her body.

"You are adventurous and brave and passionate." *So very passionate.*

He was lucky to have found and wed Delilah. Granted, he hadn't expected to wed at all with the black cloud of danger and deceit hovering over him. She was the one who should be disappointed in him. As soon as she was faced with his crumbling estate, he feared she would be doubly disappointed.

Those worries were for tomorrow. Tonight he would give her what he could afford. Pleasure.

He slipped a finger inside her and was rewarded with another moan and the rock of her hips. Without taking his hand from between her legs, he rose to his knees and shifted to kneel behind her.

He flicked her night rail to her waist. The fire cast enough flickering light for him to take in her pale curves. As one hand worked between her legs, he massaged her buttocks with the other, enjoying the sight and feel of her in every way.

She twisted to glance at him over her shoulder. Their eyes met in a moment of intensity that stilled his hands on her body.

Her hair had come out of its ribbon and cascaded over her shoulders, and her cheeks had flushed. She looked wild and on the edge of losing control.

"I want... I need..." Her voice was raspy and desperate.

"Tell me, love. I'll give you anything." As the words came out of his mouth, he recognized their truth.

He would give *everything*—his heart, his soul, even his life—to keep her safe.

"Your cock. I need your cock. *Now.*"

A slow smile spread over his face. He wouldn't make her ask twice. Loosening his smallclothes, he pulled his cock free. He'd done his best to ignore the throbbing need of his own body, but as if sensing the imminent ride that awaited, his cock grew even harder.

He grasped her hips and pulled her fully on her knees, her face still pressed into the mattress. It was an arousing, tantalizing position. Fitting himself at her entrance, he tried to take care, but as the head of his cock pressed inside her, her burgeoning climax snapped his control. Her moans were muffled in the pillow as she writhed on his cock and clamped him tightly. He could be gentle no longer. He slammed himself deep.

As her climax peaked, he pumped his hips, slowly at first, savoring the pleasure skating all the way to his toes, but soon enough, his pace grew more frantic. His spend sent him soaring into a space where he forgot everyone and everything except this woman.

She slid to her belly, and he collapsed at her side, both of them breathing hard. Silence gathered, but not an uncomfortable one. On unsteady legs, he retrieved the linen bath towel and cleaned between her legs until she batted his arm away and curled on her side with a sigh. He climbed in behind her and fitted himself to her curves.

"I apologize," he whispered. "I had no intention of taking you tonight."

"I'm rather glad you changed your mind. My bottom still hurts, but otherwise, I feel lovely." A sigh gusted out of her, and she wiggled her bottom against him. "But I'd rather not discuss what transpired. If I wasn't so exhausted, I would be mortified."

"Just so I'm clear, you don't want to discuss how you begged for my cock?" He smiled into her hair.

"Please forget that exchange ever took place." A different sort of plea made her voice rise in distress.

He nuzzled the soft skin behind her ear, the scent of her clean skin enhanced by her obvious embarrassment. "As if I could. I'll dream of you begging for my cock from this night until eternity."

"You aren't shocked?"

He was, rather, but in the best possible way. "We have only begun to explore the pleasures of the marriage bed."

She jerked around to look at him, wide-eyed.

He raised his brows. "It seems as if it's your turn to be shocked."

"Do all husbands and wives enjoy bed pleasures such as this?"

How to answer? From simple mechanics, husbands had an easier time enjoying themselves in bed with their wives—and other women—but he wasn't sure how women felt about their wifely duties. For most of the ton, marriage was an obligation to be met with a stiff upper lip.

But Delilah wasn't part of the ton, and neither was he. From the stories shared by his grandmother, his mother had been desperately in love with his father and vice versa. He didn't need stories to know his grandparents had loved one another until the very end. It had been a blessing they passed within weeks of one another. The world had seemed unbalanced when they weren't together.

Could he and Delilah form such an attachment?

"Some husbands and wives even enjoy such pleasures out of bed," he said in a teasing voice when his heart was serious. He was a coward for not speaking his heart, but there would be time. He hoped.

CHAPTER 15

*D*elilah stretched under the covers and winced at the soreness across her bottom and legs. Was it because of her hours spent on horseback or her nightly activities with Marcus? Heat burned into her cheeks, but when she sat up, the space where he'd slept was empty. Relief had her sinking into the pillows. How could she possibly face him after what she'd said?

A clock ticked on the mantel, but the room was otherwise silent. Light leaked through the heavy draperies at the window. She rolled to the edge of the bed and stood gingerly before shuffling to the window. The rain of the day before had left behind a bright blue sky and birdsong. A garden stirring in the first throes of spring spread out toward the distant shimmering water of a pond. Left behind droplets of rain shimmered on new green shoots and leaves of the vine growing over a trellis below her window.

Optimism unfurled like flowers pushing through the soil. Maybe the killer would give up on finding her. Perhaps Marcus would put aside the quest to clear his father's name. They could pretend to be a normal newly wedded couple and start their life together at Wyndam Castle. It sounded idyllic.

She stopped herself. Making future plans was a thumb to the nose at fate.

A scratch sounded on the door a moment before it opened, and Mrs. Devlin, the housekeeper, bustled inside the room.

"Ah, you're awake, Lady Wyndam. I have your clothes, dry and freshly pressed. Let me help you dress." Mrs. Devlin was brisk and efficient, making quick work of the hooks and ties of Delilah's brushed-out habit. "Your husband and Master Rafe have been cavorting in the stables like schoolboys since near to dawn. However, Lord Wyndam expressed a wish to make a start toward his estate soon."

"Thank you, Mrs. Devlin. I must say, I'm relieved with the change in weather. I wasn't looking forward to arriving at my new home feeling like a wet, bedraggled kitten." Delilah gave Mrs. Devlin a shy smile.

Mrs. Devlin did not return the smile, her brow furrowed. "You've never visited the Wyndam estate?"

"I haven't. Is there anything amiss?" When Mrs. Devlin's gaze landed anywhere but on her, Delilah gave a nervous laugh. "Is it haunted?"

"It's the oldest landholding in the area," Mrs. Devlin said. "The Wyndam line goes back centuries."

"Marcus calls his ancestral home a castle." Delilah couldn't stop a vision of an armored knight who looked like Marcus riding toward a tower to collect a favor from his lady before battle.

"A castle, yes. A very *old* castle." Mrs. Devlin shook a small smile back on her face. "You won't be but a few hours' ride from Wintermarsh. You and Lady Lily are of an age. You must come for a visit once she returns from her season in London."

"I would like that very much." Unease stamped on Delilah's

budding optimism. Old could mean historic and stately or decrepit.

Mrs. Devlin led her down the long staircase to the morning room where breakfast was laid out. "Master Rafe and Lord Wyndam have eaten. The tea is hot. You should fortify yourself for the journey and bundle up. The rain has moved on, but the breeze is brisk."

"Thank you, Mrs. Devlin." Unexpected emotion brought a lump to Delilah's throat. It was something her mother might have said. She was always nagging Delilah to eat more and put on a pelisse. By marrying Marcus, she had been cast out of a safe, familiar harbor, but Mrs. Devlin's unexpected kindness was like a comforting lighthouse in the unknown waters.

Mrs. Devlin started to turn away but then reversed to pat Delilah's arm in a way that was overly familiar for a servant, but welcomed nonetheless. "If you run into any trouble, you and Lord Wyndam are welcome at Wintermarsh anytime. Day or night."

"Lord Drummond won't want us disturbing him." Delilah tried a smile, but her lips trembled. She mashed them together and swallowed hard. Although he'd been kind enough the evening before, Lord Drummond didn't seem the jolly, welcoming sort.

"Pish. He might not host a ball in your honor, but he will extend a warm welcome to friends in trouble." Mrs. Devlin's brown eyes were sharp and all knowing. Except what could the woman actually know about their situation?

If the past week had taught her anything, it was that she should be wary and suspicious, but instead, her instinct was to throw her arms around the housekeeper. Which wouldn't do at all. She was no longer Miss Delilah Bancroft of Stoney Pudholme, but Lady Wyndam of Wyndam Castle.

Mrs. Devlin bustled off. Delilah did her best to fortify herself, but her stomach was a mass of nerves. While Mrs.

Devlin's offer of sanctuary was consoling, it made Delilah painfully aware of the troubles ready to pounce. She barely choked down a piece of buttered bread before giving up.

The front door opened, and the promised chill breeze rushed into the morning room along with a duet of male voices she recognized as Lord Drummond and Marcus. Rising, she smoothed down her skirt.

Marcus entered first, his cheeks ruddy, his smile growing wider upon spotting her. "Good morning, my dear."

Her own cheeks grew hot. Dear Lord, she had begged him for his... For his... It didn't bear repeating, even in her head. Still, her gaze dipped to his breeches before skating away.

"Good morning." She turned to Lord Drummond and inclined her head. "My lord."

Marcus and Lord Drummond seemed to have come to an understanding. Marcus smiled, and there was true warmth in his voice. "I thank you heartily for refuge last night, but we should be off. Hopefully, O'Connell will be waiting at the castle with provisions from Lipton."

"I'll be leaving for London soon, but upon my return, we'll discuss breeding Starlight with Aries." Lord Drummond directed a small bow in her direction, and she was struck again by the man's rather grim intensity. "Lady Wyndam. When my sister returns, you must come back for a visit."

"That would be most welcome." She sidled closer to Marcus.

Lord Drummond retreated to a book-lined room with a heavy, ornate wooden desk situated under large windows. Marcus led Delilah through the front door. The pins she'd used to secure her hair were no match for the whipping wind. While her hat had dried from the day before, it was bedraggled and droopy, much like herself.

Marcus led her to the stable where Starlight and another horse were both saddled, their traveling bags secured. "You will be riding Pegasus."

Delilah stopped short, examining the bay horse with white socks who was tossing its head. The name alone filled her with trepidation. "It looks rather more spirited than Pigeon."

Tom Donahue took Pegasus's reins and drew her closer to Delilah. "Pegasus is an even-tempered, docile mare. It will be like riding a giant turtle."

"I once read about tortoises in the tropics big enough to ride. I would prefer you find me one of those." Delilah tried to hide her cowardice behind a laugh. "I would much prefer to ride with you on Starlight, Marcus."

Marcus shook his head. "I—*we*—can't afford to risk Starlight going lame. Our fortunes rest with her and her progeny."

Now she felt cowardly *and* selfish. What was wrong with her? She had scaled the side of a building, bested a possible murderer with a well-aimed turnip, and married a man she'd met over a dead body. She could surely ride a horse.

"I'm sure Pegasus and I will rub along famously."

They did not rub along well at all. The problems began the moment she mounted with the help of a block. She heaved herself onto the sidesaddle and lost her balance, listing too far over before grabbing the pommel with both hands and righting herself.

Pegasus tossed her head and shuffled to the side to compensate for Delilah's clumsiness. Tom was taken off guard, and Pegasus's back end swung around with enough momentum to make Delilah clutch and pull at the horse's mane, which only made things worse.

Pegasus tossed her head and took off down the drive, the reins slipping through Tom's hands. Delilah hadn't yet notched her right leg around the lower pommel, making her balance all the more precarious. She leaned over the horse's neck, the pommel digging into her stomach. Her hat flopped into her face. For all Delilah knew, Pegasus was headed to the nearest tree to scrape her inconsiderate rider off.

As she considered her options—screaming being at the top of the list—a flash of white whizzed in her periphery. Pegasus stopped so suddenly, Delilah got a mouthful of coarse horse hair and a throbbing nose.

Mounted on Starlight, Marcus held Pegasus's reins and spoke soothing, lilting words of comfort. "It's all right. Everything is fine now. Nothing to fash yourself over."

Delilah wasn't sure if they were meant for her or the horse, but guessed the latter. She pushed herself upright and positioned her legs properly. Her wiggle on the saddle sent the horse into a shuffle, but Marcus made a tsking noise deep in his chest, and the horse ceased her restless movements.

"I told you I was useless on a horse." The humor she attempted to inject was ruined by the quaver in her voice.

"You'll learn." He seemed untroubled by her lack of horsemanship, but how could he not be greatly bothered? Horses were his passion, and Delilah had turned the most docile horse in Lord Drummond's stable into an unmanageable beast in less than a minute.

Marcus didn't return to them to the stables, only clicked his tongue, and both Starlight and Pegasus set off down the long, sweeping drive toward the main road. Delilah looked over her shoulder once, but it upset her balance enough to send a skitter of panic through her, so she focused on the road ahead.

Marcus brought Starlight closer to Pegasus and held out the reins. "Here."

"No. You keep them." Delilah maintained a death grip on the pommel. "What if Pegasus gallops off again and you can't catch me?"

Marcus's voice was gentle. "Pegasus can barely manage a trot."

Delilah's snort was indelicate, and she tried to cover it with a cough. "It was dashing down the lane with me."

Marcus only gave her a sympathetic glance from the corners

of his eyes. "I'll stay close in case she decides to bolt. Go on, take the reins."

Delilah took them reluctantly, and Pegasus tossed her head and shuffled to the side. Delilah let out a yelp. "What am I doing wrong?"

"Nothing. You're merely inexperienced. Horses prefer confident riders." Marcus stood up in his stirrups and reached over to put a hand over hers. "Loosen your grip. Hold the reins gently."

Marcus's hands were bare, and their warmth and strength seeped through her soft kid gloves, relaxing her grip.

"Perfect." He favored her with a smile as he regained his seat, and she couldn't help but admire the ease with which he moved atop Starlight, his hips rocking much like...

An invisible hand of wanting pulled the laces of her stays tighter, leaving a not entirely comfortable tension through her chest and belly. She squirmed on the saddle but kept her grip light on the reins, and Pegasus kept plodding along.

The clop of horse hooves and the calls of birds weren't enough to fill the expanding silence between them, and in that silence, questions bubbled out. "Do you have no relations left in Ireland? Aunts or uncles? Cousins, perhaps?"

"I am alone in the world, except for O'Connell." The lilting melancholy in his voice filled her with both sadness and indignation.

"You have me," she said tartly.

A look of chagrin passed over his face. "Please forgive me. Marriage has been an unexpected change in circumstances for me."

"I would like to say the same, but Mother and Father and Lady Casterly have been pushing me to marry all season." She sent Marcus a wry smile. "Just not to you."

"I fear I was a rather unpleasant shock." He didn't return her smile. "I hope one day you and your parents can repair things. I don't like being the cause of your estrangement."

Delilah wished it was only the brisk wind making her eyes watery. "I hope so too."

"Do you have a large extended family?" he asked.

"No. It was only me and Alastair."

"I can't imagine your pain." Guilt he shouldn't have to bear weighed his words.

Her brother had been the most important person in her life. His death had hurt beyond measure, and even though it had been almost two years, the raw pain sometimes took her breath away as if the news had arrived yesterday.

"The truth is important to me as well. I want the people who killed Alastair with their greed to pay dearly." Only when Pegasus began to shuffle to the side did Delilah realize her grip on the reins had tightened.

Marcus was like a statue on Starlight, staring straight ahead. "And if it turns out my father is to blame? How will you be able to stomach being my wife?"

"Whatever else I learn, you are not to blame for my brother's death." She attempted to lighten her voice. "Anyway, you are certain your father is innocent."

Doubts crossed his face like storm clouds.

Delilah preferred to judge a man by his actions and not an accident of birth. Sir Wallace, for instance, was welcomed into every ball and drawing room in London. He was every inch a gentleman by Society's standards. Yet he had spoken disrespectfully about her and would have never cared for her.

Marcus, on the other hand, had inherited a tainted title and was shunned by Society, yet he had treated her with admiration and respect. Marcus was not his father, and no matter what truths came to light, nothing would change his fundamental kindness.

Would things change if his father was ultimately implicated?

Her worry centered not on her reaction, but whether Marcus would be able to bear the guilt of association. He was prideful and his honor was also his burden.

Alastair would have liked Marcus very much, and her parents would like him too once time had softened their shock. The load on her heart lessened.

"What is your opinion on brown paneling?" She tipped her face up to the sun and smiled. Her mother wasn't here to warn her about freckling.

"Brown paneling?" Marcus sounded perplexed at the sudden conversational shift.

"Pay me no mind." She peered ahead but could see nothing resembling a castle rising behind the rolling hills. "How much farther?"

"Not far." Marcus cleared his throat, his anxiety obvious in the way he held himself.

"Do you fear trouble awaits us on the road?" She squinted at the brambly hedgerows lining the lane, sensitive to any movement. A blackbird popped out of the leaves of a tree on her right and made her start.

"No doubt trouble is on our heels, but I think—hope—we'll be safe until we can determine what secrets the book holds and how to proceed." His face remained tense.

"What worries you if not for the mysterious killer on our trail?" she asked.

"Wyndam Castle is rather…" His mouth moved silently as if testing different words and finding them lacking.

"Historic?"

"Indeed, it is. Alfred, the fourth Lord Wyndam, commissioned the build during the reign of Charles I, but it's also…"

"Quaint?"

"In a fashion, I suppose, but it also has a certain air of…"

"Coziness?"

"Decrepitude," he said at the same time.

It seemed her fears had not been misplaced. "How decrepit?"

"Besides a few rooms, the castle has not been maintained. Yet another reason I can't believe my father was bilking the Crown of a fortune."

As Delilah attempted to unpack his words and formulate a reply, he continued. "I have thoroughly investigated my father's finances. He was not a regular at any club nor at the racetrack. The rooms he rented in London were fashionable but hardly ostentatious. His stables were depleted. If he was involved in the illicit sale of tainted gunpowder, he was a pawn who earned nothing because he knew nothing of the ultimate scheme. I have to believe that."

His voice was both desperate and adamant. Who was he trying to convince? Her or himself? "Could we circle back around to the state of the castle? When you say air of decrepitude, what exactly does that entail? A bit of grime, or holes in the roof?"

"We patched the holes months ago." He waved a dismissive hand.

"But there were holes?"

His saddle creaked as he squirmed. "A few, but O'Connell and I repaired the roof and cleaned up the damage from the animals and elements. Mostly."

"Mostly." She didn't even pose it as a question. Her excitement was morphing into dread at what awaited. Mrs. Devlin's sly warnings about the castle took on added weight. "Is it haunted?"

"I haven't had a single encounter with any of the rumored ghosts in residence," he said blandly.

She wasn't sure if he was serious or teasing and was afraid to ask. Instead of focusing on the spiritual, she concentrated on the physical. "How much damage from the elements and the animals?"

"The rooms with the worst water damage have been sealed

off until I can hire workmen to make them habitable. The downstairs is quite comfortable in spite of all the stone. The vermin have mostly moved on."

Vermin? A shudder went through her that had nothing to do with the wind buffeting them. "Tell me this, will we be sleeping on cots in the drawing room, or is there a clean, dry bed to lay our heads on tonight?"

"Of course there is a bed. The west wing was spared the water damage. *Mostly,*" he added in a whisper followed by a clearing of his throat. "Ah, I see the turnoff ahead."

Crumbling stone walls that were hip high along some sections and knee-high along others lined the drive. Wild flowers grew along the edges, and woods stretched on either side of the approach. It was picturesque, and a modicum of hope reemerged.

Delilah raised herself higher in the stirrups and peered ahead to catch a glimpse of her new home. Around a bend, the castle came into view in the middle of a clearing. She gasped, not because of the general air of shabbiness, but because of the beauty of the place. It was a castle straight from her gothic novels. Full of ghosts and vermin but also romance and adventure.

Sand-colored stone formed turrets and high walls with slits for windows. She could imagine archers manning each one. The ground around the castle had settled, leaving the castle sitting on a slight rise.

As they drew closer, a wooden bridge clued her into the realization the depression had once been a moat. While she noted the repairs to the bridge and the east wing, the bones of the castle were sturdy and handsome.

Marcus led them to the stable yard. The stables too had seen better decades. The walls had been patched with different woods, lending them a quilt-like quality, but they looked snug. The chuffs of horses could be heard from inside. A dog rushed out of the stables. It was lean with a tannish coat, its tail whipping back and forth in excitement. Marcus dismounted to greet it with an equal amount of enthusiasm. Master and dog resembled one another in their lean handsomeness.

"Who is this?" Delilah asked. While her confidence with Pegasus had grown over the morning's ride, Delilah wasn't brave enough to attempt a dismount. She waited for Marcus to turn his attention from the joyful reunion to her.

"Hermes. He's an English greyhound. Fast runner when he isn't lazing around, which is most of the time." After one last affectionate pat, Marcus took her waist and lifted her down, her hands on his shoulders. Once on the ground though, he didn't let her go.

"If I had been honest about the state of my estate, would you have reconsidered my offer of marriage?" His face was solemn.

Delilah took a breath and looked around her, squaring her shoulders. Would the castle require work? An enormous amount. "My mother has treated me as if I need to be protected —even from my own impulses—since my illness, but I'm not weak. I can work as hard as you to set things to right."

"Your father mentioned a nervous disposition when I offered for you." He stepped back and examined her with an admiring eye. "If your nerves are weak, mine must have crumbled into dust. What was this affliction?"

"I contracted a lung malady after becoming lost on the moors. I was bedbound and feverish for weeks. Ever since, Mother has attempted to protect me from my baser instincts for adventure. I thought to satisfy myself with my novels. You know how well *that* worked out."

A laugh burst from Marcus before he turned quite serious once more, taking her hands in his. "I wasn't coddling you when I neglected to be open with you about the condition of the estate. To be frank, I was… embarrassed."

She blinked dumbly for a moment. "Why?"

"Because you are used to a higher standard than I can provide." His gaze shifted over her shoulder. "And I didn't want to hand you a compelling reason to turn down my offer of marriage."

His admission set her stomach tumbling. He had wanted to wed her. The newness of their marriage made it difficult to know how to respond. "My childhood was quite simple. We lived comfortably, but with no extravagance. Father did not make his fortune until I was quite grown."

He looked her in the eyes, his intensity startling. "I will turn things around, Delilah. I promise."

"You don't have to do it alone, you know," she chided softly. When she might have said more, O'Connell came out of the heavy front door, his bandy-legged gait listing him side to side.

"Ah, it's good to see you arrived safely and none too soon. Weather is turning once more. Cook has tea and cakes waiting." O'Connell plucked the leads up. "I'll get the horses rubbed down and settled."

Dark clouds from the south painted over the blue sky of their travels. A fat droplet hit her cheek and slid down to her jaw, inciting shivers.

"How is everything?" Marcus asked.

"Quiet. For now," O'Connell added the last over his shoulder with the same ominous darkness as the coming storm.

"Let me introduce you to your new home, my lady." Marcus offered his arm, and Delilah took it. Spring rains had carved trenches along the courtyard, making the cobbles underfoot uneven and precarious.

"You have a cook?" She was more than mildly relieved. While she could make tea and peel a potato under duress, she would not flourish in the kitchen.

"She's worked at the castle all her life and has been a godsend. Besides Cook and O'Connell, there's Ella, a maid-of-all-work, and Duncan, a stable boy who helps out where he's needed. No butler or housekeeper at the moment, I'm afraid."

"We'll manage." She gave a bracing squeeze to his arm. "We've survived thus far, haven't we? Given time and a little luck, we'll turn Wyndam Castle into a home for us and—" *Our children.* She stopped the flow of words, uncomfortable with how easily her mind tripped in that direction.

The heavy wooden front door had bradded metal hinges and a matching knocker in the form of a dragon hanging from the middle. Marcus shouldered the door open, and Delilah preceded him inside. While the narrowed windows had given the castle a romantic feel from the outside, the large room would remain dim no matter how bright the sunshine.

The length and breadth of the room gave her pause. Tapestries and rugs softened the unrelenting stone walls and floor. Longbows, crossbows, swords, and axes hung on either side of the large, ornate fireplace set in the middle of the long wall. A scarred wooden table with benches on either side looked small in the space, but Delilah estimated it could seat twenty with ease.

Two large comfortable-looking armchairs of a more recent vintage were placed before a fire whose heat did nothing to cut the chill from where they stood. A decanter and glasses set on a low table were positioned between, as if waiting for two knights to negotiate a peace.

Had she stepped into a storybook?

She blinked and took in the iron chandelier, empty of candles, above their head. She could see no water damage from this vantage point. Perhaps Marcus had exaggerated the situation.

"It's magnificent." Her voice echoed.

He relaxed, as if he'd been expecting her to pass a severe judgment on his home. "The great hall was built to impress and intimidate. I'm glad you appreciate the stark grandeur. We'll take tea in the drawing room. This way."

He led her to a door she hadn't noticed. She stopped short inside the doorway. This room was better lit by a large bay window looking onto an overgrown center courtyard. The difference between the barely adorned great hall and the drawing room was a jolt. It was as if they'd been transported into a different house altogether.

The ceiling had been painted in the Baroque style with plenty of naked cherubs. The floor was crammed full of plaster busts and paintings and life-sized marble statues. The mismatched tables were covered in vases and knickknacks. A path had been cleared to a settee upholstered in a fabric with large red poppies on a black background.

Marcus let out a sigh. "My grandfather fancied himself a collector. Unfortunately, it appears to be a worthless pile of imitations."

The rattle of cups on a tray grew louder, and Delilah stepped toward the settee to make room. Her foot caught on the frayed edge of the rug, and she stumbled. Her elbow jostled a bust of a young man with unevenly spaced eyes and crooked lips. It teetered for a heart-stopping moment before crashing to the floor and breaking into half a dozen pieces.

"Lord preserve us," a young girl carrying the tray said in an accent reminiscent of the farm wife who came to Stoney Pudholme during market days. "Another one meets his maker."

"One day soon, we'll clear the whole lot out. The worthless pile." Marcus kicked a piece of the plaster head out of the way, took the tray from the girl, and set it on the low table in front of the settee. Two empty vases stood on one end of the table while a flock of tarnished, brassy-looking candlesticks clustered on the other.

Marcus gestured toward the young girl. "Ella, this is your new mistress, Lady Delilah Wyndam. Delilah, this is Ella."

Ella dropped into a shallow, wobbly curtsey and grinned, a strip of pink gums showing above her white, remarkably straight teeth. She couldn't have been more than sixteen and was as skinny as a wild cat. Her bright smile elevated her from plain to pretty. "Nice to make your acquaintance, my lady. I cleaned your chambers and even put fresh linens on the bed." She offered the information as if clean sheets were an unusual occurrence.

"Thank you, Ella."

"Shall I sweep up the mess, sir?" Ella turned to Marcus and cocked her head. Her comfort with Marcus was apparent.

"You can see to it later. Run along and see if Cook needs help for now."

Her walk out of the room turned into a skip before she disappeared around the corner.

Delilah scooted sideways around the table to avoid knocking over the vase to perch on the edge of the settee, the aggressive red flowers off-putting. "Ella seems young and energetic."

"She is Cook's niece and a hard worker. There's not many who want to work at the castle." Marcus took the armchair, their knees bumping. A week ago such casual contact would be forbidden. Now she fought the urge to lay her hand on his thigh for a quick reassuring squeeze.

The china cups were mismatched but clean, and Delilah poured for them both, gratified by the hot, strong brew. Marcus shifted and worried his bottom lip. One of the legs of his chair slanted to the side with a creak as if ready to splay to the floor in exhaustion.

"The sleeping chambers," he said shortly.

"Yes?" She took another bracing sip, restored by the familiar custom.

"It's customary for a husband and wife to have separate rooms for reflection and privacy, but there's only one habitable chamber." Marcus stared into the dregs of his tea. "I can sleep in the stables with O'Connell, or we can… share?" The look he shot her through his lashes could only be described as hopeful.

Delilah's mother and father shared a chamber in their home in Stoney Pudholme, but upon their ascension into Society and move to London, they had adopted the attitudes of the ton and now spent their days and nights apart. Delilah didn't want Marcus to schedule visits to her bed. She wanted to curl into his warmth and strength and talk… among other things.

Heat crept up her neck, and she covered her discomfiture by cutting a piece of the lopsided plain cake. "Sharing a chamber seems the only practical option. Anyway, it seemed to work fine the last two nights, don't you think?"

Before she could expand on her reasoning, she stuffed a forkful of cake into her mouth. The cake might not have passed muster in London's drawing room, but it was scrumptious.

He sat back with a wickedly satisfied smile. "Eminently practical."

After the two of them polished off the tea and cake, Marcus stood and held out a hand. "Let me show you the rest of your crumbling abode."

She slipped her hand in his, and before she realized what he was about, he'd tugged her into his body, the back of his fingers brushing over her cheek.

"Thank you," he said before touching his lips to hers in a chaste kiss.

"For what?"

"For being the brave, beautiful lass I met in an almost deserted library. This place is a challenge, and so am I."

She wound her arms around his neck and gave him a kiss that wasn't chaste at all. A yelp broke them apart. Ella stood in the threshold of the room with a worn broom. Her eyes were wide, and her cheeks flushed. "Pardon me, sir. My lady."

"Come in, Ella. You can clear away the tea tray. I'm going to give my wife a tour of the rest of the castle."

Marcus pulled Delilah into the great hall. Her giggles were silenced when he took advantage of the shadows to press her into a tapestry and kiss her until she forgot her worries about his father's guilt or innocence, the coded book, and the murderer on their trail.

CHAPTER 16

*A*fter giving Delilah a tour of the few upstairs rooms that were livable and a dinner of stew and crusty bread, Marcus slumped behind the desk in the small study. It was the only room in the house bearing the fingerprint of his father.

One wall was filled floor to ceiling with books, most of which were older than Marcus. Portraits of his ancestors filled another wall. The resemblance between the solemn men staring down at him and his face in the looking glass every morning was striking. Only the hairstyles and eye colors were different.

But it was the picture above the fireplace that drew his eye time and again. Captured in the flush of love, his mother smiled at someone off to the side. She had been a beauty, with red hair and soft-green eyes. His eyes.

An armchair sat the perfect distance away so the sitter could stare at the portrait in comfort. The hours Marcus's father had spent in the chair had left a physical impression in the cushions. Marcus had left the chair empty. It felt like sacrilege to attempt to fill the space.

Marcus found himself seeking solace and searching for

answers in the study, but his father's ghost never appeared to help him. At the moment, however, Marcus was less concerned with the ghosts than with the living. Namely, attempting to remain alive. He propped his elbows on the desk and rubbed his temples. The coded book was open, and the strings of letters swam before him. The code was as yet indecipherable.

Simple alphabetic codes hadn't done anything but produce more gibberish. A numeric code hadn't fared any better. It was becoming apparent Marcus didn't have the skills to translate the book and hadn't a clue who might be able to help him. He was no better off than he had been months ago. In fact, he was worse off.

By stealing the book and marrying Delilah, he had drawn the full attention of a ruthless murderer. Retreating to the country had bought time, but how much? Hours, days, weeks? How determined was Lord W to acquire the book? If the book implicated Lord W, as Marcus suspected it did, the answer would be "very."

A scream echoed through the great hall and sent him bolting upright. The chair tipped over and added to the cacophony. He sprinted out of the study as another scream rang out from upstairs. *Delilah.*

How had Lord W managed to infiltrate the castle?

Taking the stairs two at a time, he was on the first-floor landing in seconds, his heart pumping more out of fear than exertion. The screaming had stopped, which only escalated the sense of urgency. Sprinting to the door of the bedchamber, he burst inside, heedless of the awaiting danger.

He rocked to a stop in the middle of the room. The flickering light from the fire cast dark shadows in the corners. Marcus made a quick inventory around the room. Expecting to find Lord W ready to bargain with Delilah's life in exchange for the book, Marcus was disconcerted to find... no one.

No one except for Delilah. She was on her knees with the

covers clutched in her fists to her chest, her night rail slipping off one shoulder.

"What's wrong? Did you have a nightmare?" Marcus strode to the window and peered through the gap. It was wide enough for a lean man to slip through, but reaching the window from the ground would be difficult and opening the sash from the outside nearly impossible. Nevertheless, he made an inspection, seeing nothing out of the ordinary in the slanting moonlight.

"A huge beastly rat with a long tail, beady eyes, and pointy teeth bolted across the foot of the bed." Delilah let go of the covers long enough to make fangs with two of her fingers. "It was horrible," she said on a suppressed sob.

"It was most likely a common field mouse," Marcus said with more confidence than he felt. He would not be at all surprised to discover a rat or two still making their home in the castle.

"It wasn't a mouse, Marcus. It was a rat." A tinge of outrage stiffened her voice. "You forget I was raised in a small village with field mice aplenty."

He much preferred her anger over her fear. Her stare made him fidget with a loose button on his waistcoat. "We'll acquire a cat or two, shall we?"

She let the covers drop a few inches. "Mother had an orange tabby when we lived in Stoney Pudholme. It was a brute who left all sorts of dead animals on our doorstep, but he would curl up in my lap while I read."

"I'll find a litter of kittens, and you can pick out the two most bloodthirsty of the lot." He took a step backward toward the door.

"Wait!"

He stilled and cocked his head.

"What if the rat returns with his brother and gnaws on my toes?" The look she cast him had no relation to fear. It held an invitation. A frisson of awareness zipped through him.

"Would you like me to join you in bed to protect you from beasts?"

"I expect it's the only way I'll ever find sleep."

He vacillated. If he returned to the study, it would be to bang his head on the desk in frustration. In order to tackle the mystery fresh, what he needed was sleep.

Yet, if he joined her in bed, sleep would not be imminent. He knew it, and based on her mischievous smile, so did Delilah. He stripped off his waistcoat and dropped it over a chair. His shirt followed. "Are you sure you aren't too sore after last night and the day's ride?"

"I'm a bit sore, but—" She plucked her bottom lip with her teeth and looked away in an unconsciously sensual gesture, shrugging her one bare shoulder. Her night rail slipped down another inch. "I want you."

A roar of satisfaction blasted through him like a flame through dry tinder. They had created sparks from their first moments together, and he was gratified she wanted him as badly as he wanted her.

Peeling off the rest of his clothes, he slipped under the covers. He could smell sunshine on the sheets. Or did the brightness radiate from Delilah's skin? She was still sitting upright, and he lay kisses along her bare, freckled shoulder while plucking the ribbons loose along the front of her night rail.

"I never understood." Her head fell back, giving him access to her neck.

"Never understood what?"

"What it could be like between a man and wife. How much I would crave your touch. Will it always be like this?" She lifted her face to his.

He considered the question with the seriousness it deserved. "I don't know. My Irish grandparents loved each other until the end. In fact, one couldn't live without the other."

"But we weren't introduced at a dance. You didn't set out to woo me." She clutched at his shoulders, demanding a response, her nails scoring him with bone-deep pleasure.

"Our courtship was unconventional, but never doubt that I consider myself a lucky man for having met you, Delilah." He didn't say it merely to get up her night rail. No matter the complications and worries she added to his already complicated, worrisome situation, he was a lucky man. He hadn't realized how lonely and isolated he'd been in his quest until she'd joined his cause and become his partner in every sense.

He should make love to her slowly and tenderly, but desperation beset him, hastened along by fear. Fear he might die. An even greater fear she might.

Although he didn't put voice to his fears, she seemed infected with the same driving need to prove their existence in the here and now. She pulled at the fall of his breeches. Their fingers tangled in their haste. Finally, she had him in one hand while she rucked her night rail up to her waist with the other, drawing him between her legs. She was a siren, and he was ready to drown for her.

As the head of his cock breeched her folds, her hips jerked, and he was buried deep inside her, pleasure spiraling to curl his toes. She didn't allow him to wallow in the feeling but pulled at his buttocks. His rhythm was wild and primitive, guided by her erotic sighs and moans. Rolling them over, he shimmied his breeches lower and urged her into a straddle.

"What are you doing?" She rolled her hips and rubbed herself against him.

He barely kept himself from lifting her and impaling her on his cock. "Giving you your first riding lesson. Remove your night clothes."

She drew in a quick breath before scrambling to obey him. Her night rail puddled on the dark blue counterpane. He took a moment to enjoy the sight of her glorious body above him.

Her thick, silky hair had come partly loose from its braid and pieces brushed her cheeks and shoulders. Her breasts were full, her nipples dusky and budded in her arousal. The curve of her waist and hips was decadent, and he was embarrassed at the way his hands trembled in reaction as he grasped her thighs.

She plucked at his shirt. "What about you?"

"I am your beast to command. What would you like?"

"Take your shirt off," she said huskily.

He raised himself enough to grasp his shirt. It joined her night rail. "Take me inside you."

She wriggled and spread her wetness over his cock. He let out a slow breath, trying to keep his animalist urges under control. Perhaps he truly was a beast.

She lifted off him, her gaze dropping to where she played over the head of his cock with her fingertips. It was the most erotic thing he'd ever experienced. His cock twitched against her hand, and she gasped. "Am I hurting you?"

"My cock has a mind of its own, and all it can think is how badly it wants inside your tight sheath."

She sank her teeth into her bottom lip as if uncertain, yet the sly smile overtaking her mouth said otherwise. She fit his cock to her body and lowered herself an inch at a time. Bracing her hands on his chest, she let her head fall back on a low moan that vibrated through him.

Finally, *finally*, he was seated inside her. "Now, ride me, Delilah. Ride me at whatever pace gives you the greatest pleasure."

At first, her pace was a plodding walk, rising only a few inches before falling. But soon she was cantering and then galloping hard and fast as she raced toward her pleasure, her hips rolling with a grace that was hypnotic.

His control was in tatters and fraying to the barest of threads when her body shuddered and her movements grew erratic. Muttering a curse of thanks, he grabbed her hips and drove her even harder until he too spent.

He trailed his hands up her torso to cup her breasts and glide his thumbs over her velvet-soft ruched nipples. A lock of her hair tumbled over the back of his hand in a caress. The intimacy between them blossomed from understanding and something more elusive. Something he wasn't quite ready to name.

She sank down to his chest. "Were you pleased with my performance, my lord?"

The smile in her voice made him smile in return and press a kiss into her hair. "You are a quick study. However, there is much yet to learn. It will take a great deal of practice, I'm afraid."

She rose to her elbows and playfully nipped his bottom lip with her teeth. He growled deep in his chest and deepened the kiss, one hand on the back of her head, the other grasping her bare bottom. He stirred inside her.

He broke the kiss and shifted her to his side. Taking her again so soon would be selfish on his part. She stretched like a cat, yawned, and cuddled into his side. Her breathing evened, and her body grew lax against his as she slipped toward sleep.

Unable to help himself, he allowed his hands free rein over her curves, mapping them in his mind's eye. One day soon, after the danger had passed, he would take her to bed in the afternoon. Her hair would toss red sparks, a hint at her fiery passion, and her body would be gilded by the glow of the sun.

But for now, danger stalked them, and he had to keep his wits sharp and determine a safe path forward. He slipped from under the covers and shivered as he re-dressed and then returned to the study to pore over the coded book once more, searching for inspiration but finding none.

The faint sound of Hermes barking from the stables had him stilling and cocking an ear. Probably another rat. Even so, he tucked the book into a pocket inside his jacket and snuffed the candles. The darkness lent both a sense of safety and menace.

On the balls of his feet, Marcus took small, silent steps toward the ornate entry door. The creak as it opened made him grimace. He listened but heard nothing. The quiet should have been reassuring, but instead, the hairs on the back of his neck prickled. It was too quiet.

The great hall offered little cover if indeed peril had landed on their doorstep. A quick glance up the stone staircase sent fear skittering through his stomach like thrown gravel. In sleep, Delilah was vulnerable.

Keeping to the walls, he made his way to the front door, easing it open only enough to slip through. He flipped up the collar of his jacket to hide the snowy whiteness of his shirt. Sounds erupted from the direction of the stable.

Starlight whinnied, a panicked sound as if being prodded. Hermes barked and scrabbled against the wood of a door, trying his best to protect the castle. Marcus crouched as he made his way toward the stable, pausing to the side of the wide stable entry.

A voice carried faintly out of the stable. "Stay down, old man. Answer my questions and I'll make your death quick. Otherwise…" The man sounded calm, unhurried, and slightly amused.

"A curse upon you, ye bloody bastard." O'Connell's voice was strained. The thud of a boot hitting flesh had Marcus seeing red. The last play of the game was upon him.

Marcus stepped farther into the stable. O'Connell was splayed on the ground. His chest still rose and fell, and the bands around Marcus's lungs eased. He attempted to imitate the cool tone of the man who had come to kill him and those he loved, but anger and fear added a dash of heat. "Lord W, I presume?"

"Ah, I can say the same, can't I, Wyndam?" The man stepped from the shadows. "But we haven't been formally introduced."

Recognition jolted through Marcus. It was the gentleman he had bumped into at Gilmore's soiree.

"I am Lord Whitmire." He moved with feline grace to face Marcus. The lantern hanging from the peg nearest Starlight's stall swung in the stiff breeze and cast eerie shadows across Whitmire's jawline. "You have proved an even bigger nuisance than your father."

The truth was a bitter vindication. "You framed him. Did you kill him too?"

Whitmire clucked his tongue. "No. He chose death over rotting in Newgate while his title and lands were stripped away from him. And from you."

The pang in Marcus's heart echoed in his chest. Had his father sacrificed his life so Marcus could receive a title and lands? If so, it had been a poor trade. "Why involve my father in your schemes at all? What had he done to you?"

"Nothing. He was convenient. I needed someone on the outside of government. Someone who was well-liked and had a reputation for honesty. Any of several peers would have done, but your father was the most desperate for coin. Based on my assurances, he swore on his reputation the powder was of the highest quality, demanding an equally high price. When he discovered the gunpowder was tainted and soldiers had died, he came to me, devastated and trusting me to do the honorable thing. It was really quite unfair. I didn't know the gunpowder was defective when I bought it."

"You bought cheap powder and used my father to sell it to the government at an inflated price. My father earned a commission, but the bulk of the profit filled your coffers. Is that about right?"

"Yes," Whitmire said simply.

"And the book you killed Quinton for?"

"Your father stole two personal journals from my study, intending to expose me, but he didn't understand how long and how successfully I've been playing the game. I code anything of importance. One, as I'm sure you know, I retrieved from poor Quinton. The other will be mine tonight."

"Over my dead body." Marcus regretted the bold, naive statement as soon as it left his mouth.

"I'm glad to hear we are in agreement." Whitmire pulled a deadly-looking stiletto out of his jacket. It was the same sort that had killed Quinton.

Marcus braced himself for an attack that didn't materialize. At least, not yet.

"I was surprised to hear you married the chit." The way Whitmire caressed the stiletto was disturbingly sexual.

Marcus didn't pretend ignorance. "There's no need to involve Delilah. This business is between you and me."

Whitmire hummed thoughtfully, as if he were actually considering Marcus's suggestion. "If only that were the case, but she saw me in the library with Quinton. Rather careless of me, I must say."

With a suddenness that gave Marcus just enough time to throw his hands up, Whitmire leaped forward, the end of the stiletto aimed at Marcus's heart. Marcus's wrist made jarring contact with the side of Whitmire's hand, saving himself from a quick end.

The point of the stiletto glanced across Marcus's upper arm, tearing through fabric and flesh. A stinging pain spread outward to his shoulder and hand, and with it came an unwelcome numbness. His sleeve was already wet with blood.

Marcus scrambled out of the stable and into the graveled yard. He had to fight back, but with what? His fists? Whitmire would cut him down. The wall of weapons in the great hall flashed into his head, but the blades hadn't been sharpened in decades and he had no arrow to notch into the crossbow. Plus leading Whitmire into the castle brought him closer to Delilah.

Marcus veered toward the horse ring. After patching the roof of the castle, he and O'Connell had concentrated their repair efforts on the stables and horse ring, knowing only the horses could change their fortunes.

He tripped over something long and hard. Reaching down to catch his balance, he closed his fingers around a splintered piece of rotted post. It was better than nothing. He swung the post around, making hard contact with Whitmire's shoulder. The man grunted and stumbled to the side. The knife clattered to the cobblestones.

The wood snagged on Whitmire's jacket, and Marcus yanked it free. When he did, Whitmire let out a bellow of pain. Moonlight glinted off a bent, rusty nail sticking out of the wood. Blood dripped to the ground. Hope injected strength and dulled the pain in his own arm. Marcus let out a feral-sounding yell and swung again, this time at Whitmire's head. The man blocked the swing and stepped into Marcus, grappling for the post.

Having been raised on a farm, Marcus had been involved in his share of brawls. Brawls as a means to expend excess high spirits when the brew ran out or no lasses were available for the task. The brawls had never been a means for murder. More often than not, they would end in laughter and a handshake.

This was not a brawl. This was a fight to the death, and Marcus was outmatched. His confidence ebbed, and he stumbled backward in retreat. The smile that came to Whitmire's face was chilling.

Whitmire was a man used to dispatching adversaries with an unnatural dispassion and ruthlessness. He would kill Marcus and O'Connell, then march into the house to dispose of Delilah, for he would be careful this time to eliminate any witness to his evil.

Marcus couldn't allow Whitmire to win. Iron determination drove out the fear. Fear would not save him. A clear head and dirty fighting might. Reversing course, Marcus launched himself at Whitmire, grabbing the man's injured arm and squeezing as hard as he could. Whitmire's bellow echoed around the yard.

Whitmire reared back and headbutted Marcus. His head rang, but he didn't let go of Whitmire's arm, digging his thumb into the wound the nail had made. Blood left his hand slippery and his hold precarious.

Whitmire hooked an ankle around Marcus's leg and yanked as fast as an adder's strike. Marcus landed on his back and gulped for air. Before he could recover, Whitmire dropped on top of him and pinned his arms down with his knees. Whitmire wrapped his hands around Marcus's neck and squeezed, thumbs crushing his windpipe to nothing.

Marcus scrabbled and kicked at cobbles, finding no leverage to heave Whitmire off. Black edged his vision as he crawled toward unconsciousness. He pictured Delilah in bed and the horror that awaited her as he slipped toward nothingness.

CHAPTER 17

*D*elilah woke with a start and sat up in bed, holding the sheet up to her chest. Her heart galloped along. Had the rat come back to torment her? Because no matter what Marcus said, it hadn't been a cute little field mouse but a giant toothy rat that had run across the bed. But no rat family stood ready to gnaw at her toes. Everything seemed to be in place. Except for Marcus. The bed was empty.

Naked from their earlier lovemaking, she lay back down and blinked up at the ceiling. It was too dark to see the water stains, and in the dim light from the embers, the room took on the romanticism of a storybook illustration. For the first time, she grew excited at the potential.

After only a few blinks, she pushed the covers off and slipped on a night rail and her dressing gown. Sleep would be an impossibility. She would keep Marcus company until he was ready to retire for the night. The stone floor was cold on her bare feet, but she didn't stop to dig her slippers out of her luggage.

She lit a candle in the embers of the fire and made her way into the hallway. The shadows were long and cold. The castle was her new home, and she would do her best to make it a welcoming one, but it would take work. Much work.

She stopped in the door of the study, the smile on her face falling. The room was unoccupied but had the feeling of being recently vacated. A finger of brandy remained in Marcus's glass, and a full brace of candles on the desk flickered.

Had he gotten hungry and retreated to the kitchens? Had he gone to seek comfort from Starlight? Delilah shoved the niggle of jealousy away. It was ridiculous to envy a horse.

A noise from the courtyard drew her to one of the archer's windows. Expecting to see Marcus and Starlight bonding in the night, she blinked. Marcus was on the ground and a man who was surely not O'Connell was on top of him. They were locked in a struggle, and based on their position, her husband was losing.

Fear and anger coalesced into action. Her mind whirled but was surprisingly clear. She would be no help without a plan. Her gaze fell on the glinting weapons hanging along the wall of the great hall, fixating on a short sword with a sharp-looking point. It had been made for someone her size.

She yanked it off the wall. It was heavier than she'd expected, and the edge clashed to the stone floor. Adjusting her grip on the hilt, she raised it and slashed the blade through the air. Had a former lady of the castle been tasked to defend herself or her loved ones?

Her only advantage was surprise. Her dressing gown was made of dark greens and blues, and her bare feet made no sound as she slipped out the door. Marcus still thrashed on the ground, but less vigorously.

She had no training in sword play. Should she slash or run the man through? She must act before it was too late, but she was at least two dozen paces away. Too far. She ran.

The stones cut into the bottoms of her feet, but desperation blunted any pain. She didn't attempt to be quiet now. Her goal was to get the man off Marcus. Her scream echoed against the stone walls of the castle.

The man loosened his hold around Marcus's throat and shifted to the side. She'd been aiming at the middle of his back, but instead the sword entered the man's shoulder. The sudden hindrance of flesh and muscle and bone made her stomach flop, but she kept pushing until the blade had pierced him through.

She tried to yank the sword free of the man's shoulder, but it hung on something—she didn't want to think what—and the man let out a guttural yell full of primal pain and fury. He staggered to his feet and spun to face her, jerking the hilt from her numb fingers.

Between the sharp end of the sword emerging from his shoulder and his twisted mouth, the man made a macabre picture. Used to seeing him in the elegance and civility of a London ballroom, it took a moment to place his identity.

"Lord Whitmire? But, you…" Lord Whitmire moved among the highest echelon of political circles. He was Prinny's man. Whispers circulated about his ambition to be prime minister. A darker fact registered. He was also the infamous Lord W—killer of Quinton. Traitor.

"You have caused me a great deal of trouble." He fumbled behind him for the hilt of the sword.

Delilah risked a glance toward Marcus. He was alive, although gasping for breath, his hand at his throat. A measure of relief had her knees quaking. She had no time for sentiment, because if Lord Whitmire managed to free the sword from his shoulder, she and Marcus would both die by the already bloody blade.

Already bloody. Delilah narrowed her eyes, noticing a gash on Lord Whitmire's other arm. Both sleeves of his jacket were torn and wet with blood. He was injured. Not mortally, but surely he was weakened. Delilah considered her options. She could run, but if Whitmire didn't take the bait, Marcus would be left vulnerable. On the other hand, she had no weapon other than herself.

Alastair's spirit whispered in her ear. When she was a child, she'd loved to follow her brother around and try to scare him. Her favorite method was to run out from behind a bush or tree, circle her arms around him, hook a foot behind one leg, and force him to the ground. Then she would proceed to tickle him until he gained the upper hand.

With a yell that would make Alastair proud, she ran straight for Lord W. He stumbled backward, a look of shock on his face. She grappled with him, searching for wounds as she looped her foot around his ankle. Already off-balance from his retreat, he toppled to the stones, pulling her down with him.

The hilt of the blade pushed farther into his shoulder. His agonized scream made her cringe. As it pressed forward, the edge of the blade ripped through the sleeve of her dressing gown. A burning sensation streaked along her upper arm.

"You little bitch!" Whitmire rolled to his side and tried to throw her off him by driving his knee into her stomach. Pain burst through her and stole her breath. She held onto him as if her life depended on it. Which it did.

The tang of blood, both hers and his, turned her stomach. She had no idea how bad the wound on her arm was, but her hand was tingly and weak. Although he was injured, Lord Whitmire was bigger and stronger than she was. In addition, he had the advantage of having no conscience or morals. He reversed their positions until he was on top of her.

The grimacing smile on his face reminded her of a gargoyle, fixed and stony. Only when he brought his chest closer did she realize his intention. The point of the sword extended six inches from his shoulder. He aimed at her heart, ready to impale her.

She squirmed away but didn't make it far enough. The sharp point tore through her dressing gown and poked her skin. She closed her eyes, unable to look the demon in the eyes as he ran her through the heart.

The pinching pressure against her chest eased. She popped her eyes open and stared into Whitmire's face. His mouth gaped in shock and agony. The sword was gone. Blood trickled from his shoulder onto her in a foul baptism.

Whitmire was ripped off her and thrown to ground. Marcus stood over him, swaying slightly, but with clear eyes and a set jaw. The sword point was inches from Whitmire's neck.

With his advantage gone, Lord Whitmire began to barter. "You don't want to kill me, Wyndam."

"Oh, I believe I do." Marcus's voice was hoarse but preternaturally calm.

"Only I know the key to deciphering the book. If you kill me, you'll never clear your father of wrongdoing." Satisfaction lifted Whitmire's expression.

Marcus's hesitation lasted only a breath before he drove the sword through Lord Whitmire's chest where his heart—if he had one—beat. The man blinked, his gaze falling to where the sword skewered him. Marcus pulled the sword free and blood gushed from the wound. Lord Whitmire collapsed like a rag doll tossed away by the hand of a god.

Delilah closed her eyes against the sight.

The sword clattered to the stones, and Marcus fell to his knees at her side. "Are you injured?"

"A mere scratch on my arm." Delilah touched his chest. "I was afraid I was too late."

"You almost were." Marcus touched his throat and winced before shaking his head. "Delilah. I can't believe you put yourself in such danger."

"If I hadn't, we'd both be dead."

O'Connell stumbled out of the stables, his hand pressed to the back of his head. "Laddie! The devil sneaked up on me. I'm sorry."

Marcus rose and took the old man's arm. "No need for apologies. The man truly was a devil. How's your head?"

"I've had worse getting thrown from a horse. The bounder is dead then. Good riddance." O'Connell spit at Whitmire's feet.

"Aye, he's dead." No satisfaction warmed Marcus's voice. The three of them stared at Whitmire's body for a long moment. "Wait for me in the study, O'Connell, so I can look at your head in the light. You might need to be sewn up."

O'Connell grumbled but made his way inside.

Good riddance. The words echoed hollowly, and Delilah wished she could savor their escape from death. Whitmire had been vile and evil and would have shown them no quarter, but what would happen when his allies in London found out? Would they attempt to throw Marcus into Newgate for his murder? After what had happened to Marcus's father, no one could be trusted.

"Now that Whitmire is dead, how will you clear your father's name? The book is undecipherable. What will we do?" A shiver turned into a shake until her entire body was beset.

"You're safe. We're alive. That's all that matters." Marcus squatted and drew her to his chest. She flinched when his hand bumped her injured arm. He peered closer at her wound. "This is more than a scratch. I need to see to your arm immediately."

He helped her to her feet. Her knees were wobbly, and her head swam. She might have swooned if not for the arm Marcus wrapped around her waist.

"I'm sorry to be such a weakling." She leaned even harder into him.

"A weakling?" He made a noise of disbelief. "You ran Whitmire through with an ancient sword."

"I didn't kill him though."

His sigh was heavy with emotion. "You did more than enough. You should have found a hiding place behind a set of curtains like the first time."

She ground to a stop, shuffled in front of him, and hung on to his jacket. The darkness hid his expression, but she could sense his torment at her pain. "Would you have hidden to save yourself and leave me to face Whitmire's evil alone?"

"Of course not! I have my honor."

"Honor is not exclusive to the male sex, my lord. I would never have left you at his mercy." The tart edge to her voice couldn't be helped, but it naturally softened when she added, "I only wish we could have forced him to reveal his cipher."

"*You* have been revelation enough. I thought the most important thing was to clear my family name, but everything changed the evening I met you." His tongue darted along his bottom lip. "I love you, Delilah. When I thought I was dying, my only regret was not telling you sooner."

She swallowed past a rising lump of tears. "I love you too."

"Even with everything that has happened?"

"Even through the danger and death and rats running across my bed." Her attempt at humor ended in a choked-back sob, and she buried her face in his neck, taking a deep breath.

"Come and let me tend your arm, my love."

He guided her into his study and to a chair by the hearth. The embers of the fire emanated just enough heat to make Delilah aware of how cold she was. O'Connell sat in the chair next to her with a glass of liquor.

Marcus pushed a matching glass into her hand. "Drink it all. It will help dull the pain of what is to come."

Marcus added fuel to the fire and lit another brace of candles, flooding the sitting area with light. He first examined the back of O'Connell's head. "Quite a goose egg. You'll have a splitting headache, but the skin isn't even broken."

"Told you I was fine. No harder head than an Irishman's. What about the lassie?"

Marcus knelt by her chair and tugged her dressing gown off her shoulder. She gasped as the cloth pulled at the wound and jerked away from him. Producing a penknife from his desk, he poured a small measure of the liquor over the blade and sliced through the sleeve of her dressing gown and night rail from sleeve to shoulder.

Delilah glanced down, but seeing her torn flesh and the ooze of blood made the room spin. She rested her head against the back of the chair. "It's bad, isn't it?"

"It's not good." Marcus sounded distracted and distant.

A numbness spread from her toes and fingers. Even her lips felt strange. It reminded her of the long night she'd spent wet and shivering in the bog. She'd accepted death as a likely outcome. But now, she had too much to live for. Fear quickened in her body, driving her heart into a furious pounding.

"Tell me truly. Am I going to die, Marcus?" Her voice sounded tinny and far away.

Marcus glanced up from examining her arm, his face softening, a small smile coming to his lips. "Of course not, but the injury requires stitching, and it's going to be painful."

It was his smile more than his words that offered comfort. She remembered the solemn faces surrounding her during her illness as if holding a vigil until death claimed her. He rose and pressed a bracing kiss on her lips.

"Have you experience stitching wounds?" she asked. The brief exchange of glances between Marcus and O'Connell wasn't reassuring.

"On horses. I've stitched saddles and such." Marcus cleared his throat.

"The laddie has a fine, steady hand." O'Connell waved his glass in the air, his ruddy cheeks almost matching the red of his bushy eyebrows. "

"Saddles?" Delilah sat up but sank back into the chair when dizziness overcame her. "I'm not a saddle. Or a horse."

Marcus poured more liquor into her glass and pushed the rim toward her lips. "Drink while I gather what I need."

The rim clinked against her teeth as she did as Marcus bid. "I'm so cold."

O'Connell heaved himself out of his chair, and Delilah wanted to reach for him and ask him to stay with her. She didn't want to be alone. He returned with a blanket and tucked it around her legs.

"Ach, you're in shock, lass. I've seen it happen with mares after difficult foalings. The laddie will get you back to rights in no time." O'Connell patted her knee and then her cheek, his work-roughened hand warm and comforting.

Maybe it was the pain and fear, or maybe it was the liquor, but she wanted her distracted, loving father and her overbearing, judgmental mother. With her brother dead and her parents blissfully unaware of her circumstances, she was adrift from her family. If she'd known what would happen, would she have chosen Marcus over her parents?

Delilah blinked but couldn't keep the flooding tears at bay. One trickled out, followed by another and another. The saltiness chased away the taste of the liquor on her tongue.

Carrying a steamy bowl of water, young Ella entered the study, her hair disheveled and her cap pinned on lopsided. "Oh, my lady, I'm sorry you've been hurt, but the master and I are going to set you right as rain. You'll see."

Delilah couldn't help but smile through her tears. Marcus returned, his hands full of supplies, his face serious and focused on the upcoming task. As he organized the bandages, the thread, and water, she asked, "Just how painful will it be?"

"Like the devil is breathing fire on your arm." His eyes were stamped with worry. "If I could bear your pain, I would, love."

"I know." The smile she offered was small and watery. She took a deep, bracing breath, turned toward O'Connell, and held out her good hand. "Will you hold my hand, O'Connell?"

"Aye, lass." Her hand was enfolded in his. "You squeeze as hard as you need to."

O'Connell was her family. Ella was her family. And, of course, Marcus. Always Marcus. She had followed him out of a window and had no regrets.

"Ready?" he asked.

"Do it," she said shortly.

Her mother often said the anticipation was worse than the deed.

Her mother had never had a wound sewn. The deed was far worse than she'd imagined. She made it through the cleaning with a half dozen yelps from her and more than a dozen colorful curses from O'Connell as she bore down on his hand.

With the first piercing of skin with the needle and the tug of thread, she had enough wits to yell, "Bloody hell, Marcus," before a welcome blackness overcame her, and she felt no more.

CHAPTER 18

*D*elilah sighed and fluttered her eyes open. She was in bed. Sunlight slashed through the narrow windows where dust motes danced. Calm enveloped her like the covers drawn up to her chin and tucked around her. The previous night took on a dreamlike quality. Had it all been a terrible nightmare?

She lifted her arm to push her hair back and winced. Not a nightmare, then. A muted throb had replaced the stabbing pain of the night before. The last thing she remembered was Marcus taking a stitch. She laid a hand on her forehead, half expecting a fever, but she only felt cotton headed from the liquor. Or perhaps that was due to almost dying at the hands of a madman. A madman who had been killed by Marcus. What would happen now?

She couldn't hide in bed with so much at stake. She sat up and swung her legs around, pausing while a wave of nausea crashed over her and settled to churn her stomach. She slid off the bed, her bare feet cold and sore against the stone. The shift she wore was clean and fresh. Her ruined night rail and dressing gown weren't in sight. She hoped someone had burned them to ash.

Strips of linen were tied off around her upper arm. The blood dotting the white wasn't red and fresh. She peeked underneath the bandage to see a row of neat stitches. Marcus's needlework was better than hers.

She flipped through her meager dresses and chose a simple frock with a front ribbon lacing she could manage. Woolen stockings and her half boots followed. Gingerly, she made her way downstairs, her entire body sore.

She stopped in the middle of the great hall. Was Whitmire's body still lying in the courtyard? Had the magistrate been called? Would Marcus be hauled off to Newgate? She wouldn't allow anyone to spirit him away under the guise of justice. Justice had already been served with Whitmire's death.

Voices echoed against the stone, and she followed them toward the study. Stopping in the doorway, she took in the scene. A stranger occupied one chair in front of the fireplace. She could only see part of his profile, the sleeve of a dark blue jacket, and highly polished boots, but his body was upright and expectant. In the same clothes he'd worn the night before, Marcus was slumped in the adjacent chair. Lurid bruises ringed his throat like a grisly cravat.

A third man she hadn't noticed emerged from the shadows of the corner. "Sir, Lady Wyndam has arrived." His rough-hewn looks didn't match the silk of his voice. He was tall and broad, with huge hands and piercing gaze. The air around him snapped with danger.

"Ah, Lady Wyndam, come join us. I was terribly sorry to hear you were injured during last night's ordeal." The dapper stranger rose and gestured toward the chair he'd relinquished.

Marcus stood and gave her a bracing nod. Her knees still weak, she shuffled forward. The man was small in stature but emanated a power that was even more intimidating than his companion's strength.

"I'm afraid you have the better of me, sir. I don't believe we've been introduced." Although she had a guess as to his identity.

"Sir Harold Hawkins." The man performed a small, perfunctory bow. He didn't seem the type to waste words or gestures. "I serve the Crown and have an interest in what transpired here last night."

The spymaster's name had hovered over everything that had happened since she bore witness to Quinton's murder.

Marcus gently took her hand and urged her to sit in Hawkins's vacated seat. "You shouldn't be out of bed, love. Your arm—"

"Isn't going to fall off. We have more pressing matters to attend." She gingerly sat, and Marcus followed suit. The man who had announced her shrank back into the shadowy corner to bear witness. Sir Hawkins's hawk.

Hawkins's expression didn't waver while she sized him up. A marble-like hardness emanated from him, which stoked her melee of anger and worry. This man held their future in his hands.

"Why exactly are you here, Sir Hawkins?" she asked briskly.

"The death of a peer will always warrant scrutiny, and Lord Whitmire is of particular interest to the Crown." Sir Hawkins remained calm and cool in tone and manner even as his sharp eyes searched hers for truth and lies.

Marcus remained silent, rubbing his bristled jaw, his focus on the ashes in the hearth. Was he merely exhausted, or had he resigned himself to his fate? Delilah wasn't giving up. She refused to give *Marcus* up.

Agitation had her scooting to the edge of the chair. "I was a witness, you know."

"It's my understanding you were more than witness." Sir Hawkins made a slight gesture toward her wound.

"I am referring to Mr. Quinton's murder. It was Lord Whitmire who drove a knife through his heart." It was a slight stretch of the truth, for she hadn't exactly seen the deed.

A spark cracked the stony facade of Sir Hawkins's expression. "Indeed. What else did you bear witness to?"

"Whitmire tried to kill me at a ball. I only escaped thanks to a few handy turnips." At Hawkins's continued silence, her tongue began to run away. "Then after Marcus and I managed to abscond with the blasted book everyone is so interested in, Whitmire comes here and almost kills Marcus and would have killed me if I hadn't grabbed the sword from the wall and jammed it in his—"

"Stop." Sir Hawkins held up a hand, opening then closing his mouth before asking, "Turnips, you say?"

"Yes, turnips." Delilah popped up and stepped toward Hawkins, ignoring the twinge in her arm and weakness in her legs. "My husband did nothing but defend our lives, and if you think you can pin murder on him and ruin him like you did his father, then you can... you can... stuff it!"

The thump of her heart and her quickened breaths filled the resulting silence in her head. Sir Hawkins's eyebrows had bounced higher, but his face was otherwise impassive. Instead of responding to her tirade, he rubbed a finger over his lips almost as if he were stemming a smile.

She glared at him for a moment before turning to Marcus. A tender smile had banished a portion of his worry and exhaustion. He stood and folded her gently in his arms, lightly rubbing his chin against her temple. "While I appreciate your defense of my honor more than you can imagine, Sir Hawkins is aware of the circumstances surrounding Lord Whitmire's death."

Feeling dizzy with relief, Delilah shuffled out of his arms to collapse back into the chair, but she kept her fingers tangled with Marcus's. He remained standing, his thigh warm and hard against her shoulder. She tightened her grip on him.

"Indeed, my lady, I have been attempting to ferret out the traitor in our midst for some time. Lord Whitmire was one of our most trusted agents for many years, but it seems several ill-advised investments left him vulnerable. He needed coin, and the only thing he had left to sell was his honor."

"What about Marcus's father? How was he involved?" Delilah asked.

"Ah, that is a bit more complicated, I'm afraid." Hawkins paced in front of the hearth.

"How so?" Delilah had the feeling Marcus and Sir Hawkins had already discussed the complications.

"After the first accidental deaths were reported due to powder accidents, my men uncovered a scheme headed by a man with the codename W who had bilked the Crown by selling subpar cheap powder at elevated prices. As the late Lord Wyndam had indeed formed a consortium to do just that, we had him watched. He grew paranoid and rarely left Wyndam Castle. His death was unexpected but convenient."

Marcus sagged against the chair and gripped her hand until it bordered on painful. "You might have stopped him if only you'd acted."

Sir Hawkins faced them, his face flickering with a regret she suspected was rare. This was a man not used to examining past decisions. "At the time, his death seemed to wrap up the inci-dent rather neatly. It was only afterward when someone came forward with rumors of coded books your father had acquired that I became suspicious. When Lord Gilmore approached the Crown with another shipment of powder for sale, I realized your father was not the mastermind, but a pawn."

"Can you help clear his name in Society's eyes, Sir Hawkins?" Marcus's desperation tore at her heart.

To his credit, Sir Hawkins didn't avoid Marcus's stare. "I'm afraid I don't have that sort of power. Once the rumors circulated, probably stoked by Lord Whitmire, they were unstoppable. You will have to be satisfied your father did his best to restore the family's honor after he learned the truth."

Marcus extricated his hand from hers and stalked to the window, presenting his back. Delilah shifted back to Sir Hawkins. "What happens now? I assume there will be an inquest, and we will be called upon to provide evidence."

"That will not be necessary, my lady. The truth of Whitmire's death will only be known to a select group. The rest of the world will be told he met an untimely end by unknown assailants on a road outside London. A tragedy, considering his prospects. The countryside can be dangerous, after all." The twist of his lips landed short of a smile and made the hairs on her nape stand at attention. Hawkins wielded incredible power, and she could only hope to remain in his good graces.

"And what of myself and Marcus?" Delilah's grip turned strangling on the arms of the chair.

"You will continue on with your lives here at Wyndam Castle. I believe His Lordship has plans to breed quality horses, yes?" Sir Hawkins's eyes narrowed as they flashed from Delilah to Marcus and back again. "After granting the Crown one last favor, of course."

Marcus ever so slowly spun around, his face carved from granite. "And what favor would you ask of me?" he said mockingly.

"I will need the book you pinched from Gilmore."

Marcus ran a hand through his hair, his exasperation blunting his caustic edge. "I suppose it does little good in my possession considering I haven't the faintest idea how to decipher it. Will you fare any better?"

"I have access to some of the greatest minds in England, although even then, nothing is guaranteed." Hawkins nodded once to the silent man in the corner. The man approached Marcus and waited.

"Considering you had one snake in your garden, do you trust this man not to abscond with the book?" Marcus raised a brow at Hawkins.

"You don't know me, so I won't take offense at your insinuation, my lord. This time." The man's silky voice held a warning Delilah hoped Marcus heeded.

"I trust Garrick with my life, Lord Wyndam, which is no small thing in the dangerous world I inhabit. He will see the book safely into the hands of our best cryptographer."

Marcus hesitated before reaching into his jacket and handing over the book. "May I ask a favor of you?"

Hawkins's expression never changed, but Delilah sensed impatience now he had the book. "If it's in my power to grant, I shall try. What do you want?"

"If what you discover in the books clears my father of suspicion, will you share it with me?"

Hawkins regarded Marcus for a long moment. "My men will need time to ferret out Lord Whitmire's network of connections. However, I don't relish leaving your father's reputation in tatters. I will share what I can when I am able."

"Thank you, sir." Marcus and Hawkins shook hands, but Delilah had doubts Sir Hawkins would honor any such gentlemanly agreement.

Hawkins moved toward the door, Garrick at his side more like a hound on guard than a hawk. "I must take my leave to see the magistrate."

Delilah braced her hands on the chair to stand, wincing at the shooting pain in her arm. "Won't the magistrate have questions you can't adequately answer?"

"It's shocking what a bit of coin crossing the right palms can accomplish. Both for good and evil." Sir Hawkins sounded almost sincere when he said, "I wish you a speedy recovery, my lady, and hope you can put this grisly situation out of your mind."

She sank back in the chair, closed her eyes, and allowed Marcus to see the men out the door. She ought to be thankful he was on England's side, but she could only think how easily he could ruin and discard them like rubbish if it suited his needs.

Marcus returned. Weariness lined his face.

"You look exhausted. Have you slept at all?" Delilah reached for his sturdy hand, savoring the now-familiar calluses.

He shook his head. "How can you possibly be worried about me after your ordeal? You're the one who should be in bed resting."

Her arm was stiff and sore, but she wasn't dying. In fact, a burgeoning sense of relief lightened her mood. Whitmire would never bother them again. Marcus wouldn't be dragged to Newgate and charged with his murder. She wanted nothing more than to get on with their lives as Sir Hawkins had instructed.

"I feel remarkably well considering the events of last night. My arm will heal, and I have exhibited no signs of fever." She managed a slight laugh. "My mother would be shocked at my hardiness."

"Your mother almost lost you once and lived in fear of losing you once more. She did her utmost to protect you in every way. Finally, I can commiserate with her." Marcus stretched his long, lean legs out and crossed his boots at the ankle.

"She'll be thrilled to discover the two of you have something in common." The tease in her words gave way to real trepidation. "I hope you understand I don't need coddling."

"If I hadn't already understood, your point was driven home —literally—last night when you ran Whitmire through with the sword." His huff was humorless, and a bleakness colored his voice. "I would have died at his hands without your intervention."

Delilah couldn't stand it a moment longer. She rose to sit on his lap and snuggle into his hard, warm, very alive body. "Yes. And I would have died several times over without your intervention. We are partners."

He tucked her head on his shoulder and held her close, taking care with her wounded arm. "Indeed, we are."

Delilah tried to imagine what her life would have been like had she spurned Marcus and traveled the expected path. If she had married Sir Wallace, she would have her parent's approval, a comfortable town house, and invitations to all the best functions in town. She would also have a husband who didn't love or respect her, passionless sex, and a marriage empty of any affection.

She lifted her head and cupped his cheek, smiling in the face of his somberness. "I love you, Marcus."

"Even with the dark cloud over my honor, a ramshackle castle, and a dream I'm not sure will succeed?"

"Your honor is golden and gleaming in my eyes. It may take some time, but we'll turn Wyndam Castle into a home. I have faith you'll be the most respected horse breeder in England. Nay, in all Britain." As if she were a diviner, she knew without a doubt her predictions would come to fruition someday.

"I don't deserve you, lass, but you're mine now, and I'm never letting you go." His brief, hard kiss was the seal on his promise.

EPILOGUE

*E*ighteen months later...

Tossing her head, Starlight shuffled around her stall, her distended belly rippling with the force of her birthing pains. The foal's delivery was imminent. Marcus left O'Connell with Starlight to pace outside the stable doors. He took a deep breath of crisp autumn air and tried not to dwell on everything that could go wrong, from a stillbirth to maternal death. If he did, his worries would transfer to Delilah and he would go stark raving mad.

As if summoning her with the force of his fears, Delilah stepped out of the castle with a basket hooked over her arm, peering around her rounded belly at the uneven cobblestones as she picked her way to the stables. She was heavy with child, and Marcus hadn't been sure whether she or Starlight would labor first.

He strode across the yard to offer her a steadying arm and to take the burden of the basket from her. "You should be resting, love."

"I'm tired of resting," she said with a bright grin that never failed to fill him with warmth. "I brought you and O'Connell something to eat. How is the sweet girl doing?"

"Her labor is progressing satisfactorily." Marcus only just stopped himself from mumbling a prayer. While he wasn't a particularly spiritual man, he wanted all the good luck the universe could muster focused on his growing family.

They stepped into the shadows of the stables. She halted at the stall door and watched Starlight while Marcus watched Delilah. Being with child had only enhanced Delilah's natural beauty and inherent strength. She glowed with life, and he hung on to that fact. She had survived more harrowing adventures than childbirth, but even as he reassured himself, he understood firsthand how quickly a healthy mare could be brought to death's door during a difficult birth.

"She's in terrible pain." Commiseration and dread threaded through her voice. She lay a hand over her belly, her thoughts clear.

Marcus put a bracing arm around Delilah's shoulder and nuzzled the wispy hair at her temple. "Yes, but once the foal is born, a mare recovers with astonishing speed."

"You and O'Connell have overseen many successful births, haven't you?"

Marcus let out a sigh. He and Delilah had been going round and round who would attend to her during her confinement and labor for the past month. Marcus wanted to send for a physician. Delilah had insisted Marcus and O'Connell could see to her as well, if not better, than a blood-letting, tonic-giving physician.

"Of horses. Not gently bred ladies. O'Connell would prob-ably have an apoplectic fit if he had to attend you in such a manner."

Hearing his name, O'Connell glanced over from the corner where he stood with a casualness that bespoke his comfort with the proceedings. Marcus took it as a good sign.

"Eh? I don't need to sit. I'm not that old, laddie." The indignation in his voice made both Marcus and Delilah laugh softly.

Marcus raised his voice. "Not *sit*. I told Delilah you would have a *fit* if you had to attend the birth of our child."

O'Connell shambled over to them, all the while keeping a professional, practiced eye on Starlight. "Course I wouldn't. I helped birth you, after all."

Marcus blinked at the older man. "You what?"

O'Connell's smile held a bittersweet sadness. "Aye. Your dear mama's labor was hard. The midwife had all but given up on you both. Your mama was dear to us all, as you know. Your father burst into the stables, grabbed me up by the collar, and dragged me straight into the birthing room."

"What did the midwife do?" Delilah's eyes were wide, and Marcus felt the same astonishment. He had never heard this story. Of course, his mother's death had cast a pall on any happy reminiscences.

"The midwife screamed at me to get out, but His Lordship—your father—pushed her aside, told me to wash my hands, and see what I could do. So I did."

"And?" Delilah tucked her arm around Marcus's waist for a squeeze. "Marcus is here because of your experience and skill."

"Aye." O'Connell gave Marcus a twinkly smile, his eyes crinkled under his bushy red eyebrows. "He came out backward. It took some doing to find his feet, but once I had hold, I gave a gentle pull, and out he slid, wailing and ugly as sin."

Marcus swallowed past a lump of emotion. Perhaps it was fitting. O'Connell had seen Marcus into the world and would bear witness to the birth of Marcus's son or daughter as well. The old stable master had been more a father to him than the old earl.

But… it wouldn't hurt to have at least a midwife present as well. If only to yell at O'Connell to heave to.

Starlight let out a guttural chuff and lay down on her side.

"It's time, lad." O'Connell squatted at Starlight's back end.

Marcus joined O'Connell. No directions or explanations were necessary. Marcus's first foaling at O'Connell's side had been at age ten, and since then, the two of them had watched numerous mares labor. Most had been successful. The ones that weren't still haunted Marcus.

Starlight was a first-time mother, which increased the risk for complications. She was strong though, and her instincts were good. It took another quarter hour of pain and pushing for the foal to slip out in a mess of fluid.

Marcus cut the sac around the foal and rubbed the newborn with a square of burlap. The foal was jet black like its sire, Aries, except for a symmetrical white diamond on its face. He checked the sex. "A colt."

O'Connell heaved himself to standing and wiped his hands on a length of cloth. "He's strong and fine-looking."

Marcus joined O'Connell on the periphery, letting nature take its course now mother and foal were out of danger. Starlight rose and nosed her colt, who was already attempting to stand on spindly, shaky legs.

Delilah let out a soft exclamation from where she watched at the entrance to the stall. Relief and pleasure melded as he watched the colt climb to his feet. "It's amazing, isn't it?"

"Yes, but... *Marcus.*"

The strain in her voice had him whirling. Her face was pale, her eyes wide. A streak of alarm had him rushing over. "What's wrong?"

Her hands were pressed tight around her belly, and the ground at her feet was wet. "It's my turn."

Panic beset him. "What do we do?"

A groan cut off her bark of laughter, and she hunched over her belly. "Prepare for another labor."

He took her forearms and bellowed, "O'Connell."

Grumbling a little under his breath, O'Connell left Starlight and shuffled toward them. "You don't need to yell, lad. I'm not deaf."

Marcus would have laughed if he wasn't so terrified. "Delilah's pains have started. What do we do?"

O'Connell looked at him as if he'd taken leave of his wits. "Take her to your rooms and make her comfortable." To Delilah, he asked, "When did your pains start, lass?"

"While Starlight was laboring. I thought at first they were merely sympathetic, but my waters have broken."

"You have time yet." O'Connell shoved Marcus's shoulder. "Go on then, lad. I'll get what we need from the kitchen and send Ella to Lipton for the midwife."

The next hours were a whirlwind of activity. The pain Delilah experienced cut him to the quick, and Marcus felt adrift and clinging to his sanity.

The midwife arrived and took control with a no-nonsense attitude. Understandably, she balked at having two men in the birthing room. Delilah paced while holding on to the midwife's arms. She puffed her way through a contraction, her face red, and her sweat-dampened hair clinging to her neck while Marcus hovered.

Once she caught her breath, she looked at him and smiled. "I love you, but you're driving me mad. Why don't you and O'Connell retreat to your study, and if there are any complications, Mrs. MacCready will send for you. Is that agreeable?"

The midwife gave a brisk nod. "The lady and I will manage just fine, gents. Off with you both."

O'Connell grabbed the back of Marcus's jacket and hauled him from the room. The next three hours were agonizing. When Delilah's cries crescendoed, Marcus could bear it no longer and took the stairs to their chamber two at a time.

He entered to his child's first cries, lusty and loud. Delilah's head fell back on the pillows, but her smile helped banish a portion of her exhaustion and his anguish.

The midwife wrapped the baby in linen and handed it to Delilah. "A fine son you have, my lady."

Delilah's full attention was on the babe in her arms, crying and waving his fist as if quite put out with his new environs. Marcus circled to the head of the bed as the midwife dealt with the afterbirth.

Delilah looked up and gave him a teary-eyed smile. "We have a son."

Marcus sat on the bed and covered her hand with his, both resting on the baby's chest. His screams turned into mewls as he blinked up at Delilah and Marcus with unfocused eyes. He was red-faced and covered in blood and muck, and his nearly bald head gave the impression of a wizened old man. In short, he was the most beautiful thing Marcus had ever seen.

"Edward Averill Ashemore," Delilah said softly.

They had agreed on names some months before. Edward for his father, Averill for hers. He knew the moment was bittersweet for Delilah. She and her parents had begun a tentative correspondence during her confinement, but no invitation from either party had been issued. Marcus had hoped the rift would have been healed by the time their babe was born, but alas, it hadn't.

"You did beautifully, love." Marcus kissed the top of her head. "I'm so proud of you and, frankly, in awe of your strength."

"You were right. The pain was all worth it," she said, stroking the baby's cheek.

The midwife put her hands on her hips. "We need to get the babe and the lady cleaned up, my lord. Could you send up hot water and clean linens with the girl?"

"Yes, of course." He touched the midwife on the arm. "Thank you for seeing them through safely."

The midwife's expression softened. "Your wife did the hard work. Now go on with you."

Before he stepped out the door, Delilah called his name. He turned back to her.

"Could you perhaps send a note to my parents informing them they have a grandson?" Her voice was hesitant, as if she was not sure she was making a sound decision.

"Of course." Now it was his turn to hesitate. "Would you like me to invite them for a visit?"

She gazed at Edward and kissed the top of his bald head. "Yes, I think I would."

Marcus was happy. Gloriously, shockingly happy. He had no doubt the babe would heal the rift between Delilah and her parents. While he might never fully restore his father's honor in the eyes of Society, Marcus cherished the truth. He had an indomitable woman by his side and a new son. The birth of the colt brightened his hopes for the future.

He was a rich man. Not of coin, but of everything that mattered. Since he'd met Delilah, his heart had grown and then grown some more.

With a last glance at his reasons for being, he went to do her bidding while whistling a tune.

READY FOR MORE?

ALSO BY LAURA TRENTHAM

*H*istorical Romance
Spies and Lovers
An Indecent Invitation Book 1
A Brazen Bargain, Book 2
A Reckless Redemption, Book 3
A Sinful Surrender, Book 4
A Wicked Wedding, Book 5
A Daring Deception, Book 6 (Coming Soon)

CONTEMPORARY ROMANCE
Highland, Georgia Novels
A Highlander Walks Into a Bar, Book 1
A Highlander in a Pickup, Book 2
A Highlander is Coming to Town, Book 3

HEART OF A HERO **Novels**
The Military Wife
An Everyday Hero

. . .

COTTONBLOOM NOVELS
Kiss Me That Way, Book 1
Then He Kissed Me, Book 2
Till I Kissed You, Book 3
Christmas in the Cop Car, Novella 3.5
Light Up the Night, Novella 3.75
Leave the Night On, Book 4
When the Stars Come Out, Book 5
Set the Night on Fire, Book 6

SWEET HOME ALABAMA Novels
Slow and Steady Rush, Book 1
Caught Up in the Touch, Book 2
Melting Into You, Book 3

ABOUT THE AUTHOR

I hope you enjoyed *A Sinful Surrender*! If you have a chance please leave a quick review! Although, many readers know me from my Southern-set contemporary romances, the first books I wrote were the Spies and Lovers series! I grew up reading the historical "bodice rippers" of the late eighties and early nineties along with wonderful gothic romances. Now that I have the opportunity to publish all of the Spies and Lovers series, I'm so excited! The Spies and Lovers world will be expanding soon with a new series called, Laws of Attraction!

I was born and raised in a small town in Northwest Tennessee. Although, I loved English and reading in high school, I was convinced an English degree equated to starvation! So, I chose the next most logical major - Chemical Engineering- and worked in a hard hat and steel toed boots for several years. Now I live in South Carolina with my husband and two children. In between school and homework and soccer practices, I love to get lost in another world, whether it's Regency England or small town Alabama.

My first two Falcon Football books received TOP PICKS from RT Book Reviews and a STARRED review from Library Journal. KISS ME THAT WAY, Cottonbloom Book 1, won the Stiletto Contest for Best Long Contemporary and finaled in the National Readers Choice Award. THEN HE KISSED ME, Cottonbloom Book 2, was named an Amazon Best Romance of 2016 and was a finalist for the National Excellence for Romance Fiction. TILL I KISSED YOU, Cottonbloom Book 3, is a finalist in the Maggie contest. LEAVE THE NIGHT ON, the latest Cottonbloom book, was named an iBooks Best Book of the Month and a Recommended Read from NPR. AN INDECENT INVITATION and A BRAZEN BARGAIN were both finalists for the 2014 Golden Heart® Award.

I love to hear from readers! Come find me:
Laura@LauraTrentham.com
www.LauraTrentham.com
Sign up for Laura's Newsletter
Join Laura's Facebook Squad

A SINFUL SURRENDER

Copyright © 2020 by Laura Trentham

Cover by Angela Waters

Edited by Heidi Shoham

eISBN: 978-1-946306-12-8

Printed in Great Britain
by Amazon

40543652R10138